'Red, how do you plan to apprehend the escapees?' Margaret Hunt asked.

'Officially,' Red said, 'I can only say we have a full manhunt team on their trail, and we'll proceed with due haste.'

Ainsworth of the *Dallas Times Herald* led the chuckle.

'And unofficially?'

That was like putting it up on a tee for Ted Williams. They all waited. But Red hesitated – something bothering him.

'Unofficially,' he said finally, 'I'm gonna hunt 'em like the rabid dogs they are.'

ABOUT THE AUTHOR

Dewey Gram is a journalist and screenwriter. Since 1986 he has been involved in the film industry, working closely with writers, producers and directors on a great number of films. Among his credits are *Fried Green Tomatoes at the Whistlestop Cafe*, *The Tooth Fairy* and *Breaking In*. His other novelizations include *Boulevard Nights*, *Foxes* and *Sneakers*. Before becoming a screenwriter Dewey Gram worked as a journalist for the *Sunday Times* (as their West Coast Correspondent) and *Newsweek* magazine.

He lives in California with his wife and three children.

A PERFECT WORLD

BY DEWEY GRAM

**BASED ON THE SCREENPLAY
BY JOHN LEE HANCOCK**

A SIGNET BOOK

SIGNET

Published by the Penguin Group
Penguin Books Ltd, 27 Wrights Lane, London W8 5TZ, England
Penguin Books USA Inc., 375 Hudson Street, New York, New York 10014, USA
Penguin Books Australia Ltd, Ringwood, Victoria, Australia
Penguin Books Canada Ltd, 10 Alcorn Avenue, Toronto, Ontario,
Canada M4V 3B2
Penguin Books (NZ) Ltd, 182–190 Wairau Road, Auckland 10, New Zealand

Penguin Books Ltd, Registered Offices: Harmondsworth, Middlesex, England

Published in Signet 1993
1 3 5 7 9 10 8 6 4 2

Printed in England by Clays Ltd, St Ives plc

▪ ONE ▪

*H*uraken is the Mayan god of storm. About forty times a year this tropical god collects its rage out over the Gulf of Mexico and attacks the state of Texas all along the coastal lowlands from Beaumont to Brownsville. Most of these hurricanes leave behind little or no damage. But now and then the long shadows they throw before them—the large, heavy thunderstorms that rampage across the hard flat Texas interior— spawn the deadly dark-funneled cyclones for which the state is famous, tornadoes, known here as twisters.

A late-October version of one of these thunderheads formed up somewhere past Houston in Deep East Texas. It beat its way across the southeastern lowlands, over the Prairies and Cross Timbers stretches of North Central Texas, and hit a high-pressure ridge just above Abilene where it spun into a furious, trouble-seeking black funnel cloud. A short spree of mayhem, then the spiraling storm flayed itself out against the stockade wall of the high plains Llano Estacado up the Panhandle from Lubbock.

Now it wound down to a snarl of dust in a hayfield, strange only because of the baggage it carried in its dying tail—U.S. bills of small denomination. No longer the god *Huraken*, the dust devil sprinkled small change—a single, a five, a ten, another single, about the face and shoulders of a man lying in the field. A dollar bill came to rest against his cheek.

1

The man—Butch Haynes—paid no attention. His eyes were closed. He was in another world. A large black bird circled overhead, intersecting the high noon sun, causing Butch to open his eyes and squint, adjusting to the light. The eyes were tired but relaxed, even content. Muffled voices and whispers filled the air around him, but it all seemed to come from another place. Butch ignored it. He propped an arm behind his head and rested comfortably.

More muffled noise. A larger dark object intersected the sun. Butch noted its passing, but didn't try to follow with his eyes. Gusting wind ruffled his hair and wiped a piece of straw across his forehead; the dollar bill flitted away from his cheek, floating with others in the air. The wind died. The bills settled in the dust. Butch, in his world, took no notice.

■ *TWO* ■

MADISONVILLE, TEXAS—1963—OCTOBER

It was a farmland four-corners, fewer than five thousand people. At one time straddling the main post road between Houston only ninety miles south and Dallas–Fort Worth half again as far to the north, Madisonville had entertained dreams of grandeur. No longer. Interstate 45 now bypassed Madisonville by four miles—a good four miles—good enough to leave the community mired in its Depression-era foundings and country-town feel.

On the four corners itself stood the First National Bank building, the Post Office, the old, redbrick combined City Building–Police Station, and the modest town square with the center-set statue of Sam Houston, father of everything Texan. There was something peculiar about this particular Sam Houston statue—its disconcerting blank eyes, instead of bringing history to life, suggested to some that the inmost lessons of a man's life were opaque and died with the man.

One movie theater, a Woolworth's and Clayton's Barbecue—those were the leading commercial lights of Madisonville. Gladys Perry worked at the Woolworth's during the day and at Clayton's on those nights she wasn't at service and could arrange for a fellow believer to sit her kids.

Two minimum-wage jobs the last nine years while raising three kids mostly alone, Gladys Perry was thirty going on forty-five. A slim shape, an almost pretty face, dark brunette hair that had seen a beauty parlor just that once, high school graduation. Gladys's mother before her had set the pattern: a few early years of fun and hope, youthful romance, the onset of children and work that piled up all the way to illness and an early grave. Gladys was determined to do different.

She'd leased-to-buy a house in the poorer south end, a neighborhood of plain streets behind the movie theater and the string of bars on either side of the Madisonville Hotel. Pine-slat houses, cars in the front yard, packed dirt and patches of yellow grass for lawns. But Gladys had picked out the nicest street in the neighborhood, one with some green grass, fresh paint, and trimmed hedges, and for eighteen months now she'd been making owner payments on the tiny ranch-style house on Bryant Street. Next year, she calculated, she could get the trim painted.

As the sun went down on the muggy lowlands Texas day, Gladys fed her kids and kept them behind closed doors. No way they were going out tonight. Not her kids. There was a flash weather warning—flash storms ruled east Texas. But it wasn't that. It was this night and what it stood for. She slid the tuna casserole on the table and went back to the fridge for milk.

"Judy Baumer is going as a twirler," Naomi said. She smiled at the very thought. Naomi, a grown-up ten with an olive complexion and well-brushed dark hair, had an innate sense of dignity.

"But she's so fat," said Ruth, also ten, same brunette hair but uncombed—younger than Naomi by forty-five minutes and from another universe of temperament. "She should go as a doughnut and get it over with." She looked like she was about to dip her fork in venom.

Phillip faintly smiled. He was eight, with a lopsided home-crafted mop top and brown eyes that were so large and serious he always looked a tad worried. It was a face that said even eight-year-olds knew it wasn't all just a romp in sunshine. Phillip had learned long ago to keep his own counsel around these two barracudas.

"I'd go as Cinderella," Ruth said. "Or Peter Pan."

"Peter Pan's a boy," Naomi said. "Tinkerbell's a girl. Phillip could go as Peter Pan. 'Cept you gotta fly."

Phillip half smiled at the notion, and waited for the zinger.

"Phillip could go as a bump on a log." Ruth smiled sweetly at him.

"Flash Gordon," Phillip said, thinking out loud, picking a hole in his bread. "Why can't we go? . . ." he said. "Just once?"

Gladys set the milk and margarine on the table, slid onto her chair, and stared directly at her son. She gave his hand a tap to stop the bread mutilation. "Remember the starving children in China," she said.

"We ain't like others, Phillip," Naomi said.

"Our personal beliefs lift us to a higher place," Gladys said, pouring four glasses of milk. " 'Sides, Halloween is nothing but the Devil's work."

The doorbell rang. The kids all put their glasses down and watched as Gladys got up and strode into the front hall with a sense of purpose.

Albert Reeves, a family man about thirty-five years old and forty pounds overweight smiled up at Gladys when she opened the door. Proudly arrayed before him were Superman wearing a black mask, Tinkerbell, and a dancing skeleton.

"Trick or treat!" the children yelled.

Three gypsies of varying sizes and four cardboard-box playing cards, King, Queen, Jack, and Ace, came up the walk with big paper sacks at the ready for loot. Three other parents with half-embarrassed grins lingered partway up the walk and waved.

"Albert Reeves and clan. Hi," Albert said. "From a block and a half down. We've never actually met. We oughta have a welcome-wagon for the neighborhood, huh?" He liked Gladys's slim hips and the hint of warmth behind the tired eyes and frazzled hair. He knew about her only the sidewalk scuttlebutt: she was raising her chickens without benefit of rooster. He beamed invitingly at her as though to say he was wide open to drop in for a frosty any afternoon.

Gladys stared out at the children—more were trooping up the walk—before looking back to Albert Reeves. "I'm sorry, but we don't take no part in Halloween," she said to the friendly man, pushing her hair back. She gave a small polite smile.

"Excuse me?" Reeves said. Was it safety, he was about to ask. This was a pretty easygoing, doors-unlocked, keys in the ignition kind of neighborhood. Every year it seemed the parade of kids and parents on Halloween grew bigger, the reception friendlier. In fact, it was the one time each year that Reeves, a car paint salesman, actually walked around his own community and pressed the flesh. He made a note to get out more. Phillip arrived at his mother's apron and stared at the costumed kids with relish.

Ruth and Naomi stood at the window and watched intently, whispering feverishly to each other, pointing. Ruth pushed the curtain back further to see more kids and costumes coming. It sure looked like fun.

"We're Jehovah's Witness," Gladys said to Albert Reeves. Time seemed to stop. The parents down the walk stared, then looked at each other, and shrugged. People had a vague sense of what it meant to be Jehovah Witness.

"Hey, Phillip Perry," Superman said, locking eyes with the shaggy-haired boy half hidden behind his mother.

"Hey, Billy Reeves," Phillip said with a big grin.

"How'd you know it was me?" said Superman, puffing up, making a muscle.

Albert Reeves didn't give up easy. "There's a heck of a haunted house over on Ohio Street. Don't want to miss that. Electrician and his wife put it up. Every year now. Free." He beamed and couldn't help noticing Gladys's legs.

"Go eat your supper, Phillip," Gladys said. She pushed him back from the door and moved back herself, reaching for the knob.

"Come on kids," Reeves said with a cheerful smile. "Let's go to the next house. Sorry for the bother . . . Mrs? . . ." His son Superman said, "Perry. That's Mrs. Perry."

"Nice to meet you, Mrs. Perry," Albert Reeves said and gave a grin and wink to Gladys as she was closing the door. He waved his herd down the walk.

Gladys closed the door and shook her head. He winked at her. Not too many people winked at her, even at Clayton's Barbecue. She pointedly did not look at herself in the hall mirror as she walked back into the linoleum-floored kitchen.

Reeves, joining the other parents waiting by the street, urged the crowd toward the next house. "All you spirits of darkness, cooties, bedbugs, and playing cards!" he called. "There's lots more loot out there; let's get it all!" He got a laugh from the adults. One of his kids gave him a shot with his elbow to make him shut up.

Inside the modest house on Bryant Street, Naomi carefully picked the pieces of mushroom out of her tuna casserole and stared distractedly at her plate. Ruth was uncharacteristically quiet. Phillip was in dreamland, out there on the street laughing with the other wildly attired spirits of the dark.

"Phillip, eat," Gladys said evenly.

"Mom, how come Pam Tenz's mother—?" Ruth started to say with her patented whine.

"Ruthie, Pam Tenz is no account of mine," Gladys said, "When the glory day comes, my three children will be standing before Him clean and ready, free of the taint of violence and government. That's my job on this earth."

A moment of silent eating and digesting of this wisdom.

"What if," Ruth said quickly, "we all went as Jehovah, like in our play? Then could we—"

"Bite your tongue, Ruth Perry," Gladys said. "Bite your tongue this minute. May Jehovah God forgive you. The things of the Kingdom Hall are not for the street. And you are not street urchins, not even one night a year."

The doorbell rang again. Gladys put her hand up. "Ignore it," she said. She nodded to go back to eating. The three kids looked deep into their tuna casserole. The doorbell rang insistently. It was going to be a long night. "Phillip, go turn off the porch light," his mother said.

"Yes'm," Phillip said, and rose to obey, his melancholy brown eyes seeming to say that porch-light-turning-out was a heavy burden for a boy on Halloween.

■ *THREE* ■

A pea green Chevy Impala with white trim pulled off the highway, down the drive, and up to the main gate of Huntsville State Prison. The Impala stopped, the driver's window came down.

"Evenin' Larry. Forget something?" asked the guard stepping from his office, slapping on his Department of Prisons cap. He peered in the car to make sure everything was standard. Not Larry's usual arrival time, after all.

"Heya, Julius," Larry said. "Goin' to Austin tomorrow. Gonna take some work with me." Larry smiled. He was a pudgy amiable assistant warden in charge of materials acquisition and allocation. Everybody liked Larry Seyler—everybody who went home every night, anyway. The permanent residents didn't like anybody. That's why they were permanent.

"Work work work." Julius the guard grinned. "Hey, I hear you turned double nickles, young fella."

Larry looked at him, puzzled.

"Fifty-five," Julius said. "That's worth a cold one. I'll stand you one Friday if you're back."

"I'll be back." Larry smiled. "Austin's got too many pinko kids over't the university for my comfort. Place's a hotbed. You know they got up a movement supportin' some South American pinko outlaw named Che Guevara? What won't they think of next?"

"Time we all went back to school, pard." Julius laughed, and slapped the top of the Impala with his clipboard. "Don't stay late."

He opened the gate and the Impala passed inside.

Huntsville was maximum security, as hard a place to do time as you could find short of a federal pen. Attica up in New York was hard state time; Huntsville was harder—because it was Texas. Texas, where they have that Southern penal attitude toward individuals who make any kind of serious habit of antisocial behavior: Stomp their knuckles till all they've got left is stubs to pray with.

North Block comprised four tiers around an inner court, but not the new kind where gun bulls sit in a central bird cage opposite every tier. No, Fourth Tier North, once the lock-down walk-by was over each night, was a primo place to own real estate. You could carry on romance if one of your cellmates was your flavor of fish. Or you could practice becoming a mime, say, so you'd amount to something by the time you made your date and they gave you your parole shoes. Or, you could crouch behind the cell bunks and chip at the patched concrete wall.

Butch Haynes, thirty-eight and an old hand at jailing, chipped at the wall. His tired eyes said he didn't believe for a minute he was getting anywhere, but you have to do something with your regret when you're a long-timer. Butch carried a maximum of regret, and so figured he had to take the maximum long shot at changing the unchanging parade of days. Attacking a concrete ceiling with a sharpened angle-iron was a long shot.

Jerry Pugh, Butch's belligerent rail-thin excuse for a cellmate, licked his lips constantly and kept watch at the door. Pugh, twenty-nine, but only chronologically, was nobody's first choice for a campout. Listed as "dull-normal" and "explosive" on his psych report when he came in, he was plugged into solitary for two months' observation. The prison psychologist discovered during that time that he was in fact "bright-normal"—a much more dangerous pail of worms, the psychologist noted. Describing Pugh as "alert but off-center," he had no choice but to let him into the general prison population.

There, in the general population, Pugh might not be

expected to live long, once the nature of his beef got out. He was a "short-eyes"—a molester of a kid—not an acceptable crime to run-of-the-mill Texas inmates. That and Pugh's hair-trigger temper did not suggest longevity. The cell lieutenant thought about housing Pugh on the gump tier—the homosexual tier—since the child he had molested had been male. But as Pugh did not for a minute consider himself a faggot, chances are he would ignite, eating the resident faggots alive.

In his wisdom the cell lieutenant moved Pugh in with Butch Haynes, a guy he knew was smart enough to see where Pugh was coming from. Haynes's relatively controlled nature could act as the graphite pile in the nuclear reactor, absorbing just enough of Pugh's evil rays to keep him below critical mass.

So far it had been a brilliant pairing. Butch had no time for the kind of perverted erratic criminal Pugh was, and let him know. Older and looking at longer shelf time, Butch wasn't about to risk adding time by hassling with a punk. Pugh knew he could snipe at the older con and do the dozens up to a point. But when he saw the look start to light up in Butch's eyes, he knew to back off. Any real trouble in the cell would bring down pure hurt on Pugh, and everybody would look the other way. Pugh saved his aggression for the big yard, and it was his reputation for unpredictable savagery alone that kept him alive.

Butch grunted as his makeshift chisel chipped through the thin concrete slab into an open space.

"Damn if the old man ain't right," he said, enlarging the opening, sticking his hand in, and feeling around in the dark. "Here's the vent," he muttered, enlarging the opening, running his hand over a thin metal inner wall.

Pugh turned and snaked his arm through the bars, grabbing the nervous old man sitting in the corner of the adjoining cell, listening to every development.

Pugh pulled him up by the shirt. "And this goes to the roof?" he asked.

"Used to," the old-timer said, "afore they walled it over. Goes right to the back wall, then up."

"If it don't, I'm gonna come back here and rip your tongue out," Pugh said. "And make you eat it."

"Git yer damn hands off me!" the old man squealed, trying to jerk away. "Damn hanky freak."

Pugh laughed and let him loose, and he fell in a heap, spitting curses at the younger con. Pugh straightened up and started to follow Butch behind the bunks. Butch was busy prying open a seam in the corrugated metal air shaft hidden behind the pierced wall.

"Come on," Pugh breathed excitedly. "Bend steel with your bare hands, man. I can smell it, I can lick it."

The hole was almost big enough for Butch's shoulders.

"Screw!" hissed the old man from his perch by the cell door. Butch and Pugh both hit the floor and were draped in their bunks, looking innocent, within three seconds. They waited half a minute, heard nothing. The old man burst out laughing. "Assholes," he said, making the jerk-off sign.

Pugh jumped up, moving to throttle the old-timer. Butch grabbed him and shoved him back. He motioned toward the hole in the wall. Pugh pointed at the old man warningly.

"Fuck around," he said, "I won't send yer favorite thing." He smirked at the old man, turned, and joined Butch at the escape hole.

"What's he want?" Butch said, yanking the hole wider.

"You wouldn't b'lieve it if I tole ya'," Pugh said.

Butch turned to him. "Try me."

"Later, maybe," Pugh said with a leer like a kid with a secret.

Butch shook his head, disgusted he'd given the freak the satisfaction. He lifted himself into the hole.

■ *FOUR* ■

Superman and Dancing Skeleton, freed of adult supervision, skittered through backyards and over a low rail fence to the house next door to Phillip Perry's. They moved in the shadow of the carport to the hose spigot at the corner of the house. Crouching under a bedroom window, they began to fill colored balloons with water.

"Make 'em small," Superman said. "You can't heave big ones. No bigger'n this."

"Dad said they used to fill 'em with paint when he was a kid," Skeleton said.

"Dad's full of it, case you hadn't noticed," Superman said as he tied his balloons and laid them carefully side by side. "You see the way he was looking at Perry's mother? Jeez. You'd think she was Ava Gardner, 'stead of some skinny old maid."

"What's a old maid?" Skeleton asked.

Superman groaned. "Sheeeze, Marko, the things you don't know."

"Means you don't know either," Mark said. "Hand-job."

Superman laughed. "Don't call me somethin' you don't know what it is, creep," Superman said. "You could get in some very serious trouble."

Mark thought for a moment, struggling to tie an overfilled balloon. "Then what's a hand-job?"

Superman filled a last water balloon thoughtfully. "A hand-job is when you get yer girlfriend to wash yer car for ya'."

"Really?" Mark said.

"Something like that," Superman said, "Close enough for your age."

Inside the Perry house, the twins slouched at the sink and scraped tuna casserole and washed evening dishes while Phillip dried. Gladys sat at the table, reading a religious pamphlet, policing the ritual, when suddenly several thuds resounded through the house, shaking the front windows.

"What in the world?" Gladys said, jumping up.

Phillip slid off his stool, threw down his dish towel, and raced into the living room, an austere room with just three pieces of furniture and a patterned rattan mat for a rug. The boy jounced on the slipcovered couch and pulled a curtain back. The girls headed for the front door.

"Phillip!" Gladys yelled. "Girls, get back from that door!" She pulled the girls back and huddled with them as though Satan himself might come bulldozing in.

Outside on the curb Superman lofted a balloon in a high arc toward the roof, then zinged a frozen rope toward the front door. Blam! Boom! They hit one-two.

"Bombs away!" Superman shouted.

Inside, Phillip could be heard faintly cheering.

Little Skeleton Mark heaved a water bomb with all his might toward the front door. "Here's your trick!" he hollered. His water bomb reached halfway to the front stoop and splatted along the walk. He ran up with the next one, threw it from ten feet, and hit the door. "Steeeeerike!"

At the window Phillip gaped in happy wonder at the onslaught—ready for every kid in the neighborhood to come charging, barraging his house with splats and thuds. He barely flinched as a balloon whapped the siding only inches from his face. The joy of the unexpected. His mother reached from behind, pulled him from the window, and snapped the curtains shut.

▪ *FIVE* ▪

Butch kicked the rotted wooden top off the ventilator shaft and rolled onto the tar-paper roof. He scrambled into the deep shadow of an air-conditioning unit. Jerry Pugh followed him out and scuttled to join him at the edge of the roof. From there they surveyed the yard as searchlights routinely bathed the walls in ovals of light. The two men inched over the ledge and slid down to the next roof level, then the next.

Butch saw something. He took off to his left, running on all fours along the peaked roof of a gallery joining North Block to the Administration Building. As Pugh tried to catch up, a searchlight swung toward him. He hung against the back side of the roof, the light passed, then came back again. He waited, then sprinted and threw himself up on the Administration Building roof and looked around frantically for Butch.

Butch was leaning over the front of the building, watching something. Jerry stealthily joined him. Parked directly below them, next to the entrance to the Administration office, was a pea green Chevy Impala with white trim.

"You'n'me must be livin' right, Butchie boy!" Jerry hissed.

"Let's get something straight," Butch said in a hoarse whisper. "I don't like you. Soon as we're on our way, that's it." He never looked at the younger man.

"Who said I liked you?" Jerry asked. He gave Butch the finger behind his back.

Butch slid over the edge, let himself hang down full length, and dropped softly on the roof of the entranceway.

A soft thud caused a guard in the office to look up, but only momentarily as Larry Seyler walked up to his desk and opened his briefcase. Larry opened his coat and showed his stack of files in pro forma display. "No inmates, no state secrets," he said to the night guard.

"Have a safe trip now, Mr. Seyler," the guard said. "Make 'em give us all raises, them fat cats in Austin."

"They all Jack Kennedys now, don'tcha know?" Larry smiled. "Chauffered cars, wives speakin' French to the cook. We're in the wrong business."

"From your mouth to God's ear, mister," the guard said. "You take care." He reached down and buzzed open the heavy mesh security door—the last barrier to freedom if you were a client of the place.

Larry hefted his file-heavy case and slouched through with a friendly wave. He pushed the outside door and went out into the humid autumn night air. Originally from Detroit, Larry had never gotten used to the gloopy Gulf humidity of Southeast Texas. He started sweating the instant he was outdoors and rarely showed up at a meeting without his jacket soaked through the back. He took at least two showers a day.

He stepped down the concrete stairs and moved along the flower-edged walkway toward his car, barely noticing the incandescent spotlight that raked across his face in its routine pass down the front of the building. But in the half second it took his eyes to adjust to the stab of light, Butch and Jerry leapt down and landed on either side of him. Before the pudgy man's reactions could kick in, Butch clapped his hand over his mouth and yanked his head back by the hair, and Jerry slid a practiced hand into the man's jacket. Bingo—a shiny .38 Special.

"Keep yer mouth shut," Butch hissed, pulling Larry low beside the Impala.

Jerry leaned into the man's wide-eyed face. "Gawd I'd love to blow yer head off," he said. Jerry pulled the car door open, Butch shoved the stunned man into the driver's seat, and Jerry kept the .38 pressed to his head.

"Remember," Butch said reasonably, "you got a lot to lose in the next two minutes. You got a family?"

Larry Seyler nodded earnestly at Butch, seeing in his eyes something more sane and recognizable than what he saw in Pugh's.

"You can choose yer life," Butch said.

Larry, driving with his eyes straight ahead, slowed at the gate and waved a palm at Julius, the guard. Julius opened without hesitation. He grinned down as Larry eased the Impala past. "Double nickles," Julius called. No response at all from Larry, eyes still straight ahead, sweat pouring down his overweight face. The Impala turned onto the roadway and rolled away into the night. Julius shook his head. "He don't live up that way," he said to no one, a touch puzzled. "Workin' too hard. Early grave for that one."

Stuffed and hidden on the back floor of the Impala half under the mats, Butch and Jerry let out long breaths as the car hit the main drag and picked up speed. "Double nickles?" Jerry said gleefully, easing halfway up on the backseat. "That what we put on your eyelids when you lay down for the long one, screw?" He jabbed the .38 hard into Larry's neck. Larry jerked.

"You were smart," Butch said as he slid into the front seat. "Drive at twenty-five in town and don't do nothing fancy with the headlights. Turn north on 190 and stay on it past the interstate."

"Less'n you wanna lay some flowers on the grave of General Sam Houston hisself." Jerry said. "Not five miles on up Route 19. You the one told us that durin' induction?—like we was gonna need that information." He kicked the seat back. Larry flew forward, the car lurched, the horn sounded.

"Lay off. Let him drive," Butch said. They were passing through the little hamlet that had grown up down the road from the prison. The streets were nearly deserted.

A black-and-white patrol car approached from the opposite direction as the Impala entered the main intersection. Butch and Larry slouched low. Larry slowed, put on his left-turn signal, waited.

"You're still alive," Butch intoned. "Yer kid's still got a father."

Larry's jacket and shirt were soaked through with sweat. Jerry jabbed hard through the seat back, making the driver's head jerk just as the uniformed cop pulled even and looked over. Larry quickly raised a hand to his neck and massaged, as though he had a crick. The cop looked away and drove on.

"You got real good survival instincts, Warden," Jerry said as the Impala swung left and headed out of town.

"I'm not a warden," Larry said, trying to keep the terror out of his voice. "I'm acquisitions and allocations. I don't deal directly with inmates."

"Well, welcome to Touch the Inmate!" Jerry said. "What's your name, Fatty? You got a fatass wife you hump ever' Sunday morning before church? Squishin' and gruntin' like hawgs."

Larry's eyes flitted a look of pure hatred at Jerry. And Jerry saw it. He'd made a mistake, Larry could tell right off. Dumb, he told himself. Then the sick sense came over him that the outcome no matter what he did was already written in this psycho's brain.

"Up toward Texarkana," Jerry said, "there's a little town called Uncertain. You ever hear of it?—Uncertain, Texas. Don't matter what road we take, we're headin' toward that town tonight, Warden." Jerry guffawed loudly, looking to Butch, expecting at least a chuckle.

"Jezus," Butch muttered. "Shut the hell up."

That was Larry Seyler's second mistake, though he himself didn't make it. Jerry smoldered in silence, the .38 heavy in his lap. He let Larry drive on for another few minutes until they were well into desolate bayou country, not a light as far as the eye could see. "Stop here," he said sullenly.

Larry looked at Butch in panic.

"Stop the fuckin' car!" Jerry screamed.

■ *SIX* ■

A phone rang in a dark bedroom. A dog whimpered in its sleep. A second ring. The dog, a fifteen-year-old golden Lab and an old hand at this, nudged his owner. The phone rang a third time. The golden Lab leaned over and growled directly into his owner's ear.

"Thanks, Chuck," the man said, ornery, reaching for the phone and clicking on the table lamp. The light revealed the bedroom of a quintessential Texas Hill Country bachelor—walls adorned with shotguns, modern and vintage, a mounted deer's head, a fanged boar's head, a six-foot sailfish, and two framed dog pictures, both Labs.

Red Garnett, sixty, red gray hair, lean face with high forehead, swung his legs off the bed and reached for his pants, assuming the worst before hearing even a word of what the phone caller had to say.

"Hullo . . . uh-huh . . ." His face grimaced at the news. Some news was worse than others, even at 3 A.M. He pushed the slobbering Chuck back and snagged his socks off the floor and pulled them on while talking. "How big a jump they got? . . . Uh-huh. Files on the way? . . . Anybody call John yet? . . . No, I'll do it. Night calls for anything but quail huntin' he gets mean . . . Yup." He went to hang up, then asked another question. "By the by, the guy in the next cell you said knew all about it—what's he have to say? . . . Yeah, well *he's* the lucky bastard, he's gonna die in his bed."

The pea green Impala sat empty in the parking lot of Five-Mile Market, a little roadside convenience store just east of the town of Madisonville. The open-late store was on the town end of a string of honky-tonks stretching several miles to the south, and it caught the eye of a steady stream of returning beer drinkers with late-night munchies. The balding man who ran the place, a lifelong shrimp fisherman from Port Aransas who had retired here to be near his in-country relatives, considered himself lucky to have found this lucrative spot. He'd had a string of a half dozen very good years and saw no reason they shouldn't continue. Tonight the string ran out.

A gunshot tolled inside the store and echoed in the cooling night air. A car with three teenage boys pulled in the parking lot at that precise moment. It is a given that the sound a gunshot makes is familiar to every boy growing up in Texas. The boy driving, registering the sound, chose not even to look inside the store, instead swung his pickup back onto the highway and accelerated away—discretion the better part of munchies.

Butch, behind the counter at the cash register, looked down at the floor and then over at Jerry, giving him a cold stare. Jerry smiled back, grabbed a girlie magazine, and leafed the pages with the .38. He was wearing Larry's plaid jacket.

Butch jimmied the register, grabbed a bundle of bills, looked down at the heap on the floor again, and hopped over the counter. He headed for the door.

"Hey, wait up!" Jerry yelled. He grabbed two more magazines, scooped up a pocketful of Brach's candies, and hurried after, splatting through a pool of blood on the floor, with a quivering hand extended into it.

Texas Rangers headquarters was a long low, brown-brick building set back from the road on a modest rise, surrounded by carefully trimmed green lawns. The brass-doored main entrance, crowned by the Texas Rangers shield and flanked by two stately flag poles, projected an air of grave officialdom. A trooper stationed at the door jotted down the name of every man who entered at this ungodly hour. Then the trooper snapped off a straight-backed salute. Be righteous and on the right side of the law, all ye who enter here, his very posture charged. Lights showed only in one wing of the building.

Inside was cinder-block walls and concrete floors painted with everlasting rubberized green institutional paint—all except Red's office. If you took away the huge ranch-style desk and changed the dark green carpet to dark brown, you'd swear you were back in the man's Hill Country bedroom—same mounted heads on the walls, similar fish, same golden Lab draped along the couch.

"I understand your concern, Governor," Red said. He sipped coffee with one hand, worked a gold Liberty dollar across his knuckles in a magician's exercise with the other, and talked on the phone tucked in his neck. "Cons are creatures o' habit. Like old coyotes, they'll crawl back into familiar holes . . . Uh-huh . . . That's my job . . . Yeah . . . Sure yer' right. Listen, you go back to bed and I'll call you in the A.M. with an update. I'll have the complete files by then. Hell, maybe even the perpetrators. Say hullo to the Mrs . . ."

Red sighed, put the phone back on the hook, and stared at it until it rang again. At the same moment four deputies trooped into his office, one carrying a big county map book, and another, Tom Adler, still knotting his tie.

"Forget the tie, Tom," Red said. "This one's gonna be hair, teeth, and eyeballs—ours if we ain't careful."

The phone rang again.

"They armed?" Adler asked.

Red looked at him deadpan. "Does a bear? . . ."

The phone kept ringing. Red closed his eyes, trying to will it away.

▪ *SEVEN* ▪

The windup alarm clock clanged hard at 5:30 A.M. Gladys Perry opened her eyes, reached out, and touched it to silence. She groaned, forcing herself upright, unwilling but programmed. She rose, starting the ritual she followed unfailingly every morning. Had she faltered just this one morning, had she stayed in bed, slept in like the sinner she'd have known herself to be, much that followed would have been different, much anguish sidestepped, much occasion for grievous acts avoided. But venal reality has a way of creeping up the walk of the most steadfast and true among folk. Job, the sufferer, knew that. It has nothing to do with deserving.

Gladys slippered through the living room where all three of her children slept on the pull-out couch. The twins snoozed on soundly as Gladys snapped on the kitchen light. Phillip, half awake, turned fitfully away and buried his head.

The green Impala with white trim crept along Bryant Street on the south end of the town of Madisonville. It rolled without lights in the predawn past the Reeves house where Superman and Dancing Skeleton were snug in their beds—where Albert Reeves just then awoke with the priapic urge to dominate the nearest female, but instead went into the bathroom, urinated, and went back to sleep.

Butch drove, Jerry hung out the window scouting the block. They sure hadn't picked a wealthy neighborhood.

"There's a Buick," Jerry said quietly.

"Don't want a Buick," Butch said. "Want a Ford."

"Fords leak oil," Jerry said. "A car's a car."

Butch put on the brakes and brought the car to a halt. "Then take the Buick."

"Soon as we cross the state line I'll do just that," Jerry said, giving Butch a long look. He cracked the door open. "I'm tired of riding around. I'll check down the block . . . for a Ford!" He got out, slammed the door, and walked away lighting a cigarette.

Butch leaned down and peered at the gas gauge—almost empty. He tapped it with one finger. It didn't budge. He sighed and looked around. Jerry, across the street in the driveway of a darkened house, checked a car door—locked. He walked back to the street, grinning at Butch, heading for the next house around the corner.

Butch turned the Impala key to off and climbed out. He closed the door behind him without a sound and started down the block.

Jerry spotted a light on in the back of a house on Bryant, the only sign of life in any direction. He squinted and headed for it like a moth.

Happy to be out and night-prowling, Jerry Pugh would've been happy if dawn never came. He was raised on the east side of Houston along the industrial Ship Channel in sight of the chemical-plant cracking towers—a fulminating, satanic vista at night. It had been both his norm—the eerily lit, smoking, flaming spires—and a kind of unattainable grandeur. Yet it wasn't the inferno on the horizon that shaped Jerry Pugh's destiny so much as the flash fires in his head. He lacked what developmental psychologists call impulse control.

Jerry's style with toys was to see how much stress it took to demolish them, with bikes, how many crashes to cripple them—normal boy stuff but without guilt or governor. He broke a neighbor boy's arm so badly he was declared off limits by all surrounding families for a summer. His fourth-grade teacher refused to have him in class unless he had permission to hit him back.

When puberty washed over him, Jerry Pugh capered right to the edge and stayed there. He tried to discourage a would-be stepfather with roach poison in his corned-beef hash. The unsuspecting man, an oil-field driller who had just moved to Texas from Louisiana, went into convulsions but recovered. Nothing could be proved against Jerry, but nothing had to be proved from the driller's point of view; he was convinced. He was on the next Greyhound back to the relative safety of a Morgan City offshore oil rig in the hurricane belt.

Petty theft, lying, reflexive violence—Jerry was a juvenile delinquent. At fifteen, on the occasion of his killing a neighbor's dog by taping its mouth shut until it expired from overheating, his mother sent him to Artesia Hall. There was a name to conjure with in Texas schoolboy history. It sent chills through the spines of even hardcases like little Jerry Pugh. A school for "troubled" kids forty miles north of Houston in the middle of a dismal swamp full of alligators, snakes, and bobcats, it had a reputation for working wonders.

"Dr." Leo Murphy, the smiling, round-faced headmaster at Artesia Hall, could have sprung full-blown from Dickens's darkest imaginings. He was held up by his defenders as avatar of the honored Texas belief that it took good knocks to form character. The doctor in the privacy of the night in the middle of his swamp would instruct his charges by dragging them around by their hair and making them stand in garbage cans filled with ice water while staffers scrubbed them with wire brushes. Straitjackets for intractable cases. A lot of kids shaped up just to get sent home alive. Jerry, unable to grasp even the idea of shaping up, slipped away into the swamp and never saw the doctor or his mother again.

He lied about his age and joined the army. He got cashiered for chronic insubordination and suspicion of the rape of a townie. And after several years as an off-and-on grave digger and practically full-time mean drunk, he permanently maimed a hearse driver for repeatedly driving over his dirt piles. He tried to eviscerate the driver with his shovel and came close before he was pulled away. He was sent to Huntsville. He got out once and vio-ed himself back in before his parole papers reached Austin.

■ *EIGHT* ■

Gladys stepped into her slip and snapped her bra and cracked eggs into a skillet, almost in one motion. She salted, stirred, popped bread into the toaster all by rote. On the counter she lined up three lunch boxes and put the same thing in each one, a little assembly line—piece of fruit, jelly sandwich, dill pickle in waxed paper, thermos of milk, a few loose Good 'n' Plentys as a surprise.

From behind the fence through the opened screened windows, a pair of eyes watched Gladys work—watched as Phillip scuffed into the kitchen, dressed only in cotton briefs and a striped T-shirt.

The boy pulled butter from the fridge, dragged a chair from the kitchen table and performed one of his morning helper chores, buttering the toast for his mother.

The eyes moved closer to the house.

Gladys leaned down and gave Phillip a kiss on top of the head. "Thank you, Phillip. Go wake up your sisters." Phillip dutifully stepped down and padded back into the living room to wake the harpies.

Grabbing plates and silverware, Gladys spread them around the kitchen table. She straightened up and grabbed paper napkins from the sideboard.

"I like mine over easy," a voice said through the screen door. Gladys practically jumped out of her clothes—a face was pressed against the screen, a man brandishing a pistol. She collected herself as best she could, trying to catch her breath.

Jerry motioned for her to open the back door.

She went over to do so, eyeing the wall telephone on the way. The man slid in, looked around the room, and sat down at the kitchen table. "Coffee?" he said with a smirk.

Butch silently footed down a shadowed driveway and circled a shiny white Ford. He noticed over in the middle of the block one back porch light was on. The black of night was beginning to hint at the watery gray of dawn as he turned back and tried to jimmy the car door lock. He had no luck. He rose and looked off toward the light on the back porch. One street over, a screen door slammed and a dog gave a few happy barks as he ran into the yard for his morning business.

Jerry stuffed a piece of buttered toast into his mouth, grinned at Gladys, and made a motion to the counter. "Little on the bland side. Gimme that ketchup." He waggled a finger at the bottle on the sideboard. A grim-faced Gladys picked it up and held it out, leaning it toward him as though he were radioactive. When she got close enough, he grabbed her wrist and pulled her onto his lap with a snort of laughter. He laid the cold gun muzzle against her breast and nuzzled her soft hair back from her neck. He whispered in her ear, "Don't got a man around here, do ya?"

■ *NINE* ■

Fred Cummings, a seventy-year-old retired chemical plant worker who lived alone in the house behind, put on his glasses and reached the coffee can out of the fridge. He made his moves slowly, with hands that shook badly—legacy of years working with neuro-active chemicals at the pesticide companies down in Houston. As he measured out coffee, he glanced over at the Perry's house. He leaned closer to the window and looked again, all the while sprinkling coffee on the counter.

Gladys, trapped on the convict's lap with the .38 stuck in her side, submitted expressionlessly while he ran his other hand freely over her body, up under her bra. Her mind worked feverishly, looking for a way to ease this vicious parcel of unbalanced male chemistry out of her and her children's lives, as she'd had to do at other times, with other men.

"Feed me, sweet liberty," Jerry said and laughed, a man in hog heaven, a man who'd gone from bleak masturbatory fantasies to a live warm pliant woman on his lap in the space of hours. Gladys raised a forkful of eggs to his mouth. He licked around them lascivi-ously, then gobbled with gusto.

Phillip shuffled into the room and stopped dead in his tracks.

"Well, lookie here, you do got a man!" Jerry said, smiling at Phillip while he kissed Gladys's neck and licked around her ear. Phillip barrelled across the room and threw himself at Jerry, who backhanded him with the gun, sending him sprawling.

Butch blasted through the door in an instant. With a swift kick to the side of the head, he knocked Jerry senseless onto the floor against the cabinets.

The gun slid across the floor and landed at Phillip's feet. The boy stood frozen against the sink, watching the tall cropped-haired man in the white prison shirt and pants squint at him, pick up a piece of toast, turn it over, and take a delicate bite.

Gladys picked herself up and moved to the archway to the living room where Naomi and Ruth in their pjs had appeared. She gathered the groggy girls behind her, trying to back them out of the room.

"I'm bleedin'!" Jerry howled, sitting up, patting at his ear, looking at blood on his fingers. "You happy?"

Butch gave Jerry a short stare and knelt down to eye level with Phillip, who was still halfway across the room. Butch peered at the gun by his feet and then at Phillip. "What's yer name, boy?"

"Ph . . . Phillip." Properly scared shitless, trying not to burst into tears.

"Well, okay, Phillip," Butch said. "Reach down and pick up that pistola."

"Give it to me," Jerry piped up, rising to his knees, reaching out.

"Shut yer mouth," Butch said without turning to look at the younger con. To Phillip he said, "Pick it up and bring it over here."

The boy reached down and slowly picked up the gun by the handle. He took one step toward Butch, then another. Gladys, petrified, let out a sudden sob. Behind her, Naomi was whimpering and Ruth staring wide-eyed.

Phillip, knowing he'd fall apart if he looked at his mother, instead kept his eyes fixed on Butch's and proceeded forward. He arrived at arm's length from the man, holding the pistol out toward him by the handle.

"Now say 'Stick 'em up,' " Butch said with a serious tone.

Phillip hesitated, then said, "Stick 'em up . . ." And added, "Haynes"—reading the label stitched on Butch's prison-issue shirt.

Butch laughed out loud and sat back on his haunches. "Pretty good, kid," he said. "Pretty sharp."

A noise outside brought him back to his senses. He grabbed the gun from Phillip and spun to see Fred Cummings standing outside the screen door, shotgun more or less leveled, but shaking violently.

Before the old man could utter a syllable, Butch grabbed Phillip, yanked him close, and aimed the .38 at Cummings's face. Jerry jumped up and grabbed Gladys. Naomi started screaming. "Jeeeeeez . . ." Ruth said, finally getting scared.

"Put the gun down, old-timer," Butch said, lining up the .38. "You couldn't hit me anyway. You'd sure as hell shoot the boy."

The phone rang.

"Leave it be," Butch said, standing to full height, holding the boy at his side.

"Look here, you boys ain't gonna . . ." Cummings started.

"You deaf?," Jerry screamed, pushing Gladys in front of him as a shield. He was no reassuring sight with his eyes bugged out and blood running out one ear.

"Mama!" wailed Naomi.

"It's all right, honey," Gladys said in a trembling voice.

The phone continued to ring. Cummings, his shotgun vibrating in palsied spasms, looked from one con to the other, at a loss what to do. He knew he should do something, he had the firepower here. He'd regret ever afterwards if he blew this chance.

"Set it on the ground," Butch said in no-nonsense tones, pointing once, looking the old man straight in the eye. Butch Haynes generated maximum conviction at such moments with his unblinking stare. He'd have made a great platoon commander in the infantry—were there ever an army for incorrigible lone wolves. The old man obeyed, laying the firearm on the back porch with a clatter.

The phone was still ringing.

"Shut up!" Jerry yelled. In one fluid move he ripped the phone from the wall. The silence was deafening. Naomi whimpered again.

Jerry yanked Gladys with him toward the back door. "I vote we bring her with us." The old man stood like a statue outside the back door, watching, shaking.

"No," Butch said.

"How we gonna get outa here without a hostage, tell me that?" Jerry said. "The whole goddamn neighborhood's awake." He pointed at Fred Cummings. "We got Paul Revere with his dick in his hand."

Cummings narrowed his eyes at Jerry.

"We'll take the boy," Butch said. Silence. Gladys didn't register it. Then she did. She lunged forward. "Nooooooo!!!"

Jerry hooked her and flung her aside. She stumbled onto the floor and landed under the sink. The twin girls began instantly to howl.

Phillip wound up and slugged Butch as hard as he could. Butch picked him up, directed Cummings into the kitchen with a wave of the gun, and nodded for

Jerry to lead. The younger con bumped Cummings aside and slipped out the back door. Butch followed.

"You'll get him back," is all he said to Gladys. Carrying Phillip, he emerged from the house and raced after Jerry toward the Impala.

"Phillip . . ." Gladys cried, scrambling up and running after.

Butch flipped the gun to Jerry and stuffed Phillip into the front passenger seat. He leapt over the hood, grabbed Gladys, and laid her down firmly in the grass and slid into the driver's seat. He keyed the engine and the car surged forward with a squeal.

Neighbors, aroused by the uproar, came out of their homes clad in robes, pjs, curlers. Jerry leaned out and fired a shot over their heads, sending them to the deck or scurrying to safety inside. "Ain't you folks ever heard of sleeping in?" Jerry hollered. He fired another one for good measure, taking out a big plate-glass picture window where a light had just winked on.

Fred Cummings, armed with his over-and-under, locked and loaded and raced from behind the Perry house across the yard, determined to recoup. He squared away as the Impala raced by. Gladys screamed, "Noooo!" He fired a blast.

The side windows of the station wagon parked in front of him shattered and fell away like so many chiclets. The wagon's owners rose from their cover behind a bush and looked at Cummings in disgust. "Nice shootin', Fred," the man said.

Gladys ran a ways down the street after the car, but stopped. The Impala slowed, signaled properly for a left turn far at the end of the next block, and disappeared.

Gladys uttered a strangled cry and ran back to the house to her girls.

■ *TEN* ■

The sun was high and Texas Ranger headquarters was bustling—cops, civilian staffers, technicians and reporters. A prison break was always big news in Texas, where the tradition of cussed individualism bleeds into the myth of the larger-than-life outlaw. Billy the Kid lives on in Texas. Every fugitive, in the eyes of the story-hungry press, would be either a renegade folk hero in search of redemption or the meanest Big Bad John ever to fly over prison walls— until proven otherwise. The tale spinners were gathering in the briefing room to learn which opening slant to take on this fugitive story.

Red Garnett had on the same clothes as the night before, as he suspected he would for some time to come. "Yes, Johnny, I do understand that . . . ," he said into the phone while he shuffled through the files before him, looking for something.

Tom Adler, Red's deputy and boy Friday, warmed up Red's coffee with a jolt from the chief's favorite plaid thermos. Adler was a heavy-set, forty-five-year-old boy scout with crewcut hair whose top three values were loyalty to the chief, loyalty to the chief and, yes, well . . . The always helpful aide had more the look of a certified public accountant than a Texas Ranger, but his face was as amiable and approachable as Red's was chiseled and hard. His job was to run interference for the Chief, knock down the high hard ones before they took the boss's head off, and carry water at all other times.

Tom Adler was glad to do these things. He had lost both his parents in a house fire when he was five and had done his growing up in series of foster homes that were paid to keep him. He never felt like more than a boarder in those places, and in fact he wasn't. Now his home was the Texas Ranger barracks, and he loved it. One of the rare things that could scrape his bark off was an attack on the chief, frontal or sneak. Then the steel would come out, and Adler had been known to leave blood and patches of fur in his wake.

Now he reached into the pile on the desk and pulled out the two files the chief desperately needed.

The jabbering on the other end of the phone continued as Red squinted to read the files. The first was Jerry Pugh's, complete with grinning mug shot in the upper right-hand corner. Red traced a forefinger down the top rap sheet with practiced familiarity. Like a forensic archaeologist, he could put flesh on a man's life by looking at the bones of his crimes and punishments. He gave a quick glance through the accompanying narrative bio, presentencing summaries, and parole reports before turning to the next file.

Robert "Butch" Haynes, it said on the flap. Red scanned down the rap sheet . . . something familiar about it. He focused on the photograph—something definitely familiar. The quacking coming from the phone continued as deep memory synapses tried to reconnect. The rap sheet, the picture . . . the grim visage of a younger con facing hard time. Red knew this guy. It was coming back . . .

"Red? Red, you there?" came the voice over the phone.

Red kept staring at the photo, oblivious. Tom Adler leaned over and whispered, "Red?"

"Huh?" Red said to Adler, glancing at him.

"He's talkin' to ya," Adler whispered.

Red came to. "Yeah, John. Jus' thinkin' is all . . ."

Adler knocked his watch crystal with his knuckle and whispered again. "Press has been waiting almost an hour, Red."

The chief, trying to focus on the voice on the phone, was further distracted by someone standing expectantly in his door, waiting to be acknowledged. Red impatiently motioned her in—a young woman with giant blond curls and long legs—and nodded her to sit there on the couch with Chuck while he tried to finish the call. He pushed Adler's watch out from under his nose and looked at the file and jawed into the phone. "Yeah . . . clear as a bell . . . *Mi sabe*." He hung up the phone, took a draw on his coffee mug, and focused again on the file. He seemed lost in time.

Sally Gerber, the fashionably curly-headed visitor, was twenty-eight and attractive in a straightforward, no-nonsense sort of way. Maybe even pretty, if she ever wore any makeup, but definitely too round of face and baby-cheeked for someone who was dressed up as though, and acting as though, she was in the chief's office for business. The fact was, she was about to check in for a position if she could ever get Red's attention. She stared straight at him, waiting.

"What'd he say?" Adler asked.

"Who?" Red said, distracted.

"The guvner, Red," Adler said.

Red closed the file and looked up at Adler dyspeptically. "Reminded me it's an election year." He turned his attention to Sally. "You drink before noon?"

"Uh . . . no," she said, confused about what that might have to do with the price of eggs.

"Good," Red said. "Last one I had was on a liquid diet."

"Last what?" Sally asked, afraid she was getting the drift.

"Secretary."

"Penny Munroe," Adler added helpfully, nodding. "Tippler."

"I believe you have me confused," Sally said, sitting up straight on Red's couch, eliciting a growl from Chuck, the Lab. "I'm here from Huntsville, assigned by Governor Connally." She looked at Red expectantly, waiting for the dime to drop.

Red *was* confused. He turned a blank expression to his aide. "Adler . . . What is this?"

"Rings a bell, Red," Adler said, searching the cluttered desk for something, moving files around. "Believe they sent something about you this mornin' . . ." he said to the young woman. He gave her a glance while rifling through Red's things.

"Who sent?" Red said, annoyed at Adler's mess-making. He whacked at his hand, trying to make him stop. Adler pushed the chief's hand away and kept burrowing and came up with a telex message sheet.

"Guvner, Red," Adler said. "Here it is." He read the message himself. Red grabbed it from him with a scowl.

Sally, losing patience, weighed in. "I'm Sally Gerber, criminologist with the State Prison System." She leaned forward and offered her hand.

Red, perusing the telex with growing puzzlement, ignored it. Adler somewhat reluctantly stepped in and shook her hand—the gentlemanly thing to do, though he wasn't sure if he was supposed to like her or not.

"It's a relatively new procedure," Sally said, "but I was assigned by Governor Connally."

" '. . . to work with State law enforcement officials'," Red recited from the telex, " 'in all affairs where penal matters coincide with those of the State Police.' It don't say nuthin' about—"

"It includes parole and work-release programs as well as penal escape situations," Sally said.

Red looked at her with deep suspicion, which he was about to voice when the phone buzzed. Adler picked it up and spoke without even listening: "On our way, Marge."

He hung up the phone and turned to Red. "Gettin' antsy, Red," he said, grabbing Red's coat and string tie from a brass rung on the wall and handing them over. "You scheduled it. This a bread 'n' butter story for these boys. They're salivatin'."

Red took his coat from Adler and grumbled, "I know what's bread 'n' butter and what's gonna be too dead to skin. That's us if we get crosswise on this." He cinched his tie and hunched into his coat, staring at Sally the while, as if she might come into focus if he looked at her hard enough.

"The idea is," she started up again, "that an understanding of the particular behavioral case histories should, in parole situations, help the subject to avoid habitual traps. And, in penal escape situations, could conversely identify those selfsame traps as an aide to apprehension." She looked at Red with her most open expression.

Adler stared at Sally, then turned to Red with a "never heard the like" look of amazement on his face.

Red, snugging his perfecto buff-colored ten-gallon Stetson on at just the right angle and slipping a firearm inside his western-cut blazer, looked a sight more roguishly handsome than Sally had bargained for. She followed with her eyes as he started for the door. Before he got there, he turned back and fixed Sally with his trademark one-brow-cocked stare. "In the first place, Miss Gerber—"

"Sally, please," she said.

"—In the first place, Sally, it ain't a 'penal escape situation.' It's a manhunt. Fancy words twisted in circles don't do nuthin' to help."

"And what does?" Sally said.

"A nose like a Blue Tick, a medulla with an antenna, and one helluva lot of coffee." And with that, Red was out the door.

Sally watched him go, without moving a muscle, but Adler could see many wheels turning furiously inside.

▪ *ELEVEN* ▪

It was hardly spacious or posh, but it was only thanks to Chief Red Garnett that the press had a briefing room at all, with their own coffee urn and feed bin of kuchen and sticky buns. Texas journalists were like journalists the country over, but more so. They were chronically underpaid, underappreciated, and hungry as refugees. Feeding them before talking to them was halfway home in the struggle to get favorably angled stories. Red knew that as well as anybody. Red Garnett hadn't gotten to be chief because he was always, like today, late. He'd made chief because he'd figured out how to make people glad to see him when he did show up. With his arrival now they shouted his name and converged toward the podium as though he were John F. Kennedy himself.

"Listen up," he said, Stetson still impressively in place. "I'll only say it once. At approximately ten o'clock last night, two inmates over to Huntsville, Robert 'Butch' Haynes and Jerry David Pugh, escaped through an air shaft, grabbed a prison employee's car, and got out through the main gate. At approximately one A.M., we believe they robbed a market down the road from Madisonville and killed the store's owner."

A chunky seen-it-all-a-dozen-times reporter for the *Dallas Times Herald* named Aynsworth bellowed at Red. "Is the prison employee with them?"

"Was when they left the prison, Hugh," Red said. "Nobody at the Five Mile Market was alive enough, time we arrived, to say if he was there, too."

He pointed to a woman reporter who was calling his name.

"What's the rap sheet on these guys like?" asked Margaret Hunt of the *Austin Democrat*.

"Long as Christmas Eve to a kid," Red said cordially, in as good humor as the occasion allowed. "Haynes was doin' forty for armed robbery and Pugh was ridin' twenty hisself for attempted manslaughter and assorted parole vios—"

". . . Lemme finish, Billy," Red said. "This mornin' another hostage was taken . . . from a private home in Madisonville. A boy, age eight. Grabbed him off the breakfast table."

"Any sex offenses on Haynes or Pugh?" Aynesworth asked.

"Yer askin' if they're preverts," Red said. "Well, one is . . . Pugh. Raped a paper boy."

"Would there be any details available on that offense, sir?" a new young reporter named Jack Cowley asked nervously.

"There would not, sir," Red said. "Name suppressed on account of the victim's being a minor, and details withheld so's not to put a crimp in his comin' young manhood." Cowley buried his head and scribbled gratefully.

"Red, how do you plan to apprehend the escapees?" Margaret Hunt asked.

"Officially," Red said, "I can only say we have a full manhunt team on their trail, and we'll proceed with due haste."

Aynsworth of the *Dallas Times Herald* led the chuckle. "And unofficially?"

That was like putting it up on a tee for Ted Williams. They all waited. But Red hesitated—something bothering him.

"Unofficially," he said finally, "I'm gonna hunt 'em like the rabid dogs they are." He turned to go, and every hand in the place shot up and questions flew like bullets.

Red turned back to the lectern. "That's all I've got but I'd like to introduce ya to Miss Sally Gerber. She's straight from the governor's office. Knows all about psycho-logical profiles and the like. You prob'ly have some questions for her." He stepped to one side, then turned back to the lectern. "Jack, go easy on her." He bestowed a quick grin on the neophyte and walked out of the room.

Sally stood there, taken aback. Then she warmed to the idea and stepped smartly to the podium for her first press conference. Heck, she'd take on the tough questions. It was a chance to shine. She smiled out confidently at the crowd.

They looked back at her. Every raised hand dropped. Silence. Not a question. A few cocked their heads as though racking their brains. The pride of usually famished jackals was at a loss what to do with this . . . Shirly Temple.

Red, listening from a few yards down the hall, sighed and walked away.

In the press room a reporter near the back at last raised his hand and smiled.

Sally looked to him. "You have a question?"

"Yes I do," the reporter said. He was a dark eyed Texas Ranger type, lanky and handsome.

Sally smiled a bit and put on her serious face, waiting . . .

"What are you doin' tonight?" the reporter asked.

Sally, slapped in the face, glared at the guy and stomped from the room.

"I'm serious!" he called after her.

■ *TWELVE* ■

Butch tooled the Impala across the Texas afternoon with Phillip beside him, the boy still in his briefs and brown striped T-shirt. Jerry, in the backseat, gazed out the window like a kid on his first car ride, dreamy, checking everything out—tickled pink to be out here in the clear.

Both cons had got out of their prison whites into more suitable road clothes—jeans, T-shirts, plaid cotton sport shirts with short sleeves rolled. Clothes were the easiest things in the world to come up with if you're anywhere near a bus station. Butch and Jerry knew.

A short jog southwest, and Butch had pulled in around the corner from the Greyhound terminal on the Texas A&M campus in College Station. Jerry went in first. From among the sparse middle-of-the-night crowd, he picked a young guy his size with a duffel bag. He snatched up another duffel bag from a snoozer on the other side of the terminal, waited for the first guy to put his down, then switched and walked back to the car. Enough clothes in there for both him and Butch. They ditched the bag and their prison whites in a construction dumpster and headed back north.

BLAM! . . . Jerry, pistol aimed out the window, aimed and fired. A tall aluminum water tank sprang a violent leak. Jerry laughed like an eight-year-old.

"We got a handful of caps and yer shootin' water tanks," Butch said. "He's a smart guy, huh, Phillip?"

Phillip didn't move or change expression. The gunshot had yanked him brutally from a trancelike reverie he had sunk into where he was almost feeling safe.

Blam! Blam! Jerry fired twice more for the hell of it, this time inside the Impala, and exploded two holes

right through the roof. Jerry grinned and reached up
and gave Phillip's head a rough tousle. He reached
around the seat with both arms and commenced to
tickle the kid, trying to get a rise. Phillip looked
terrified, fighting back tears.

Butch reached over and shoved Jerry back in his
seat. Pugh sat weighing the gun, watching Butch's
eyes in the rearview. "What's yer beef?" he asked.
"We got us a hostage here, ain't we?"

Butch said nothing, just drove.

"You got any kids, Butchie boy?" Jerry asked, up
to something.

Butch gave him a flat look. "Tell me you do," he
said. The thought of little versions of this backseat
vermin made his skin crawl.

"Me, I'm too young and restless," Jerry said. He
poked Phillip's seat back with the gun. "Feature me
out in the yard tossin' the ol' pill around . . . You
though, Butchie . . ."

They rode in silence, Butch thinking. "Ever hear of
that co-ed prison? Fort Worth. Experimental prison?"

"I heard about that," Jerry said. "Didn't last too
long, did it."

"Why d'ya think?" Butch said. "I did some jailin'
there. We was like rabbits. We got so we could do it
under a leaf while guards were mowin' the lawn." He
snorted. "I mighta got one girlie too big for her
clothes."

Jerry gave a sly smile. "Well, there it is. You got a
little Phillip runnin' around somewhere, don'cha. That
explains somethin'. Daddy Butch."

"Nice try, Pugh," Butch said. "Two guards and
another short-timer were skinnin' her, too. Then the
prison made her take care of it. There ain't no little
Butch Haynes and there ain't ever gonna be. Not in
this world."

Pugh looked back and forth between Butch and the

boy. Okay, maybe barking up the wrong tree there. But still, Pugh didn't like the feel he was getting.

■ *THIRTEEN* ■

Red strode out of the rear door of his headquarters and headed toward a silver-bright Airstream mobile home parked at the back of the lot. Several reporters and photographers stationed by the back door sprang after Red, shooting questions. Adler stepped in, holding up his hands. "All right, that's it, boys," he said, bringing the onrush to a halt. "Chief's got work to do." He pointed inside. The reporters retreated obediently to the back door, but didn't go inside.

Adler caught up with Red as he moved over next to the mobile home, walking along it, checking it out. Checking out the big red GMC pickup truck attached to pull it.

Arch Saunders, a fifty-year-old sharp dresser and full-time smiler, stuck his hand out to Red. Saunders was a special aide to the governor in charge of everything—picking up the governor's dry cleaning, arranging private conferences in the Bahamas with devoted constituents, arranging key political events like President Kennedy's fence-mending trip to Dallas coming up next month.

"So whattaya think?" Saunders asked, presenting the mobile home for Red's consideration. It was trimmed in red, white, and blue banners and bunting. On the front, sides, and back were large decaled plaques—the governor's special Lone Star seal.

Saunders followed Red as the tall man walked around the showpiece, rapping the paneling, kicking a tire.

"Uh-huh," Red said.

Saunders motioned for the governor's personal photographer to move in closer and get pictures. Saunders moved in tight to Red and posed as the camera clicked.

"We are very proud of this baby," he said. "Governor Connally special ordered it so state officials and dignitaries can ride in the parade in Dallas. You know President Kennedy's coming?"

"So I hear," Red said. So everybody in the state had heard.

"Latest technology," Saunders said proudly. "Oversize engine in the pickup, completely stocked kitchen and sleeping quarters, gun racks, fridge, stove, built-in hi-fi with custom speakers—the works. Even got a hot-line phone straight to the governor's office. Never out of touch with the machinery of government. Like Kennedy's got that briefcase so he can tell SAC to pulverize Moscow in seconds." He laughed heartily—nothing like power.

Red gave the vehicle a kind of seal-of-approval pat. "Fine piece of machinery," he said, and nodded to Adler, who scurried away.

"What's more," Saunders said with enthusiasm, "soon's it gets back from Dallas, it will be at your requisitioned disposal. They call it a Recreational Vehicle, but it's perfect for lots of situations—headquarters on wheels."

Red smiled, ambled over to one of the banners, and ripped it off. "We'll take it," he said.

"Uh, Chief? . . ." Saunders said.

Red ripped off another banner and headed around toward a third.

"I think you misunderstood, Chief," Saunders said, "I meant to make it clear that—hey what the hell? . . ."

Adler and three or four other deputies were packing equipment, guns, and files out of the building, across the parking lot, and into the mobile home. They were

coming back out of the mobile home with the unnec-
essary stuff cluttering up the inside—mattresses,
throw pillows, a circular hassock-footstool thing. The
men stacked the excess stuff in a pile in the parking
lot.

The energetic young official photographer continued
taking pictures—joined now by a couple of enterpris-
ing news photogs and several smiling reporters who
were all smelling one of Red's famous one-sided dust-
ups. Red decided to do something, people screamed
and flopped in the dirt and cried—Red let 'em, then
went on with his doing.

Another of Saunders's aides, a bright-eyed cow-
licked country-boy type named Dick Suttle, was evinc-
ing severe misgivings. He paced from the driver's
compartment of the pickup back to the open door of
the trailer, then back to the front—watching every
move anxiously.

"Whattaya doin', Red?" Saunders bleated. He
lunged at the photographer. "Stop taking pictures!"

Red did away with a parade banner along the vehicle's right flank. Saunders, hustling along behind, tried
to reinstate it. "It's jus' not possible, Red," he said.
"The governor's gonna ride it in a campaign parade
tomorrow. Kinduva shake-down cruise so to speak."

"Guvner hisself," Red said, "told me this manhunt
was top priority."

Adler came out of the building, carrying Red's favorite desk chair. He was followed by a law enforcement officer none of them knew, a good-looking, crop-
haired cop in his late twenties. Too good-looking, with
graceful, athletic moves, cocksure. His name was
Bobby Lee. He appeared to be a civilian—dark suit,
white shirt, narrow tie.

"S'cuse me," Adler said, stepping between Saunders and Red by the door to the silver trailer. To Red
he said, "This here's Bobby Lee. The F.B.I. sent him
over. Said you called in for a specialist."

Red nodded to the cocky young man, who nodded back once. Red knew what kind of specialist he'd ordered up, knew what Bobby Lee's know-how was and why they needed it. Wasn't anybody else's place to ask, and Bobby Lee sure wasn't volunteering anything. He just looked all-knowing and stepped up into the motor home, carrying a leather case as his only baggage.

"Please, Red," Saunders said, "you gotta believe me . . ."

Red looked up and saw the cow-licked Suttle getting in the driver's seat of the GMC pickup.

"Who are you?" Red asked.

"Dick Suttle," said the young man, round-eyed and bushy-tailed, "the driver."

"Not anymore." Red said. "Bradley."

Bradley, a tall, lean Texas Ranger, was a bit older and a lot less bushy-tailed than Suttle, and deeply devoted to motorized transport. A childhood accident had turned him away from his first love, horses. He moved to the front of the Airstream.

Suttle shrugged, but looked sorely wounded. He got out begrudgingly and moved to step away. Saunders grabbed him and stopped him. "This man stays with the vehicle wherever it goes, Red! He lives with the machine."

Red peered at Suttle. "You know how to operate the gadgets?"

"Yessir."

"Grab a seat," Red said. He walked back to the living compartment and put a leg up, about to board. Sally came chugging from the building, weighed down with two file boxes, making a beeline for Red. She was ticked off about something.

Saunders quickly made a final plea. "Please, Red. "I'm beggin'. I mean, what am I supposed to tell the governor?"

Sally arrived next to Red, loaded for bear . . . but

before she could spit out a word, Red spoke. "Tell John that Miss Gerber here checked me out on it." Red whistled and the engine revved. Red stepped into the vehicle, flipped the steps up, and pulled the door closed—Sally and Saunders standing there watching. The motor home pulled away.

"Not a scratch! You hear me, Suttle?" Saunders yelled, running beside the passenger-side window. "Not a scratch!" Suttle stared at him out the window.

Saunders stopped, breathing hard. Sally stalked up next to him, burning, overloaded with files.

The motor home stopped about twenty yards down the way. The door opened, and the steps popped out. Sally walked toward the vehicle, but just as she arrived at the door the sound of laughter filtered out of the interior and the vehicle slid forward another twenty feet.

Sally blew the hair out of her eyes and waited to see what these juveniles would do. She cautiously started forward, the file boxes getting heavier by the minute.

When she got close, the RV started creeping forward again. Sally, boiling mad, her golden curls wilting in the scalding Texas sun, stopped and crashed her file boxes to the ground.

The recreational vehicle stopped—laughter from inside and a few unintelligible jokes. Somebody said, "Okay, okay!" followed by more laughter.

Red stepped out the door, turned his gaze back inside, and the laughter and comments stopped on a dime. Smiling slightly, he turned to Sally, walked to the file boxes, picked them up, and walked back to the motor home. At the steps he turned and looked to Sally, who was stewing, holding her ground. "You comin' or not?" Red asked.

Sally hesitated only a moment before walking straight to Red, grabbing back her file boxes and entering in front of him.

Inside, balancing her boxes, Sally glared at the faces

turned up toward her full of the most innocent looks. Adler hid his grin behind the act of messily gorging on the cinnamon roll. In the corner a nasty smirk from the unknown Bobby Lee. And following up, a smiling Red.

Bradley stuck his gas foot on it and the vehicle took off. Sally lost her balance, and one of her boxes bounced to the floor. Adler and Bobby Lee both jumped forward to lend her a hand, but she gave them the evil eye.

"I've got it," she said levelly. She knelt down to retrieve the file box and felt eyes on her. She turned to see the gaze of all the men fixed on her raised skirt, her exposed bit of thigh. She calmly stood up and looked at Adler, who had a piece of cinnamon roll dangling on his chin. "You've got shit on your face," she said.

Bobby Lee guffawed as Adler wiped at his face. Red couldn't help but smile as he walked back to his office at the rear.

▪ *FOURTEEN* ▪

The Impala blasted along a country road, kicking up dust and dispersing crows through never-ending farmlands. This eastern reach of the Blackland Prairie had just yielded up a particularly rich fall harvest. The growers hunkered fat in their homes, laying aside seed and machinery money for next year and apportioning considerable remaining chunks of cash to the retirement kitty and the winter-trip-to-Memphis kitty, or maybe even the New York-to-see-some-shows kitty. It had been a year to savor for these farmers and family folk and their hired hands. None of them had an inkling of the peril pounding along the dirt roads in their direction. Most of them wouldn't even feel the cold wind as it passed and blew on into the next county. Some would.

Phillip had never been this far from home. Truth be told, he was enjoying, in a petrified way, a sudden strange feeling of freedom. The unfolding farms and fields were a boy's kaleidoscope, and nobody'd said no to him for a whole day.

"You know what run up through here a hundred years ago, Phillip?" Butch said as they tracked up a broad valley.

"Dinosaurs?"

Butch chuckled. "I mean this road we're followin'. Was part of the Dodge City cattle trail. Right up through here—thousands of cattle on their way to Kansas."

A silence. Pugh was snoozing in the back. Phillip stared on up the highway. "I guess I'm gonna be ready to go home soon," Phillip said.

Butch looked at him—scrawny kid still in his skivvies. "Soon. But not yet, Phillip," he said. "We got some things to do yet."

The Impala came up fast on a one-light township. It slowed before the main part of town and slid to a stop near a pay phone booth.

Jerry lurched upright in the back. "Why the hell we stoppin'?"

Butch looked at him in the rearview. "You said you had a cousin near here."

"So?"

"So give him a call. See if we can shack there till things cool down."

Jerry thought deep about this suggestion for a few seconds, then leaned forward and in one quick swipe snatched the keys from the ignition. He laughed raucously and crawled out of the car, then sauntered to the phone booth.

"Why'd he take the keys," Phillip asked, watching Jerry pore through the thin town directory.

"So I won't leave him," Butch said through gritted teeth, watching the highway in the mirror.

Even Phillip recognized this as an interesting idea. "Would you leave him?" he asked, a tad hopefully.

"Oh yeah," Butch said matter-of-factly.

Jerry ripped the twenty-page phone book in half, slammed out of the phone booth, and strutted back to the car, a sour smirk on his face. He slid in and tossed the keys to Butch. Butch looked at him—useless. They drove off.

"Musta' moved," Pugh said. "Prolly couldn't'uv heard 'em anyway. Goddam ear's still bleedin'." He gingerly touched his sore ear. "You ever try that shit again—"

"What?" Butch said sharply.

"What?" Pugh said.

"You were in the middle of threatening me."

"Ain't a threat. It's a fact." Jerry'd been waiting a year to use that movie line. He fixed his mouth in the proper leer.

Butch reached over, took Phillip's hand, and put it on the steering wheel. "Here kid, take the wheel."

Phillip, freaked at the prospect, nonetheless hunched up and did his best to see over the dash and keep the wheel straight.

Butch turned back over the seat to confront Jerry. "In two seconds I'm gonna break your nose. That's a threat." Before Jerry had time to get out a complete snicker, Butch hit him full in the face and grabbed the gun. Blood spurted from Jerry's nose. The injured con cupped his hands over the wounded organ.

Butch spun and took the wheel back from a frightened Phillip. ". . . And that's a fact."

Jerry might have risen up in outrage, and flesh and

fur would fly while the car went careening end over end into a ditch—kind of what Phillip was holding his breath against. Instead, Jerry slunk back down in his seat, little boy like, wearing a look of pure hatred. "I'm gonna kill you for that," he said.

"And that's a threat," Butch said. "Beginnin' to understand the difference?"

Hard to say with Jerry. He was too busy mopping to talk—blood down his chin onto his shirt, blood oozing anew from his ear. One thing was certain. Evil rage was mushrooming wildly in the dark, looking to vent.

The Impala suddenly braked. An isolated rural store tucked in the corner of a giant corn field caught Butch's eye. He pulled in the dusty turn-out.

"Okay, Phillip, listen up," Butch said. "I'm gonna run in here and get some smokes."

"Get beer," Jerry said sullenly through his hands.

"Here," Butch said, handing Phillip the revolver. "Hold it like this . . ." He wrapped the boy's small hand around the grip and put the forefinger where it could do some harm. "And point it right between his eyes."

"What the hell?" Jerry said, dropping his hands, letting blood run out on his pants.

"If he so much as moves, you pull the trigger," Butch said to Phillip. "Here, keep your finger on it."

Jerry started snickering, then laughing maniacally, his head thrown back. Butch reached over and cocked the .38. Jerry's head snapped up and his guffaws stopped short. "Yer a fuckin' crazy man!" he yelled at Butch.

"And that's a fact," Butch said. "I believe yer gettin' the hang of this." Butch stepped out of the car, reached back in, and realigned Phillip's gun right at Jerry's nose. He admired the angle, then stepped away and disappeared into the store.

■ *FIFTEEN* ■

Butch passed under a weathered sign over the door on the little store that said UVALDE SUPER MARKET. Inside it was half a dozen narrow aisles with almost nothing on the shelves—wrapper bread, Chef Boyar-dee spaghetti, Tru-Aide orange soda, Laredo white beans. No attendant. Butch looked around, waited, finally yelled. "I'm payin'!"

"Jesus Kee-ryst!" The short man behind the counter lurched to his feet. He'd been there all along under a wide-brimmed fishing hat. "You learn to talk in a sawmill?"

"Where's yer sodees?" Butch asked.

"Hot over by the front window. Cold in the back, in the cooler," the short man said. "I make gourmet sand'iches," he added hopefully.

"What kind?" Butch said skeptically as he rummaged through the cooler.

Phillip's slightly shaking hands held the pistol pointed directly at Jerry's head.

"You ever shot a gun before, boy?" Jerry asked. "A real one?"

Phillip gave no answer. He concentrated hard on his task, then stole a glance at the store, anxious for Butch to return.

"Powww! . . ." Jerry said. "Real gun'll knock you flat on your ass. Plain powerful. Ain't no BB-gun."

"Be quiet, mister," Phillip said in a tight voice.

"Naw, you ain't never shot no gun before," Jerry said. "Livin' in a house with three split tails . . . no Daddy around. You'll prolly grow up queer, you know that?"

A bead of sweat rolled down Phillip's cheek. Queer he wasn't sure of—it was bad, he knew that much. But daddy taunting at school was the one thing made him feel sick. He wasn't going to fold now, though.

"Now I'm gonna lean up real slow, okay?" Jerry said, raising his hands and tilting slowly forward. "So we can talk." He edged up off the backseat.

Phillip's hands trembled, his business finger tightened. He felt he owed it to somebody to pull the trigger if the man pushed too far. He wasn't clear who he owed it to—Butch?—his mother?

"There we go," Jerry said. "Now we can have a man to man. You are a man, ain't ya?"

Inside the Uvalde Market Butch dumped a six-pack of RC Colas, a half dozen Moon Pies, a fistful of beef jerky, and some gum on the counter. The owner, with the euphonious name of Alphonse LaRue Shales, known as Alf, pushed forward a platter of ready-mades—roast beef, sausage, tongue sandwiches on hard rolls. "All with my special guacamole vinaigrette," Alf said. He waved the horseflies away and beamed. Butch lifted the hard roll and squinted at the tongue—bone dry, shriveled, blackening around the edges. He gave Alf a level look. The man shrugged and whisked the sandwiches under the counter.

Jerry's chin rested on the front seat of the Impala and his arms were draped over onto Phillip's side. "Those are cute little underwears you got there, boy." Jerry grinned. "Say, does your mama sew yer name in 'em, initials or anything?" Jerry's hand slowly reached down to the white briefs.

Phillip's hands were shaking, but the .38 did not waver from the man's face. The boy's jaw firmed into a hard line.

Jerry snaked one finger in the front elastic waistband and slowly pulled it open. "What'cha got in there?" he asked.

Phillip did not look down, but he looked seriously close to unglueing.

Jerry, holding out the waistband of the briefs, sneaked a peak. "Kinda' puny, ain't it?" he said, looking hard at the thing.

Phillip looked straight down. Jerry in a flash grabbed the gun and had it reversed and pointing at Phillip's nose by the time the boy looked back up.

"The hand is quicker than the eye," Jerry said, flicking open the gun to check. He spun the barrel—empty slots.

"That sonofabitch," he said. "Hell's bells, no shells."

Butch put several more items on the counter.

"That be all for ya?" owner Alf asked.

"This and a carton of Chesterfields," Butch said. He looked up at the shelf behind the counter. "Are those .38 shells? Gimme a box."

The owner put the shells and Chesterfields on the counter, stubbed out his own cigarette, and tallied with yellowed fingers on a notepad. "That comes to four dollars eighty, with deposit."

Butch reached in his jeans pocket and pried out the wad stolen from the convenience store. Alf took note. Butch selected a five and placed it on the counter.

"Land's sake," the man said, bagging the goods. "What line of work you in?"

Butch picked up the shells and put them in his pocket. "Used cars," Butch said. "Buy 'em, fix 'em up. Sold a Cadillac down in Madisonville this mornin'." He gave the owner a pretty fair business-man-to-businessman smile.

The man smiled back. "Don't say."

Jerry had Phillip in the backseat with him, gun hand around the boy's neck. He pulled the sobbing boy to him and rested his face on the boy's neck. "Come over a little closer," Jerry said and groaned. Phillip seized the moment, twisted, and bit Jerry as hard as he could on the ear. The con screamed and dropped the gun. Phillip grabbed it up, lunged for the car door, and scrambled out. He ran howling, gun and all, into the corn field.

Jerry, both ears now bleeding, pain aggravating his every move, crawled out of the backseat and staggererd toward the field.

Phillip, sobbing, swiping away the tears that were obscuring his vision, ran for his life through the tall corn—taller than he was by a foot. He plunged forward, sure he had to keep running or die.

Jerry was now in stride, grinning maniacally, cutting through the field. He stretched up and searched, whistling as if summoning a lost puppy. "I'm gonna find you, boy," he called. "You best come here."

Phillip caught his foot and fell, then lost his grip on the gun. He scrabbled around looking for it, found it, got himself up and running—and running—interminably. He fell again and couldn't get up, worn out, done. Tears coursing down his face, he balled up on the ground, trying to make himself invisible.

Butch, coming out of the store with his grocery sack, saw the car doors open. He dumped the sack in the front seat and looked to the field. He saw the corn rustling far out in the middle, flashes of the top of Jerry's head. Butch took off at an angle at high speed.

Jerry stood his ground, listening, heard nothing. He moved forward, crouching, eyes peeled for the small form.

Phillip lay still. He heard the corn stalks rustling at a distance, closer, then nearby. He turned slowly toward the sound, squared his body, and pointed the revolver, finger squeezing . . .

Butch's face appeared through the corn stalks. He motioned for the boy to stay put, then held his hand

out for the gun. Phillip passed it over and watched as
Butch dug in his jeans pocket . . .

Jerry, frustrated, kept stalking, searching with his
eyes. "Hey, boy. Hey, boy," he whispered. "You
better hope I don't find ya." He spotted something—
a dash of color—and began to crawl faster on all fours.
He punched through a thick thatch of hay and looked
into the barrel of the .38 and the eyes of—

Butch, squatting on one knee, leveling the revolver,
and squinting down the gun sight with one eye closed.

Jerry froze like an animal caught in headlights, then
laughed. "What'ch gonna do? Bop me with it?"

Butch opened his free hand and showed fresh-
bought cartridges from the box. Jerry's grin dropped.

"Butch, come on!" Jerry pleaded. "Me'n you are
friends!"

"Thick as thieves," Butch said.

Phillip ran for his life back toward the store. Many
yards behind him in the cornfield, he heard the harsh
pop of a single gunshot.

■ *SIXTEEN* ■

Phillip ran to the car and hid behind the tire opposite
the store and field. He scrunched his back against the
tire and hugged his knees.

Across the way Butch emerged from the field, walking purposefully, a job done, on to the next thing. He
looked around for the kid.

Merchant Alf, having heard the gunshot, came out
to see, armed and ready with a baseball bat.

Butch, arriving at the car, spun on the old man and

leveled the revolver at him. "You got a phone?" he asked.

"Naw," the man said, letting the bat fall to the ground, holding his arms out away from his side in as submissive a manner as he could manage from a standing position.

"Then go inside and lie down till we're gone," Butch said.

Alf spun on his heel and did so smartly, no argument here. The door closed behind him and a big CLOSED sign appeared as if by magic in the window.

Butch walked around to the driver's side and saw the shivering Phillip hunched by the back wheel. "Well . . . Get in," he said.

Phillip, relieved to be riding with Butch and not Jerry, crawled in under the steering wheel and huddled by the far door.

The Impala pulled back on the highway and headed out in the direction of the setting sun.

The Governor's Special, now the Red Garnett Special, barrelled up Ranch Road 39 roughly in the direction of the Confederate Reunion Grounds at Tehuacana. Not that the escaped cons were headed there, but Red had instincts about the kinds of roads and the general drift guys like these were likely to follow when they bolted north-wise out of Huntsville.

The Airstream was now a humming, functioning mobile headquarters for Texas law enforcement. In the GMC pickup truck Red's man, Bradley, piloted, but riding shotgun at his elbow, flinching at every swerve, watching every reaction of the Airstream behind, was Saunders's man, Suttle.

Back in the Airstream, Adler was monitoring the shortwave radio with headphones and was simultaneously tacking up a detailed Texas road map. Bobby Lee sat inscrutably in his corner.

Sally wrote notes to herself on a legal pad at the

"kitchen" table. In the rear section Red sat in his designated chair before a table—his minioffice.

"Got a spot on 'em," Adler called from his short-wave station. He listened. "A store right outside of Ben Hur. About twenty miles from here." Adler set down the hand mike and stuck a tack in the map and stood back.

"All right," Red said, walking forward. "Push the roadblocks on I-35, 84 and 6 to the north and west by fifty miles."

"Ya figure they're that far along?" Adler asked.

"Hell, I dunno and neither do they," Red said. "They're jus' happy to be out. It's a high-speed Sunday drive to them."

"Sunday drive," Adler chortled as he sat back to start transmitting messages to the roadblock crews. "I like that. Never heard you use that one before, Red."

Sally, watching Red's every move, had a troubled look on her face. Red noticed.

"Somethin' eatin' you?" he asked.

"It's . . . perhaps premature," she ventured, "but do you have an auxiliary roadblock plan for when they split up? Say south on 6, south out of Waco on 81?"

Everyone stared. Bobby Lee looked askance under his eyelids. Nobody *ever* questioned Red Garnett.

Adler turned from his electronic gear. "What makes you so sure they won't stay together?"

Sally hesitated. Red waited, a touch annoyed, like the rest of them. "You got somethin' to say," he said, "spit it out."

Gathering herself, Sally spit it out. "Their situation is one of accommodation. They won't be together long."

Silence.

Sally continued. "Haynes and Pugh are opposites," she said. "Haynes is a criminal's criminal—armed robbery, mano y mano confrontation, what his sort thinks of as stand-up stuff. Pugh on the other hand has a rap sheet littered with molestation and petty crime. Sneaky, sleazy, slipping-around crimes for the most part. They'll split sheets soon."

"They got hostages," Adler said, submarining her theory. "They gonna flip a coin to see who gets who?"

Red walked to the sink. He rinsed a cup and a spoon.

"It's happened before," Sally said. "Who knows what exactly will happen, but it's a dilemma they'll address soon." She looked over at Red's back. "That's why we should address it now."

Red turned, drying the cup with a dish towel, looking over Sally's head out the window instead of meeting her expectant gaze. After a couple beats he said, "*We* don't have a dilemma. And neither do they. They'll keep one hostage . . . and get rid of one if they haven't already."

"Okay, two are hard work to handle," Sally said. "Which one do you get rid of?"

"If they run into a snafu—a trap, a standoff," Red said, still not looking at her, "who's John Q. Public more likely to give a rat's ass about? An innocent boy or a goddamn bureaucrat?" He put the cup back in the cupboard and hung up the dish towel, the slightly impatient expression on his face saying, Why am I saddled with Criminology 101 in the middle of a manhunt? He picked up the spoon and dried it on his shirt as he walked back toward his office.

The others chuckled with varying degrees of relish at their boss's handling of this female upstart in their midst. Sally's face glowed a bright red. Her eyes tracked the tall man like a rifle scope, all the way to the back of the RV.

▪ *SEVENTEEN* ▪

Red, in his office chair, poured Geritol from a bottle into his coffee and stirred it with the clean spoon. He didn't even look up when Sally appeared in front of his table. Her hair was pulled back, a stern expression on her face.

"We need to talk, Chief Garnett," Sally said.

"Call me Red," he said, stirring, not looking up.

"Red." She glared at the top of his graying head. "Why are you so hell-bent on embarrassing me?"

Of all conversations on earth, this was Red's least favorite sort. He would prefer sticking bamboo shoots under his fingernails. He did not have the knack. Twice in his life he had approached the doors of matrimony only to fall back when he failed to successfully negotiate the shoals of a key heart-to-heart. He tried. There were kinds of things he could say and kinds of things he couldn't. The women saw into the future and sent Red home to his Hill Country domicile to spill it all to his dog.

"I'm hell-bent on one thing," he said testily. "You hang around long enough you'll find that out. Till then a tough backside and a sense of humor will get you through a lot." He studied the whirlpool in his coffee.

"I have a fine sense of humor," she shot back. "But the one thing I won't do is be your straight man so you can play hero to a bunch of morons who think you're some kind of hillbilly Sherlock Holmes."

Red, taking it calmly, sipped his Geritol-laced coffee . . . and groaned, his face contorted. "Awful," he said. "Arthur Godfrey says it keeps ya young—I'm not sure it's worth it."

"Did you hear a word I said?" Sally demanded.

At last he looked his tormenter in the face. "Yes, I did," he said.

"Good. I'd like an answer." The comely woman's face was red with indignation, several sweaty golden ringlets flying free.

"What was that question?" Red asked matter-of-factly.

A strangling noise jumped from her throat. "Aghh!" she said. "It's like driving a swarm of bees through a snowstorm with a switch! Why are you trying to embarrass me?"

"What'd ya expect ya signed on for?" Red said.

Sally turned and saw Adler and Bobby Lee watching intently, enjoying the hell out of this. She abruptly closed the partition and squared off with Red.

"You think I'm what?" she asked. "Some dumb schoolgirl who wandered into the boy's locker room? Well, you're wrong. I don't mean to boast, but I happen to be one of the two most intelligent people involved in this fiasco."

Red eyed her appraisingly. "I didn't ask your IQ, girl. Asked what you expected."

"I expected to be allowed to do the job assigned to me by the governor." She stood over Red with the look of eagles.

Red appreciated at least that about her, the grandeur of her female hauteur. Some women could pull it off. "Now the governor," he started, "I happen to like the governor, hunt quail with him every year. But deep down he and I know that win, lose, or draw this is my ship, not his." He sat back in his chair and put his boots up on the table, boot soles in her face. It was a test. A man in Texas would take that as an affront, a challenge. He'd either knock the offender's boots off the desk or finesse it, walking around the desk and sitting on it next to the feet. If he didn't have the chops to do either, he'd have to walk out.

Sally didn't do any of the above. She just went on declaring, "The governor as chief executive officer of this state bears ultimate responsibility for—"

"Bullshit," Red said, taking his boots down off the desk; if she didn't recognize the game, what fun was it? "Responsibility lies with the one that loses sleep, the one with the most ulcers. This mess turns bloody— and it might—all it's gonna cost the governor is a few votes! Me, I'm the one that's . . ." He caught himself about to get too personal and stopped. He took another swig of his youth brew and grimaced.

Sally picked up on his discomfort over what he was about to say. "You're the one that's what?" she said, softening her tone ever so slightly.

Red sidestepped. "Tell ya what," he said. "You think I'm makin' a wrong turn you speak up. Might not agree, but I'll listen. As far as stepped-on toes and wounded pride, I'll buy everyone a drink when we head for home. Not until. I got more to worry about." He stood up. "That sound fair to you?"

"Yes," Sally said.

"Well, okay then," Red said, looking down at her.

Sally turned to leave, reaching for the door.

"So who's the other one?" Red asked, head tilted up, looking down his nose at her expectantly.

"Other one?" she said.

"If yer one brain," he said, "who's the other?"

"Haynes," Sally said. "He was tested in prison."

Red didn't change expression. She looked at him and walked out.

▪ *EIGHTEEN* ▪

Once out of Ben Hur it was ranch roads and county spurs all the way across to just north of Gatesville, where Butch jumped onto State Route 36 and blasted north. Small woodlands alternated with prairies; buf-falo grass and bluestem surrendered to shinnery and Black Jack oak. To a sheltered eight-year-old it was a smorgasbord, a world unseen, and Phillip was trying hard to decide if he ought still be too scared to enjoy himself. Between swigs of RC—never RC at home; cider, OJ and milk, none of which had been offered him this day—between hits of RC, Phillip stole glances at his captor.

Butch peeked over at Phillip occasionally, too, and when the boy finished off the bottle, Butch reached in the sack for another, popped the top on the dashboard and handed it over.

"Thankyew," Phillip said. He took a slug. "You gonna shoot me?"

"No," Butch said. "Me'n you are friends." Butch could tell from the look in Phillip's eyes that the boy considered that a mixed blessing. Phillip had to assume Butch and Jerry were friends. "If I was choosin' a runnin' buddy, I'd take you over Jerry Pugh any day of the week."

"You shot him?" Phillip asked. He watched Butch over the upturned RC bottle. They were just passing a four-corners where a bunch of kids Phillip's age were milling around a school bus.

"Yes, I did," Butch said.

A long silence. They drove on through untenanted dust-blown fields. Butch had a sense of the boy's bleak uncertainty. Hell, he remembered. His mother off with men, with strangers, consigning him to a girlfriend or to a public park for an afternoon or a movie that made no sense to him. Spending whole days with his mother and a man who never spoke to him, who sat across from him in a diner and talked and laughed with his mother and never so much as acknowledged his existence.

The sight of this ragamuffin Phillip sitting there stiffly with his kitchen-scissors haircut and forlorn underwear had childhood incidents scrolling out of

Butch's brain that even the blank days of jailing hadn't let loose.

"Hey," he said. "Ya know how you can tell yer in Texas?"

"How?" Phillip said. He looked over at Butch. A good joke is gold to an eight-year-old.

"Well," Butch said, "ya go west till you smell shit. Then ya know yer in Oklahoma. Go south till you step in it, then ya know yer in Texas." He watched the boy.

No laugh, but a smile. And silence. "Pretty good," the boy said at last.

Butch had scored. He could tell Phillip was committing it to memory for school telling. Any joke with poop or pee or butt in it was a sure laugh for a boy his age.

"Why did the guy from Oklahoma cut a hole in his umbrella?" Phillip said.

"I don't know," Butch said deadpan. "Why?"

"So he could see if it was raining," Phillip said.

Butch gave a short laugh, Phillip a broad smile. They drove on into the heart of Texas.

■ *NINETEEN* ■

The Law Enforcement special motor home slid to a stop in the gravel parking lot of the Uvalde Super Market outside Ben Hur. The big vehicle joined state and local police cars and milling officers and onlookers. The door swung open, the steps came down, and Red descended into the hot afternoon sun. He advanced a few steps and put his Stetson on. His seconds emerged after him and stood a respectful distance behind.

Striding up to meet Red was the local law, head high, proud as a peafowl with two tails. He stuck out his hand, making no move to strip off the standard opaque aviator shades. "T. Ray Hutcherson, Limestone County Sheriff," he said. He was a big rangy Texan, a handsome specimen but middle-aged, going soft around the gut. Red noticed the man wore four different flashlights around his middle. He decided not to draw attention to it.

"We got a positive I.D.?" Red asked.

"Positive as you can get," Sheriff T. Ray said. He tilted back on his heels and got his fingers out and ready to tick off the items. "There's the .38 shells he purchased and the piece he showed. There's the eyewitness description"—he hooked a thumb at Alf Shales sitting mopping sweat from his head by the market door. "The car, of course. And the boy. Just the one hostage now, but he's the one all right. Little Billy-Bob 'bout yay-high, and no trousers. Lookin' miserable, but no signs of foul play."

Sheriff T. Ray took his time lighting himself a cigarette, relishing the moment. He plainly had more to tell, and Sally, all ears and impatience, started forward to urge the blowhard on. Adler grabbed her arm, pulled her back, and froze her with a look.

Red knew better than to hurry a good ole boy like this. It'd just hurt his feelings and he'd likely get sulky.

"We don't get important crimes too often," T. Ray said, taking a meaningful puff. "Mostly car theft and cow tippin'. And you know cow tippin' is nigh hard to get a conviction on, less'n the perpetrators actually kill the cow they tip *and* get caught at it." He chuckled dryly, knowing that Red and all the other boys listening knew that happy combination was rare, knew it was a thankless crime to investigate. "We tried fingerprints," T. Ray said, "but you try liftin' fingerprints off a cow." He chortled.

"Now the present matter," the lawman said, "is

crime worth investigatin'." His manner brightened. "Not five minutes before y'all drove up," he said, getting to the part he'd been saving, "we found somethin' else."

Using one of his quartet of flashlights as pointer, T. Ray ran the beam, barely visible in the bright sun, from a fingertip up the arm and to the face of Jerry Pugh, lying still in the gently moving cornfield. A clean bullet hole had given Pugh a third eye and extinguished his largely unpleasant sojourn on the planet. His anguish could not have stretched more than a couple of heartbeats; his execution had been swift and nearly painless—far nearer to painless than the evisceration he had performed with his shovel on the hearse driver years before.

T. Ray brushed the late-summer flies away from the neat bullet hole. "Pretty as a new-laid egg," he said. Sally, walking around the periphery, gave a look of disgust and came no closer.

"Least now we know who's in charge," Red said. He got off his haunches and started back through the cornfield, making big zigzags, watching the ground, watching where the stalks were bent.

"These hardtime cons," T. Ray said, hurrying alongside, "what makes 'em go off is always a riddle. Two guys live together, plan together, break out and ride into the sunset, and then, Pop! No sign of a war. One of 'em just says, come out in the cornfield, I want a divorce. And the other one goes right along. You figure."

Red already had. He'd seen the converging paths through the corn and had a pretty good idea what led up to the gunplay. Sally appeared at his side. He sighed and got ready to explain.

Sally spoke first. "Haynes was stupid enough to leave Pugh and the kid alone together while he went shopping. Then he had to shoot Pugh to stop him from sodomizing the boy in the field."

"Very good," Red said.

"Something doesn't add up," Sally said. "And I guess it's that IQ report on Haynes."

Red just shook his head. He kept plowing through the corn toward the mobile headquarters.

"What?" Sally said. "Why are you shaking your head? Haynes is a very smart guy, all the files say. That was not a smart move."

"Unless he was looking for an excuse," Red said.

"An excuse?" Sally said. "A guy capable of being this brutal doesn't need an excuse."

Red walked on in Buddha-like silence. Sally matched him stride for stride, glaring at him, waiting for a reply.

Sheriff T. Ray dropped back. He'd got lost forty yards ago.

Red reached the door of the RV. "Read your files again," he said. "This guy does not go off without provocation." He was about to swing up the steps when he stopped himself and stepped back. He folded his hands patiently and let Sally enter first.

▪ *TWENTY* ▪

"You don't need to decide for years," Butch said. They were back on a cross-county dirt road, slewing over ruts, throwing up an impressive rooster tail of red dust, making time. "Yer age, hell, I never did decide what I wanted to do," Butch said. "Knew what I didn't wanna do—most everythin'."

Phillip tugged at another RC. "I'm s'posed to spread the word when I get grown," Phillip said. "Be a Bible missionary."

Butch looked at him. "That sound interesting to ya'?" he asked.

"Naw," Phillip said.

"A guy I knew at the dance hall was an inventor," Butch said. "That was interesting. He had this idea— you know what a howdah is?"

Phillip said, "Uh-uh."

"A big basket people ride in on the top of elephants," Butch said. "In India."

"A howdah?" Phillip said.

"This guy," Butch said, "took a fuselage. He worked on fuselages at Martin-Marietta, airplane bodies. And he made a howdah for the top of his Cadillac. Cut a hole in the roof so his family could crawl up there and see the sights as they drove through the country. It had windows and everything. He thought howdahs for cars would catch on and he'd make a million." He chortled. "Guess what?"

Phillip said "What?", but only after a long pause.

"You seen any howdahs on cars lately?" Butch said with a grin. He looked at Phillip and saw the boy was suddenly somber. "Whattaya thinkin' about?" Butch said.

"Nuthin'," Phillip said.

"If I guess you tell me?"

Phillip nodded.

"You thinkin' about yer mama," Butch said.

Phillip sat still, staring ahead. That was it.

Butch brought the Impala to a stop. He pointed to the horizon. Desolate. "I hear ya, Phillip," he said, "but look around. I can't very well leave you here, can I?"

"Here" was a fork in the county road in the middle of nowhere.

"Lemme ask ya something," Butch said. "You right- or left-handed?"

Phillip meekly held up his right hand. Butch

tromped on it, and the car roared off down the right-hand fork.

"Then that's the way we'll go," Butch said. "You ever ridden in a time machine before?"

Phillip shook his head.

"Sure you have," Butch said. "Whattaya' think this is?"

"A car."

"Yer lookin' at this thing bassackwards," Butch said. "This is a twentieth-century time machine. I'm the captain and you're the navigator." Butch pointed through the dash. "Out there . . . that's the future." He tapped the rearview mirror. "Back there . . . that's the past. If life's moving too slow and you wanna project yerself into the future, you step here on the gas. See?" The Impala surged forward, fishtailing wildly on the dirt track, enough for a little thrill.

"And if yer enjoyin' the moment yer in," Butch said, "well hell, just step on the brake here and you can slow it down." He stabbed the brake and brought the car to a skidding and dusty halt.

Phillip, his eyes wide, was clutching on to the door strap to save his life.

"This is the present, Phillip," Butch said. "Enjoy it while it lasts." He laughed uproariously and stepped on the gas. The Impala spun out 360 degrees worth, kicking dirt in all directions. "Yessir," Butch hooted, "time travelin' through Texas! We got to find us a Ford. My daddy always drove Fords, you know that?"

Phillip hung on, half exhilarated by the rocket ride, half paralyzed with fear. Thoughts of his distant comforting mother were driven from his mind.

■ TWENTY-ONE ■

The Red Garnett Special remained on the road outside Uvalde Market, parked off to the side. The state and local police cars had cleared out. An occasional customer chugged in and did business, unaware of the import of the bulky vehicle outside, unless Alf chose to tell the story one more time.

Which he did every time—with elaborations. Though the adrenaline rush from looking down a .38 and from the official brouhaha that followed was long since gone, Irish courage had replaced it. Alf, saucing heavily on Jose Cuervo, was ready to refight the battle. He was also ready to pass out.

A couple of cowboys who came in for six-packs of Lone Star got the whole story, updated version. Waving a World War II Luger he had dug up in the back room, Alf illustrated how close Butch Haynes had come to surcease. "Had the sucker in my sights," he said, drawing a bead on the gumball machine between the cowboys. "Hadda back off 'counta the kid. *Bing!* Sayonara Haynes." The cowboys looked longingly at the beer in the cooler behind Alf and his gyrating pistol.

Bradley, killing time in the cockpit, idly twisted knobs.

"Intercom speaker system," Suttle said edgily as Bradley twiddled a dial next to the radio. "You can get and give instructions to and from the rear of the vehicle."

Bradley was interested. "How's it work"? he asked.

"You push the power button," Suttle said. "But if you've got the volume turned up—"

Bradley reached right in and pushed the power button. The vehicle-wide sound system gave a protracted shrill, window-rattling squawk, then started creaking tinnily.

"—you'll blow the speakers," Suttle said.

The speakers were blown. In the back Red cringed, his ears still ringing. He turned to stare at the front of the vehicle.

"The things prolly got a warranty, man," Bradley said quietly to Suttle. "You oughta make a list of all the things that are wrong with it."

Red made his way over to the map. He placed thumbtacks at certain crossroads, indicating police roadblocks.

"That oughta put his pecker in a sling, huh, Red?" Adler said. Then he remembered Sally, sitting right behind him. "Sorry, ma'am," he said. He actually blushed.

Sally didn't. She ignored the remark. "Shouldn't these be roadblocked as well," she said, laying down the thick county map book she'd been studying and pointing to several other unmarked roads.

"Sooner or later he'll get on a main road," Red said. "We don't got the manpower to block every farm-to-market." He indicated Gatesville on the map. "Haynes did some early jailin' and some work-release hereabouts. Knows every cow path in these counties."

"That wasn't in the files—the work release," Sally said, surprised. "Where'd that come from?"

Red didn't answer, just stared at the map, lost in thought.

"In a perfect world, Miss Gerber," Adler said, "we'd lock arms and thrash the bush till he turned up."

Sally glanced at Adler, then went back to studying Red. "In a perfect world things like this wouldn't happen in the first place," she said.

Adler heard something on his headset. He turned to Red. "Locals are heading in toward Killeen. Got an eyeball report from a farmer—the Impala."

Sally chimed in without being asked, "Really? Aren't you surprised they're still using the same car? I mean after what happened here they oughta know it's hot."

Both men looked at her.

She backpedaled quickly. "Unless of course they've already ditched it. Maybe that sighting is old, or inaccurate." She made a mental note to stop doing her thinking out loud.

"Wanna follow?" Adler said to Red.

"Let's sit tight," Red said. "Till things jell. It's peaceful here." He settled back on the banquette opposite the map when three gunshots exploded inside the store. Rounds pierced the roof, sending the flock of resident crows beating madly up and away from the fire zone.

Adler and Sally scrambled to the RV door to see the two cowboy customers backing out of the store empty-handed—no Lone Star. They slammed into their pickup and took off thirsty.

Red, Adler, and Sally walked cautiously inside. There was Alf Shales facedown across his glass-topped counter, gun extended toward the door. The glass creaked. Red and Adler dove out the door, Red yanking Sally along with them, sending her thick map book flying. The glass counter shattered under Alf's weight; the gun went off as Alf plunged insensate to the floor. Red, Adler, and Sally peered back in the door.

■ *TWENTY-TWO* ■

A farmer was taking in grain with a combine in a small field as the Impala rolled by on the rural road. The farmer, traveling on the out row, didn't notice when the Impala stopped at the entrance to the long dirt driveway leading to his farmhouse. A four-year-old Ford car, yellow with a white slash down the side, and an ancient Dodge pickup sat in the shade of a line of windbreak trees alongside the house.

"Okay, Phillip," Butch said, "we're gonna do some car shoppin'. You ever play cowboys 'n' Injuns? See that Ford sedan? Now I want you to sneak on over there like an Injun and take a peek and see if the keys is in it."

Phillip hesitated, staring out at the yellow Ford, weighing the right and wrong of what he was being asked to do, as far as he could understand it. The moment dragged on.

"Don't have to if you don't wanna," Butch said. "But I'd appreciate it . . . You bein' the new navigator and all."

That did it. Phillip opened the door and slipped out and started down the driveway.

"Hey, Phillip," Butch called. "Check for a radio, too."

Phillip signed that he heard and scampered down the dirt drive, a waif right out of Dickens, off to do Fagin's bidding—droopy dirty underwear, scratched up muddy legs, bloody skinned knees from crashing through the cornfield.

The farmer, turning at the end of his row, was too far away and too involved in his driving to notice Phillip circling around his car and peering in the driver's window.

Keys dangled from the ignition, Phillip saw. He

looked around furtively at the house, then at the distant combine. He checked the pickup truck just to be thorough and saw keys there, too. He ran pell-mell back to the Impala and leaned in the passenger window. He said in a loud whisper, as though the farmer might hear, "It's got keys and a radio. I checked."

"Good man," Butch said, sizing up the distance from the Impala to the Ford, and from the combine to the Ford.

"Can we stop at a gas station," Phillip asked, his voice at a certain telltale pitch. He was fidgeting from foot to foot and holding himself.

"What for?" Butch said, looking over at the boy.

"Number one," Phillip said.

"This here's nature, Phillip," Butch said as he climbed out of the Impala. "Pee in the ditch."

Phillip hobbled to a bush and relieved himself while Butch jogged down the driveway toward the Ford, tossing the Impala keys into the field as he went.

The farmer, finally noticing the activity down by his house, let his combine grind to a halt and watched carefully for a few seconds.

Phillip, legs straddled in front of the bush, was ready. Despite his prior urgency, he was having a hard time getting the flow going. He wiggled his tool, set his legs a little wider apart, and looked off across the field into that middle distance where men look when they are waiting for relief to come.

Butch slid into the Ford, pumped the gas a couple of times and turned the key. The engine grumbled and died.

The farmer, fearing what in fact was happening, dropped from the combine and started striding, then trotting toward the stranger messing with his Ford.

Phillip to his great comfort finally started to pee. Intermittent dread of this friendly but scary man had tightened him up, made him hold it far longer than was normal or healthy. Now it came in a torrent, and his sense of gratitude was unbounded. His whole body started to relax.

Butch cranked the starter again and again, but the engine didn't catch, only whined and coughed. "Start, you sonofabitch!" Butch growled at the Ford. It was flooded.

The farmer, a weathered old boy who'd seen at least seventy years on this land, ran faster, already half a field closer. He grasped the full picture now. "Hey, that's my car! Hey!" he shouted, stumbling over the clods of tilled soil.

Butch punched the gas pedal to clear the flood, and the engine finally roared. He threw it in reverse and peeled out backward into the road, skidding to a stop beside the ditch were Phillip was in full release with no sign of let-up.

"Get in the car, Phillip!" Butch called.

Phillip continued with great satisfaction to pee.

The farmer, only forty yards away, raced right at them, arms pumping, eyes afire, nostrils flared like an angry bull.

Phillip suddenly saw the onrushing man and tried to hurry and finish, but the RC kept coming, one last bottle's worth.

"Phillip!" Butch yelled. "Get in the car!"

Phillip raced for the car, pulling his skivvies up and spraying the landscape as he went.

He leapt into the open passenger door at the same moment Butch floored it and the enraged farmer arrived and snagged onto the closing door.

The car fishtailed down the road, gathering speed while the farmer held on for dear life and possession of his automobile. "Stop the car!" he screamed. "Are you outa yer mind!" He grabbed at Phillip, who did his best to dodge and fend off the grasping hand.

Butch reached under the seat and gripped the handle of the .38. Phillip saw what was about to happen. He pounced on the farmer's hand and bit it as hard as he could.

"Aaaaaaaayyyyy!" The scream erupted as the farmer released his grip on the door and fell backward, somersaulting into the irrigation ditch.

Butch shoved the gun back under the seat. "Goddamn boy," he said, watching in the rearview as the farmer flopped around in the irrigation ditch, pulled himself out and slumped on the roadside. "How many RCs did you drink, anyway?"

"Four," Phillip said. He spun around to watch the farmer also, exhilarated and fearful at the mayhem they were leaving in their wake. He looked at Butch in wonder.

Butch shook his head and laughed. "One thing's for sure," he said. "You got one helluva set of chompers."

A man's approval. It was manna to him. For biting a farmer? What would his mama say? He knew exactly. He was a poor weak stem blown this way and that by the winds of Satan. For the moment he didn't try to sort it out; he sat back and let himself be buffeted.

▪ *TWENTY-THREE* ▪

Bradley Haskell, officer in charge of driving, waited with the others back in the Airstream. He tried several times to light his cigarette with the built-in lighter in the motor home, but got no heat. He shoved it back in disgust. "Lighter don't work," he grumbled to Suttle. "Put that on the list." The inactivity was getting to Bradley; he was bored and testy. "Let's ride," he growled under his breath, staring out at the highway.

Bradley's tall, lean Texas Ranger look gave little clue to his background. He'd grown up a rich kid on the Haskell Ranch in the Wild Horse Desert of South Texas, next door to the King Ranch, though much smaller in size. Bradley's mother, Cora Lee, had inherited the lioness's share of the family cattle wealth.

A rough and tumble kid and an accomplished horseback rider from age three, Bradley had taken to junior-circuit rodeo riding at the minimum age. He was fearless, but not overly discerning, and when at age twelve he sneaked a ride on a huge horse named Stalin, he got thrown badly against a metal light pole. The result was a severely broken leg and an embolism that settled in his lung and nearly killed him.

In the hospital Bradley's mother, in the process of divorce from Bradley's father, was comforted by a middle-aged gentleman who was visiting a friend in the next room. Within months this gentleman, an oil wildcatter and hustler named Henry Latimer, had wooed Cora Lee into making him her financial counselor. Before two years had passed, he was trustee of her entire fortune. A year after that Cora Lee died, and Bradley found himself a mere tenant on his family's huge estate. It had passed over to a private foundation in the iron-clad grip of Henry Latimer. Bradley was out.

Someday, the lawyers told Bradley, he might get part of his mother's estate back if the lawsuits went well. In the meantime, they told him, get a job.

Bradley joined the Marines and later became a Texas Ranger. He wanted to stay as far away from horses as possible—it was, after all, the four-footed Stalin who had led his mother down the path to the clutches of Henry Latimer. In the Marines Bradley made himself into a motor-vehicle specialist—hell, one day maybe he'd own a stable of race cars—and he never mentioned his monied background or potentially posh future, although he did have a certain air about him.

Yet he kept his tastes simple—some Scotch whiskey, an occasional cigarette to pass the time. He held up his Marlboro to Bobby Lee, who was sitting alone in the corner of the main room.

Bobby Lee shook his head. No, he didn't have a light, and he didn't have the time of day to worry about it either. He went back to smiling cynically at Sally. He didn't see Bradley give him the finger.

Red, watching the silent exchange from his office, knew that if they didn't get rolling soon he'd be refereeing chicken fights in the ranks.

Adler, with his headset on, suddenly jumped on the radio and turned up the volume. "Highway 16 north. Four miles south of Desdemona," he repeated as he heard it. "Got it." He called back to Red. "They stole a vehicle. Farm in Eastland County."

"Bradley," Red said, standing and stretching, "fire it up."

Bradley and Suttle both gladly jumped up, ran out of the Airstream and climbed in the big red pickup. Bradley fired it up and headed the RV out onto the highway, going west.

Back in the Airstream everybody was happy to be underway.

"Man, that's halfway to Memphis," Bobby Lee said to Sally. "That boy's been flyin'." Everything was halfway to Memphis with Bobby Lee, no matter what the direction. When he did well with a woman, which was surprisingly often, Bobby Lee said he'd got halfway to Memphis—or all the way, depending.

Red walked up next to Adler and looked over his shoulder at his notes. "What kinda shape's it in?"

"What's that?" Adler said.

"The Ford he stole," Sally said, not looking up from her files.

"Owner told the locals they only drove it to church," Adler said to Red. "But it does have a bad emergency brake." He gave Sally a look. "How'd ya know it was a Ford?"

"He likes Fords," Sally said, matter-of-fact.

Adler raised his brows and turned to check the big map. "Looks like you was right, Red," he said. "He's off the farm-to-market and onto a spur. Whattaya wanna do?"

Red scanned his options on the map. "Beef up the I-20 roadblock," he said.

Adler listened into his headset again, gathering more news. "What's that?" he said into the mouthpiece. He turned to Red. "The locals wanna know if they're to take a clean shot if they get one."

Red stared out the window for what seemed an eternity. Finally he said, "No."

Adler pulled off his headphones and looked quizzically at Red. Sally looked up from her files and watched the tall man at the window.

". . . come back . . . ? Come back, Mobile One," the voice on the radio said. "Adler, are you there?"

"Tell 'em what I said," Red said to Adler without shifting his gaze from the passing landscape.

Adler grabbed up the headpiece and spoke into the mike; "Uh . . . no."

"Was that a negative?" the radio voice came back.

"No!" Adler confirmed. "Er, yes. No means negative. Same thing. Over."

Red saw Sally peering at him over the top of her file. He glanced around at the other sets of eyes doing the same. "I don't want some half-ass Sergeant York taking pot shots with a deer rifle," Red said. It came out a touch defensive. He glowered. He wasn't used to being pecked at by ducks.

Bobby Lee smirked mysteriously at the whole exchange.

"It's the only thing to do," Sally said. "He's got the child with him."

Red snapped her a look that said, "Don't defend me."

"Whattaya figure there, Sally," Bobby Lee said. "That he'll just give up? Walk in, hand over the kid? Say, Here, take my firearm?"

"Maybe, maybe not," Sally said.

"Well now, there's a safe bet." Bobby Lee laughed.

"I'll give you a safe bet," Sally said. "The boy's in better hands now than he was."

Red wished he could agree with her, but . . . "The third eye Pugh's sportin' on the way to the morgue shouts otherwise," he said.

Sally flashed Red a look.

Bobby Lee got up and moved past Red on his way to the toilet. "Then why not shoot to kill?" he asked casually.

Red stared as the younger man passed and paused at the door to the toilet, waiting for an answer. Red didn't give him one.

Bobby Lee shrugged and turned his eyes to Adler. "This thing workin' yet?"

"Yeah," Adler said. "You gotta jiggle the handle."

Adler again turned his full attention to the radio and listened intently. In a moment he pivoted and reported to Red. "They've forwarded the stolen vehicle license to the roadblocks," he said. "You still wanna go to that farm?"

Red pulled out a pouch of Red Man chewing tobacco and mulled over the question while he fingered a wad and slapped it in his cheek. "Yeah," he said after a chew. "I got a hunch."

■ *TWENTY-FOUR* ■

Sailing north on 16, the Ford had cut under I-20 west of Mingus. Butch immediately veered west again on a county blacktop, then jogged north and west yet again on a farm-to-market. He'd been lucky so far. He hadn't picked any uncompleted farm-to-markets that just petered out in the middle of a field somewhere. A real Texan was always ready for the nowhere road. It was a tenderfoot, rationalist's mistake to assume a Texas road had to go *from* somewhere *to* somewhere.

"You got blue eyes don't'cha, Phillip?" Butch said. "Never met a brown-eyed Phillip before. Who you named after?"

"My daddy," Phillip said. The boy was startled to be asked about his daddy just then; the man was on his mind. He'd allowed himself to think about him more on this trip than he ever did.

"You and your old man get along all right?" Butch asked.

"Yeahsir," Phillip said.

"Toss the ball around, play grab-ass in the yard, that sorta thing?" Butch said.

"Nawsir."

Butch looked at him. "Why the hell not?"

"He ain't around, really," Phillip said.

"Well, he is or he ain't," Butch said. "When's the last time you saw him?"

Phillip shrugged.

Butch accepted that without comment. He swung the Ford off the farm-to-market onto 180 going west and picked up his speed. The Ford was in A-1 condition, Butch thought, as though the old farmer drove in only on weekends, maybe just to church.

"Me'n you got a lot in common, Phillip," he said. "The both of us are handsome devils, we both like RC

Cola, and neither one of us has an old man worth a damn.''

That hurt. That was a sucker punch. What the heck, the boy thought, glaring at Butch, his old man *was too* worth a damn. ''My mama says he'll prolly come back,'' he said. ''Prolly when I'm ten or so.''

''Well . . .'' Butch said, ''she's lyin' to ya pure and simple. He ain't never comin' back.''

Disappointment registered on Phillip's face.

Better get used to it, kid, Butch thought. ''Guys like us, Phillip, we gotta be on our own. Seek foolish destiny, that sorta thing.''

The Ford sped on, doing just that. Following an instinct, Butch veered temporarily southwest on Texas 351. It would take him into and through metropolitan Abilene on I-20, a highway so big and busy they wouldn't roadblock it short of somebody trying to shoot the president. And Butch Haynes had no illusions that his own importance, or even that of little Phillip beside him, measured up to anything so grandiose.

Five miles up ranch road 126 west of Abilene, Butch pulled the Ford off the dusty byway into a one-pump gas station, a dilapidated mirage in the middle of the prairie. There was no apparent reason why a gas station should stand at this spot, except that drivers like Butch somehow found it and justified its existence after the fact.

There were no cars around the building, indicating life. Butch pulled up to the pump. Suddenly, as though materialized from the heat haze, a fifteen-year old boy in overalls appeared at Phillip's side window. The boy leaned down—he was so buck-toothed Phillip and Butch both looked again.

''What can I do ya' for?'' the boy asked, his speech somewhat twisted by his teeth. Withal, his personality seemed unaffected; the boy smiled the friendliest smile at Phillip a boy could ever want to see.

"Tell him your name," Butch said, giving Phillip a poke on the arm.

"Phillip," Phillip said.

"Fill-er-up it is," the boy said and turned to start pumping gas.

"See there?" Butch said. "All you gotta do is say your name and people are waitin' on you hand and foot. Like a goddamn king or somethin'."

Phillip couldn't help smile at the notion. He went with Butch around the side to pee in a proper toilet. Phillip came out first and stood watching the boy attendant cleaning road bugs off the windshield.

"Yer so buck-toothed you could eat a apple through a keyhole," Phillip said to the boy. "That's my daddy's joke. He's away travelin'."

The boy looked at Phillip in disbelief. His face contorted, he dropped the nozzle and walked away fast. "Shit," Phillip heard him say.

Butch, coming out, heard it, too. "What's wrong with the kid?" Butch asked Phillip. Phillip told him.

Butch picked up the hose and continued pumping the gas. "There was this career criminal—well, like me, I guess—I knew at Brownsville," Butch said. "They operated on him, this experimental program, pinned his ears back. The idea bein' he was a lifelong criminal 'cause he hadn't had a fair shot, havin' stick-out ears and all." He pumped a little more. "This kid ain't even a career criminal."

Phillip listened while watching the buck-toothed kid out behind the station running and kicking at the dirt, running and kicking at an imaginary soccer ball.

"Here, Phillip," Butch said, pulling some bills off his wad and handing them to the boy. "You go pay him."

Phillip walked uncertainly toward the older boy—he was suddenly conscious he was no prize himself in his dirty underwear. He held out the money to the boy. "My daddy ain't travelin' a'tall, he's gone," Phillip said. "He'd prolly whup me for sayin' that to ya'."

The boy took the money from Phillip. His eyes were red. "That's okay," he said. "Who's 'at yer with? Yer uncle or somethin'?"

"Naw. He just took me, kinda," Phillip said. "From my mama."

"Like adoptin'?" the boy said.

"Not exactly," Phillip said. "More like—I can't think of the word."

"Well, have a good one," the buck-toothed boy said as they walked back toward the car. He waved and went inside.

Phillip got in the car. They got back on the road, heading north. Phillip was thinking deep. After a while he turned to Butch and said, "What happened to the guy with ears? I mean, after?"

"Oh . . ." Butch said. He'd been hoping Phillip wouldn't want to know. "He went and asked this woman for a date, you know, he'd always liked her and never dared. She said sure. He got all het up, had to get him some money and new clothes—robbed a store." He shrugged. "Back in the can."

Phillip pondered Butch's complicated world as the car plunged into a sudden dust squall and out the other side.

▪ *TWENTY-FIVE* ▪

The Law Enforcement Special was pulled off the road opposite the drainage ditch where Phillip Perry relieved himself for the first time since leaving his mother's East Texas kitchen—a long way for a boy to travel on one bladder, a third of the way across Texas. And a long shakedown cruise for the governor's recreational vehicle, which sat with its hood open, hissing and steaming.

"You responsible for engine maintenance on this thing?" asked Bradley, leaning into the motor, helping Suttle tighten the fan belt—both men trying not to get burned on the hot metal.

"Uh, yeah," Suttle grunted. "I'm the full-time driver. Got checked out on all the systems at the assembly plant—sent me all the way to Detroit. Governor likes things done right, no screw-ups." He pulled his head out.

Bradley was shaking his head, "Too bad."

"What? Why?" Suttle said.

Bradley reluctantly said, "You notice the thing goin' into second?"

"No. What?"

"You notice how it keeps wantin' to slip a bit? Doesn't grab right off?" Bradley said. "Feels to me like somebody's been a little heavy-footed with the clutch."

"No way," Suttle said. "I been the only driver, and I sure ain't . . . Probably just needs adjustin'. Ya know, new vehicle."

"I'd take care of it if I was you," Bradley said gravely.

Up the farmhouse driveway, a white-coated figure hurried out of the house and over to the waiting ambulance. He swung the back door open, then hustled back up the steps and helped a second attendant wheel a gurney out. Strapped to it was the farmer, conscious, staring at the sky, leathery face creased with pain. The farmer's wife, a thin aging woman clutching her Sunday missal, sobbed and attended to her husband.

Red, leaning on the trunk of the Impala, watched

the attendants loading the old man into the ambulance. The wife, before climbing in next to him, carefully removed her muddy farm boots and gave them to one of the attendants. The man gently closed the rear door and walked up to the driver's compartment, tossing the old woman's boots on the yellowed grass as he went.

The ambulance drove away. Sally, exiting the house, picked up the woman's small boots and walked over toward Red. In the field local sheriff's deputies, walking four feet apart, scoured the ground, looking for something—the kind of something no one wants to be the one to find.

Adler, striding in from the search, headed for Red and Sally at the Impala. Red chewed his Red Man, spat downwind from the others, and sniffed the air. Something decidedly unsavory.

"No bodies this time," Adler said. "Thank Gawd."

"You got the keys to this thing?" Red asked, standing away from the Impala.

"Uh . . . naw . . ." Adler said. "They musta walked with 'em."

"Get me a crowbar," Red said. He half turned to Sally. "You might wanna wait in the boat."

Sally, surprised, said, "No thank you."

It was black as night inside the Impala trunk. A crowbar cranked at the lid until it blasted open like a booby trap. The faces of Red, Adler, and Sally reflected what they saw inside and what they smelled. Sally spun away in nausea and disgust. She hurried toward the house, clutching the old woman's boots to her breast.

In the trunk lay the crumpled, bent, bloody remains of Larry Seyler, deputy warden in charge of acquisitions and allocations for Huntsville State Prison—the original hostage. He had just turned fifty-five, double nickles, when he died. He had three teenaged boys at home, waiting to learn his fate. They had first-tier tickets to the Longhorns game on Saturday, for one thing. For another, they liked their old man. They wanted him coming home every night so they could go on kidding him about his dangerous desk job.

"There's our bureaucrat," Red said, sick at heart.

"Prob'bly made him climb in the trunk himself, then shot him," Adler said. It was a fair surmise, given the spatter pattern.

Red took off his Stetson, spat out his chaw, turned, and walked toward the house. Sally was bending over by the outdoor spigot, ostensibly scrubbing the mud off the old lady's farm boots. Actually she was heaving, repeatedly, and trying not to broadcast it.

Red stopped a few feet away and looked across the field. "It's sure nice to know the boy's in good hands," he said to no one in particular.

Sally straightened up, ready to smash him with one of the boots. But Red's face was soft; he was holding out his handkerchief to her. She took it.

"Gallows humor, Sally," Red said. "Without it, we'd all be heavin'." He put his hat on and walked slowly back toward the RV.

Sally dried her hands on the handkerchief, then her face, watching, furious at the horror of life, and mystified by the man under the hat.

■ *TWENTY-SIX* ■

Seven hundred twelve people made Noodle, Texas, their home. To get a feel for Noodle, it might help to know that the population had neither grown nor shrunk by more than forty or fifty people since the town sprang up during the big cattle drive days of the 1880s. Boys went off to the two great wars, but many of them survived and came home and established families in the county. Poor folks left during the Depression, but poorer folks came and claimed their houses. The oil boom made many Texas towns bigger and richer, but Noodle hovered always around seven hundred good souls.

The oldest store in Noodles—fifty-three years old to be exact—was Friendly's Drug and Dry Goods Store. And all of the folks who worked there, whether they'd admit it or not, were proud of the store's claim, lettered across both front windows, of being "The Friendliest Store in Texas."

Two friendly customers, Butch Haynes and his young charge, rolled down the main street of Noodle in the Ford sedan and pulled into the side alley next to the store.

"You ready to get out of those skivvies and into some britches?" Butch said.

Phillip nodded.

"Well all right then," Butch said. "But first we gotta come up with some A.K.A.s—fake identities, ya' know. Names to call each other when we're around other folks." He turned the engine off and sat back, in no hurry.

Phillip looked like he liked the idea, thought it was funny.

"Go ahead and think one up," Butch said. "Whatever name you want."

"Any name I want?"

As townsfolk Boody Johnson and Vernon Whiteside came out and Butch Haynes and Phillip Perry went in, Lucy, the thirty-year-old schoolmarmish clerk, was replacing a handful of shoe boxes on a shelf. She noted their entrance.

"Well, hello there and welcome to Friendly's," she said with her slightly pursed smile.

Butch immediately wrote this dame off as not his

type. She was more interested in Phillip anyway, who was cowering self-consciously half behind Butch and half behind a cardboard display that said, CAST YOUR VOTE FOR FRIENDLY'S FRIENDLIEST CLERK.

"Looks like the little fella needs some pants," she said, leaning down.

"As a matter of fact," Butch said, "shoes and skivvies, too. He'll tell you his size. Go with the lady, Buzz."

Phillip, still in a daze, his eyes wandering around the rich variety of goods, didn't recognize his self-chosen new name.

"Buzz!" Butch said.

Phillip snapped to, cracked a smile at Butch and followed Lucy to the children's section of the store.

"Buzz," Lucy said. "What a cute name. Like a bee."

Butch, heading for the back of the store, gave a wink to the clerk at the cash register as he passed—Paula, her name tag read. More his type—about twenty-five, country cute, no lipstick, a smile as broad but not quite so pursed and pasted-on as Lucy's.

In the hardware section Butch proceeded to the aisle that held rope, nails, tape. He grabbed a shank of rope and jerked it taut, testing.

At the end of the long counter near the back of the store was a large glass window backed by a small, slightly raised office. In there sat Mr. Willits, forty-five, the bespectacled, anal-retentive owner—watching every move of every person in his store.

In the children's aisle Lucy held jeans up to Phillip's waist. "It's be easier if I knew your size," she said. "But we'll get it right."

Phillip's wandering eye caught on something—a circular rack with shelves, a Halloween costume display. The sign above it read, MARKED DOWN—GET THE JUMP ON NEXT YEAR. Hanging prominently on the display was a Casper the Friendly Ghost costume.

Phillip was mesmerized by the display, oblivious to Lucy's chatter.

Butch, testing a roll of electrician's tape, tore off a strip, attached it to the back of his hand, and pulled. It held tight.

Lucy, looking for sneaker sizes, selected a box, pulled it out, and turned to find Phillip gone. She looked behind her and smiled. There was Phillip wearing the Casper mask.

"Why look," she said. "It's a friendly ghost. Say 'Boo'."

"Boo," Phillip said, unconvincingly.

"That's not very scary, Buzz." She smiled. "But you'll have a whole year to work on it if your daddy lets you have it. Good price, too. What'd you go as this year?"

"A bandit," Phillip said, admiring himself in the floor-length mirror.

▪ *TWENTY-SEVEN* ▪

A local police car cruised slowly down Main Street. The driver, Officer Terrance Sweeney, noticed the Ford in the alley, didn't recognize it as from the area and came to a halt.

Terrance, number two man in a two-man department, was in his first month on the job. He was all of twenty-one, having struggled valiantly, on-again, off-again, to get through Texas A & M, until he'd finally flunked out last year. He squinted, mouthed the numbers on the Ford's back plate, and checked it against a notepad on the dash.

"Aw, shit . . . ." Terrance said. It was a find—and an

opportunity to shine professionally—he was deeply ambivalent about.

Butch made his way to the register with his handful of supplies. Paula gave him her Friendly's smile that shaded into a real one. Butch pulled a pair of sunglasses from the rack and tried them on.

"Whattaya think?"

"Look good," Paula said.

Butch added the shades to his pile and handed the goods over to the woman.

"Will that be all for you, today," she said, falling into her reflexive smile.

Butch nodded. "You folks are about the grinningest bunch I ever seen," he said.

Paula laughed, then dropped her grin. She looked behind her to see if Mr. Willits was watching. She whispered, "Old Man Willits holds a contest ever' month. The friendliest clerk gets a $20 bonus." Her eyes pointed toward the door. "There's a ballot box at the front."

In another time and another place, Butch would have registered his vote by taking Paula to Abilene and buying her a fine cowboy hat and a night of Texas two-step or even something fancier if she could keep up with him. But his options didn't include that just now. In fact, his options were narrowing even as he was admiring Paula's fresh-faced look.

Behind the glass Mr. Willits flipped the channel to the one network affiliate they got in Noodle and picked up the beginning of the local news broadcast.

". . . the hunt continues for Butch Haynes," the newscaster said, "who escaped last night from the maximum security unit over in Huntsville. Haynes, six-one, 185 pounds, with short brown hair and medium build, is considered armed and dangerous. He was last seen . . ."

At the checkout counter Paula rang up Butch's items

as Lucy and Phillip emerged from an aisle and dropped jeans, sneakers, underwear, and T-shirts on the counter.

"Here's the clothes," Lucy said to Butch, "but Buzz has his heart set on a Halloween costume for next year. It is half off." She smiled seductively.

But Butch was only half listening. His antennae were up, his face a mask.

Behind the glass Mr. Willits was tensely alert, watching Butch, listening to the end of the newscast.

". . . Haynes is believed to have an eight-year-old boy with him as hostage . . . ," the newscast went on.

Butch, locked eyeball to eyeball with Willits, spoke to Phillip without looking at him. "We'll get it next time. Go get in the car, son."

Willits was so excited he was starting to hyperventilate.

On Main Street, Officer Terrance judiciously backed his black and white a good distance down the street and stopped the car on an angle across the intersection to block it.

"Okay, Pete," he said into his radio, "I'm all set down here. You?"

"Ten-four," came a voice over the radio. At the other end of Main, another black and white was sliding into blockade position. The driver, Pete, looked enough like Terrance to be his older brother or uncle. "Let's just keep him tied up till the state boys get here," he said hopefully. He lit a cigarette nervously. He'd been a peace officer long enough to know this was the kind of occasion unlikely to end peacefully.

In the RV poised at the Desdemona crossroads, Adler took the radio message and gave the table a sharp, triumphant rap with his fist.

"They got him penned down in Noodle, north of Abilene," he called back to Red.

At a nod from the chief, the Red Garnett Express roared to life and headed west at maximum lumbering speed.

At Friendly's, Paula bagged the items, unaware of the dumb show taking place over her head. Willits goggled fixedly at Butch as though memorizing every line in his face. Butch stared back and shook his head slowly. Don't even think about it, was the message in his eyes.

Phillip, walking obediently toward the front entrance, hesitated before the Halloween display again. He stopped and ran his forefinger over the Casper package. He walked around the back of the display, admiring other costumes.

Butch took his change from Paula, then stuffed a $20 bill in her blouse. "You are truly the friendliest clerk I ever met," he said. She gave him a warm thank you grin as Butch beat a hasty retreat for the door.

To his back disappearing out the front entrance she called in afterthought, "Thank you for shopping Friendly's!"

▪ *TWENTY-EIGHT* ▪

Before he was two steps outside the store, Butch had made the two black and whites hanging way back down the block and seen the two youngish cops crouched in them, staring. Butch slid into the middle of a group of old-timers and moved down the street with them at a leisurely pace.

Phillip, still in the store, hovering behind the Halloween display, was unable to tear himself away. He looked up and saw Butch was gone. He checked around to see if he was being watched, debated for moment, then grabbed a Casper costume carton and stuffed it under his T-shirt. He moved quickly toward the door, his face flushing crimson as he pushed through onto the street. He was electrified and terrified at having committed his first genuine criminal act. He looked back and forth guiltily.

Butch, noting the unchanged positions of the black and whites, slid away from the old-timers and into the alley. He hopped into the Ford and looked in the backseat for Buzz. No Buzz. No Phillip. He pounded the wheel and started the car. He checked the rearview, and there was Pete, the older of the two cops, in his black and white, pulling into the alley behind the Ford, his cherry-top spinning.

Butch's exit to the street was blocked. So he did the logical thing. He threw the Ford into reverse and floored it.

Pete, taken flat by surprise by this instant escalation, jammed the cruiser into reverse. The Ford rammed the police car, pushing it backward at a fast pace into a lightpole and a pickup truck. The pickup truck's owner, lugging a fifty-pound bag of mulch from the feed store, screamed as his truck slid toward him, bulldozed by the police cruiser.

"Dammit, Pete!" he shouted, dropping his mulch and scrambling backward to get out of range of the wildly careening caravan.

Phillip, ambling away from the store entrance, saw the mass of metal come shooting out of the alley. The Ford stopped, went into forward, and blasted right back into the alley in a hail of dust.

Driving like a maniac, Butch power-slid around the turn into the back alley and stepped on it. Immediately, he mashed the brakes and brought the Ford to a squealing stop. Trash barrels, a pile of boxes, discarded tires, and a kids' bent and broken swing set—the alley was a dead end.

Butch ripped the car into reverse and squealed all the way back to the alleyway flanking Friendly's.

Phillip stood frozen in front of the store, at a loss for what to do. Should he run? Which way? Should he drop the package that was now burning a hole in his hand?

"I knew something was wrong from the get-go," Lucy chirped knowingly as she and Paula watched the developing chaos from behind the safety of the glass door.

"Look," Paula said, "he left his little boy."

"And, look!" Lucy said. "The little rascal has . . . He's no better than a common street—"

"What?" Paula said.

"He's got that Casper costume," Lucy said with indignation. "He stole it."

Suddenly, the Ford shot into view from the side alley, screeching out into Main Street. Butch made a wide skidding turn, clipping off a parking meter in front of Deason's Book and Card Shop opposite, straightening out and heading down the main drag at a fast clip. An elderly gentleman hollered to take cover and a group of six or eight citizens who happened to be standing in front of Connie's Beauty Parlor hurried inside. Seeing this, a dozen other people from up and down the street followed them into Connie's tiny emporium. They were so packed in, all they could see were the photographs of idealized hairstyles marching in rows above the chairs.

Terrance Sweeney, hunkered in his black and white, couldn't believe what he saw coming at him. He rammed his car in reverse and backed down the street at forty miles an hour.

On the radio Pete was shouting at him, "Get the hell outa there! We can't lose both vehicles."

Terrance sped backward, miraculously avoiding other cars, and turned down a row of grain silos. But Butch was gaining, he was right on his nose. Terrance turned and looked into Butch's grimacing face and girded himself to be run down. His black and white ran into a grain shed.

Butch crimped the wheel and mashed the brakes, sending the Ford into a dusty 180. He ended up facing the other way and tromped on it, speeding back the way he came.

Phillip, antsy as hell in front of Friendly's Drugs and Dry Goods, felt stuck as a bug in tar. He couldn't come or go, and he couldn't see this whole thing ending any way but awful. He was about to give way to crying when he suddenly became aware of several sets of peering eyes behind him.

Lucy pounded on the glass. "Buzz! You little shit," she said. "Shoplifting is a crime!" She shook her finger at him as marms through the ages have been unable to resist doing.

Butch spotted Phillip and, checking his mirror, aimed straight at Friendly's front door. He skidded to a halt and spoke straight to the boy.

"Up to you, Buzz . . ."

Phillip spun around to the store. Lucy had her finger raised. Paula looked bemused, expectant. Phillip, legs wobbly, teeth chattering, was frozen.

"You'll never get away with this, little mister!" Lucy shouted.

Phillip fled from her carping voice, dashing to the Ford and making a swimmer's dive into the open passenger window.

Before peeling away, Butch pulled the .38 from under the seat and fired once into the glass door above Lucy's and Paula's heads. The door and surrounding windows shattered into a million pieces, sending Lucy, Paula, makeup, panty hose, grins and all tumbling into a heap on the floor.

The Ford raced down the street. Pete, about to emerge from his patrol car, dove to the floor as Butch sideswiped the black and white for good measure and fishtailed out of town.

Pete crawled out again. His radio squawked, "Pete? . . . Pete? . . . You Okay?"

From the other end of the street, Terrance was radioing his older relative from the floor of his vehicle.

"Say what you want," Paula whispered hoarsely without raising her head, "I'm keepin' the twenty."

Nothing moved along Main Street for a full two minutes as the dust settled and people prayed they'd seen the last of the cyclone. One by one, folks began straggling out of Connie's Beauty Parlor and peering up and down the peaceful street.

■ *TWENTY-NINE* ■

Two farm boys, ages six and seven, were making ready, moving up to the side of the road. It was a county graded dirt road running along the back side of their father's farm and stretching straight to the afternoon horizon. Tow-headed Frank tossed an egg from hand to hand while acting the lookout. Willy, even more pale-haired than Frank, crawled through the barbed wire fence, dragging a bundle behind him.

"Hurry up," Frank called. "Someone's comin'."

Sure enough, far off on the horizon a hail of dust signaled the approach of a vehicle, coming at speed.

"Come on, come on!" Frank said excitedly.

Willy crawled into the ditch next to Frank and pushed his bundle on ahead.

"Stick it in the road," Frank said. "Hurry up."

Willy scurried out into the road with his bundle—a scarecrow complete with floppy fedora and weathered red bandana. He'd liberated the figure from its duty station in the field. He hurriedly propped the scarecrow up, facing traffic, with a forked stick and raced back to the ditch where Frank was holding out a paper sack with seven fresh hen's eggs.

"We got seven," Frank said. "I get four because it was my idea, and you get three." They divided the eggs up.

The car—or cars, it now looked like—drew closer.

"Here they come," Frank said, adrenalin pumping, heart pounding. "Aim for the windows and get ready to run."

The first car crested the last small rise and bore down on them at surprisingly great speed, followed by another car and another and another—all with lights and sirens wailing. Highway Patrol.

"Oh shit!" Frank said, his heart seizing up in his chest.

Blam! The cars did not even slow at the sight of the scarecrow, but blasted right through it sending hay, hat, limbs and all flying every which way. Could it be Frank and Willy were not the first farm boys to think of this gag?

The scarecrow's coat flapped down in the ditch next to the boys. They let out a unified sigh of relief, looked at each other, threw down the eggs, and hightailed it for home.

■ THIRTY ■

The Ford pulled into a field and parked not thirty yards off the road behind a dilapidated old shack. The car sat in the shadow of an earthen berm topped with a thick growth of mesquite and shinnery oak.

Butch reached in the backseat for the bag of clothing. "Here," he said to Phillip, "take off them nasty skivvies and put on yer jeans." He pointed off to the north. "Gonna chill down. See that?"

Phillip looked. A distinctive, steel blue bank of high clouds rose sheer in the far blue sky.

"Blue norther," Butch said. "My old man got caught in one with his shirt off. Up by Mineral Wells—dropped fifty degrees in a half hour. He was workin' out on the dam. Darn near froze his titties off."

With Butch eyeballing the cold front, Phillip tried to slip the Casper costume box from under his shirt down by the door.

Butch saw the move. "Whatya got there?"

"A ghost suit," Phillip said, by now mortified by his larceny. He pulled the package back on his lap.

"From the store?" Butch asked. "You kyped it?

Phillip nodded, expecting the worst.

"Well, hell, Phillip," Butch said. "Put it on."

"You ain't mad?"

"Let's unnerstan' each other here," Butch said, picking up the box and turning it over. "Stealin's wrong, okay? But if there's somethin' you need bad and you ain't got the money, then it's okay to take a loaner on the item." He handed the box back to the boy. "It's what ya call an exception to the rule."

Phillip took one look at him and tore into the box, ripping the costume out, shaking it open, examining it reverentially. He scrambled out of his old T-shirt and started to strip off his skivvies, then balked. Froze in position.

Butch noticed. "What's wrong?"

"Nuthin'."

Butch saw that Phillip's hand were folded together covering his crotch. "What?" he said. "You don't wanna get undressed, is that it?"

Phillip shrugged.

"You embarrassed 'cause I might see yer pecker?"

"It's . . . puny," Phillip said in a small voice.

"What?" Butch said.

"It's puny."

"Well hell, lemme see," Butch said. This was nothing if not serious.

Phillip still hesitated.

"Go on," Butch said. "I'll shoot ya straight."

Phillip gingerly pulled off his underwear. Butch smiled a broad grin.

"Hell no, Phillip," he said. "It's a good size for a boy yer age."

Phillip looked at Butch, a weight he hadn't comprehended as such was lifted miraculously from his shoulders. He smiled, remasculated, and started to put on his costume.

As he scrambled into the outfit, he caught sight of an armadillo scooting out of the mesquite, lumbering across in front of the car. "My daddy makes real good armadillo chili," he said.

"Don't say," Butch said appreciatively. He settled back watching, as though they had all day to kill in this spot.

Phillip got his arms in and excitedly tugged the zipper up the front. "My daddy says armadillos are buzzards that died and their wings fell off."

"No shit?" Butch said. "That's real deep, like Indian lore. What's yer daddy do?"

Phillip shrugged. He gazed down, thoroughly taken with his getup.

"Spiffy, Phillip," Butch said. "I bet next year yer gonna—" He stopped suddenly and sat up and listened. "Here they come," he said.

The sirens' wail preceded them, but by only a few seconds. The same four Highway Patrol cruisers that nailed the scarecrow came howling out of the east and blasted past at ninety-plus, sending the armadillo scurrying back into the thicket.

Behind the weather-worn shack, in the slight natural depression that decades of wind turbulence had sculpted out of the dust, the Ford lay invisible from the road.

As soon as the patrol cars passed beyond the next rise, Butch started up the engine and humped it to the road and took off in the opposite direction.

"Vultures is armadillos with wings, huh," he said, rooster-tailing it along the dusty road toward the now fading blue norther.

"Buzzards," Phillip said, sitting up proudly in his first-ever brand-new store-bought Halloween outfit.

Buzzards . . . vultures? One and the same, Butch thought. But the day a boy corrals his first forbidden dream is not the day to pick nits with him.

■ *THIRTY-ONE* ■

Sally stared at Butch Haynes's picture in his file, as though protracted looking would yield up secrets to his psyche and future movements. She turned to the second page—another photo of Butch, this one taken at age fourteen. Good-looking kid with some rough edges.

She traced down the list of youthful offenses and the disposition of each. Apart from the one serious incident involving the shooting of a man when Butch was only a boy—a shooting deemed by local authorities to have been accidental—Butch's early transgressions were minor. Shoplifting, pilfering, petty larceny, underage drinking. Probation, probation, three months in youth camp, charge dismissed. All unremarkable, until an arrest at Palo Duro Canyon south of Amarillo on 5/12/42. Offense #514. Technically, that was "vehicular misappropriation" in the criminal code—better known as joyriding. Arresting officer: T. Lamar. Sentence: Four years in a juvenile-authority state prison farm. Four years?

Sally read a rap sheet like an auditor reading a financial statement. What was absent was often more important than what was stated. Something was absent here. In 1942 Butch Haynes made a big jump, not so much in the kinds of criminal acts he was committing but in the kind of jailing he was doing. Why? The record was silent.

The radio spoke up, and Adler bent his head and scribbled. He shouted back to Red, "Haynes bought some tape, rope, and some clothes for the boy."

Red, staring out the window, came to and moved over behind Adler at the map.

Sally smiled to herself. She was right. Haynes was looking after the kid. A portion at least of the boy's peril had been struck dead in that cornfield. No one acknowledged Sally's correct call, though everyone knew it. Not the operative style of this crew, she was well aware. As Red had said, when the thing was over, he'd buy them all drinks. Not before.

"One puzzler, though," Adler said. "They say the boy could have gotten away, but didn't."

"Probably scared to death," Sally said. "Remember in his eyes, Haynes is an adult. As long as the man's treating him square, a child his age could fall under the adult's influence pretty rapidly."

"You don't know the half of it," Adler said. "The kid stole a Halloween outfit."

"Holy Jeezus," Red said. "They're a team."

Adler eyed the map. "Guess you called it, Red," he said. "With the pit stop in Noodle, looks like they're headed for the Panhandle."

Red sighed and groaned. He dug in his hip pocket and pulled out his pint and slugged it straight—and made a face—Geritol.

"What?" Sally said to Red.

"There's more roads than people in the Panhandle," Adler said.

"How's that happen," Sally asked.

Bobby Lee, who sat off by himself, whittling a stick and leering at Sally, spoke up. "Poor counties," he said. "They tend to half finish roads then start on another one. No interstates."

"But if anybody knows them backward, it's Red," Adler said. "Him and Tommy Lamar spent a few years up there. Palo Duro, huh, Red?"

Red didn't respond, just stared at the map.

Sally remembered something from her reading. She opened the file and went immediately to it: Butch Haynes's arrest back in 1942 in Palo Duro. Arresting Officer T. Lamar . . . Tommy Lamar, Red's then partner. Offense: Joyriding.

Now was as good a time as any. She had picked up this technique in graduate school. It might help to get them all involved. It might make her a laughingstock. What the hell . . .

"Okay, so . . . I'm Robert Haynes," she said. "Called Butch by everyone. I was born in Amarillo, but grew up in the French Quarter of New Orleans. . . ."

Everybody was looking at her—getting involved, but they didn't know in what.

"What's she doin', Red," Adler asked sotto voce.

"I killed a man when I was eight," Sally said. "Wanna know why?"

Silence. Nobody was willing to stick his neck out and play along with this egghead game.

Red turned from the window and gave Sally the benefit of the doubt. "Yeah, why?" he said. "Why'd ya kill him?"

"He beat my mother to a bloody pulp on more than one occasion," Sally said.

Adler, now that Red had parted the waters, felt free to wade in. "How'd ya kill him?"

"Shot him with a pistol," Sally said. "A little old .32. There was one in every room in the dance hall— that's what they called it, but it was a whorehouse. Every working room equipped with a hidden .32 for the girls' protection. It's where we lived. I knew where every gun was hidden, I was that kinda kid. Curious about things."

Red moved away from the center of this conversation. He stationed himself before a side window of the motor home, staring out as it ate up highway.

"What's an eight-year-old doin' livin' in a whorehouse?" Adler asked.

"Good question." Sally said. "Ask Mom."

"Hadda be the 1930s, right?" Adler said over his shoulder. "Depression. People doing whatever for money, living wherever? She was lucky to have a roof, ya ask me."

"Authorities didn't do nuthin—about the killin?" Adler asked.

"The gentleman I shot was no gentleman," Sally said. "He himself was wanted by the locals for one thing and another, and mean as a ferret—needed killing, the madame told the sheriff. So there was an exchange of gratuities, and the whole thing got shoved under the rug, Cajun style."

"No shit," Adler said. "They didn't put him in a foster home or nuthin'?"

"Hey, this is 1933, Louz'iana," Sally said. "They put me in school. Which is one place I haven't spent any time yet—eight years old, not a day of school. But I can read. Taught myself, reading dime novels. Black Mask and ones like that. Pestered the working women till they helped me with reading just to get rid of me. Anyway, I'm in school, I'm three years behind, but I catch up."

"Sounds like things are goin' okay now," Adler chimed in, looking up from the doodling he was doing while monitoring the radio.

"They were," Sally said, "For a while. I'm not doing what you'd ever call great at school. I still read only dime novels. Mom is actually making good money for those days. Buying a little house in the Quarter. I've got good shoes, clothes. I'm thinking, I'll grow up, own some buildings, take care of Mama in her old age . . . Then, I'm twelve, Mama dies."

"What happened?" Adler asked. "Killed in the whorehouse?"

"Yeah, but not what you're thinking," Sally said. "Delilah Jane Haynes hung herself in the bathroom of the brothel. Could have saved herself the trouble. Post-mortem check uncovered last-stage syphilis."

"Not easy when you're twelve," Bobby Lee said, remembering his own teen agonies.

"Flattened by it," Sally said. "But never showed a mark. Quit school, worked at the whorehouse. Tried to buy the whores with it. Some of 'em let me—I was precocious."

"Where's yer father?" Adler asked.

"Nobody knows where the hell he is—today, I mean," Sally said. "He ditched my mother and me when I was six. We were living in Amarillo. He was a small-time felon when he wasn't working construction. He got a job building a dam on the TVA—an Indian reservation somewhere—and didn't come back."

"Until . . ." Red joined in. He still had his back turned, looking out watching the countryside roll by. You could tell by the cock of his head he'd been listening the whole time.

"Until he popped up again after Mom died," Sally went on. "He'd just been paroled from a place in Alabama for what they called 'strong-arm', larceny from the person with aggravated force or fear. Or—"

"Or robbery," Red said.

"—As I was about to say," Sally said. "He moved us—the two of us—back to Amarillo. A year later I'm in trouble again."

"Yeah?" Adler said. "That little .32? Kill somebody else?"

"Took a joyride in a Ford coupe that I just couldn't resist," Sally said.

"Hell, ya wouldn't call that trouble," Bobby Lee said.

"That's what I thought," Sally said. "Judge gave me four years in Gatesville, toughest juvy farm in Texas. Worse than Huntsville for minors."

"They used to call it Gladiator School," Bobby Lee said. "Instruction in the basic skills of makin' yerself an enemy of the people."

"Well, now we know where the son-of-a-bitch learned to be a criminal," Adler said. "Seen that before, ain't we, Red?"

Red didn't answer. He seemed to be in a faraway place. Sally watched him closely.

"So, Butch," Bobby Lee said, back to being smart-ass. "Why don't you tell us where yer goin', save us the trouble o' huntin' you down?"

"The destination he's not gonna bother to tell us directly," Sally said. "Better we answer the question, 'Why there?' and we'll know where."

"Shit," Bobby Lee said, tired of the game. " 'Cause I'm runnin' and they're chasin' and I'd jus' as soon go north as south as east as west. It's a fun lil' parlor game, lady, but right now Butch Haynes don't have the slightest idea where the hell he's headed."

They all glanced at him. Bobby Lee had a way of laying down his position that curdled the milk. Maybe he was right and maybe he was wrong, but either way, the game was over. They all drifted back to their own musings.

Bobby Lee was wrong, Sally knew. But her instinct about this collection of boy's club lugs was not to press it. In her mind she marshaled a line of reasoning she'd present to Red the first time she got him in a receptive mood. It went like this:

Butch Haynes wasn't driving aimlessly, he was going somewhere. A con who breaks away from a forty-year prison beef has got to be a motivated felon. He knows the odds are he's on a short leash. He'll go straight after what he wants most, the thing he thinks is most important to him in life, the thing he missed most desperately while locked up.

What did Butch Haynes want? Freedom? The pile of money he'd stashed somewhere that would buy it for him? A woman—sex, warmth? Or maybe it was revenge—someone from his past seriously needed to die? If they could figure out, from the facts and the between-the-lines secrets of the file, what Butch craved, they could get there first, or at the very least, clear the human breakables out of his path.

■ *THIRTY-TWO* ■

Casper the Navigator rode shotgun in the Ford—mask on, outfit fully zipped, map in hand.

Butch was looping back to an east-west spur to pick up 83 north. He'd thought better of heading too directly toward his goal; a tangent was in order.

"An inch is twenty-four miles," Butch said. "Hold yer pointin' finger along the line of the road. You got three lines on yer finger, don'tcha? Each one's an inch. So how many inches to Childress?"

Phillip held one finger to the map, then another. "One, two . . ." he said. "Six."

"Yer a helluva navigator, Phillip," Butch said. "A lot smarter than Jerry. But I guess that's not sayin' a lot."

Through the eyeholes of his mask, Phillip spied a

fantasy highballing down the road at them. "Lookie there!" he said.

It was a hulking, swaying building, a gleaming glass and metal domicile sailing along on about a dozen wheels Phillip had never seen anything that massive in flight.

Inside the GMC pickup, Bradley, driving, tinkered with the windshield wipers. There appeared to be a crossed wire or short in the system. The blades flipped around erratically, not only not sweetly coordinated in their movements but now and then disappearing completely from view, rotating all the way around, wiping the hood below the windshield and reappearing on the other side.

Suttle, napping, awoke to Bradley's laughing out loud at the wipers' antics.

"What the hell'd you do to them?" Suttle asked.

"Man," Bradley said with a chuckle, "only God can make wipers do that."

Butch, smiling at Phillip's excitement, honked the horn twice as they approached the RV and waited for a retort.

Bradley looked to Suttle. Suttle nodded okay. Bradley lay on the air horn for two solid blasts. Greetings to the yellow Ford.

Phillip laughed and waved and saw Bradley and Suttle wave back as the two vehicles whooshed by each other.

Sally, staring fixedly out the window, roused herself to glance at the cause of all the horn blowing as it sped by. The driver of the car was indistinct, but there was no mistaking Casper the Friendly Ghost. And there was no mistaking the color and make of the car.

She turned quickly to Adler. "You said the boy stole a Halloween costume," she said. "What character?"

"Uh . . . I believe it was Casper," he said. "Casper the Friendly Ghost. Lemme check my notes here . . ."

"That was them!" Sally shouted. "They just passed us."

Red stared at her for a split second, then hollered, "Turn this thing around!"

Adler jumped to the intercom and relayed the boss's orders to Bradley. "Turn it around!" he barked. "That was them!" Adler lurched back to the shortwave to call in the sighting.

Bradley in the pickup started looking frantically for a place to turn the double vehicle around.

"It's a skosh narrow here," Suttle said nervously, examining the drainage ditches on both sides of the two-lane blacktop.

"Red says turn," Bradley said, "we turn."

"We won't . . ." Suttle said. "We can't . . . I wouldn't! . . ."

Bradley braked sharply, and the trailing Airstream bucked and started to indicate it had its own ideas about how quickly to stop and turn.

Adler, on the shortwave, turned to Sally. "They want to know if the boy looked okay."

"He was laughing and waving," Sally said.

"Don't say that," Red snapped as Adler was about to relay the message.

"What do I say?" Adler asked.

Up front, Suttle groaned, "We'll never make it!" "Be careful!"

But Bradley was not raised to take advice from little old farm boys. He continued to brake hard.

■ *THIRTY-THREE* ■

It was a stately room with a remarkable and intentional similarity to the Oval Office in Washington—the same array of tall French windows behind the broad desk, the same dignified official seal on the wall, the same flag stanchions flanking the window casements. The seal and the flags, however, were not presidential but gubernatorial, and the office was in the statehouse in Austin, Texas.

Pictures of tall silver-haired John Connally with family and with a formidable range of major political players graced the walls. The governor himself was not in evidence.

Gladys Perry, agitated, intimidated, and near tears, sat looking small and alone, in front of the governor's big desk, waiting. A secretary brought her a glass of cold water and tried to comfort her.

All those in the room and the press massed outside the door were waiting for the next update from Mobile One, scheduled to come in the next two or three minutes.

It was apparent to every politico in the statehouse that this was the kind of explosive news event the governor did not need, just weeks before President Kennedy's high-profile precampaign visit. It was an unusual visit to begin with, laden with political significance.

The Texas delegation, normally a Democratic stalwart, was split into two camps and needed uniting and bolstering as Kennedy's reelection year approached. The chief executive's high, early visibility in Texas would guarantee Connally the clout to crack the whip over the delegation in the coming battle.

Connally's braintrust was even now throwing a tantrum in the governor's inner office. This manhunt with its grisly murders, defenseless boy hostage, distraught mother holding vigil surrounded by those slightly off-center, let-the-world-go-away Jehovah's Witnesses, had already dragged on way too long. A quick resolution with the boy safely in his mother's arms was what would play well on statewide news.

But a quick and happy resolution appeared more and more unlikely. To the contrary, the suspense was building dramatically, and the national press and television networks smelled blood. The backroom boys reminded John Connally how the lead story on the network evening news would go:

"Texas today supplied the nation with one of those brutal dramas that only Texas, with its wide-open spaces and tradition of reckless frontier criminality, seems regularly to produce . . ."

The secretary stuck her head in the door and summoned them for the mobile update. The governor and his somber pals trooped in. The governor went straight to Gladys Perry's side and held her hand.

"They say the boy looks A-Okay," announced Willard, the governor's aide with the phone to his ear.

He listened some more, then spoke again to those gathered in the governor's office: "A high state official on board, a 'Sandy Garber'—uh, a gentleman from the Texas State Prison System, I believe—got a good look at the boy and attests to his well-being." The aide listened again. ". . . And they are pursuing the suspect with all deliberate speed . . . but cannot predict when it will all end."

Connally strode forward. "Gimme the phone, Willard . . ." He grabbed the phone and barked into it, "Red . . . Put Red on. . . ."

He pulled the phone over to the windows, turned his back on the room and spoke low into the mouthpiece. "Listen to me, Red . . . Yeah, it's me. Now's yer time to earn that genius-lawman reputation you wear around like a halo . . . 'Preciate that, understand

every bit of it, you know I do. You're a good ole boy
on a bird hunt, Red, you're my kinda man. I know you
won't let me down . . . You got it . . . You gimme a
good outcome, and you got one in the bank with me
and Jack Kennedy hisself.''

He handed the phone back to Willard and turned to
Gladys Perry with a warm, empathic look. He walked
back to her and squatted down and put the gentlest of
hands on her hands. "He'll come through this fine,
Mrs. Perry," he said. "This whole nightmare will be
over and done with very soon, and you'll be home
with your brave boy. I promise."

Gladys turned her head and pulled her hands from
under the governor's. This whole thing made her un-
comfortable. "Governor, I apologize," she said, "but
I can't be involved in your politics. My beliefs forbid
it."

Connally's aides' eyes bugged, but the governor was
turned away, singaling to his staff photographer to
come closer and get a shot. He turned back to Gladys
and again put his hand on her hands. The photographer
flashed his picture.

"Scripture says a Christian must keep separate from
the world," Gladys said, agitated. "War and death and
kidnapping are what come from mixing in worldly
things. I came here to ask you to stop this big chase
and let the Lord find my boy when and how He
chooses."

Connally nodded thoughtfully, hearing what she was
saying, picking up the thread. "The Good Lord is on
the side of the law and this administration, ma'am,
make no mistake about that," Connally said, seem-
ingly not at all alarmed at how this visit was going.
"All my forces are at your disposal—that's why your
state government is here, for just such emergencies. I
want you to know that I personally okayed the use of
a—"

" 'A man's own folly wrecks his life, and then he

bears a grudge against the Lord'," Gladys said, tearing up despite herself. "Proverbs 19:3. It is my early mixing in the world that is punishing my boy now. I bear no grudge, but you can't help me. Please."

"Even as we speak," Connally said soothingly, "a brand-new, high-tech mobile command post is being used at my direct authorization to conduct this manhunt. God's earth does harbor wickedness, Mrs. Perry, we can't get away from that knowledge. And part of my job as governor of your state is to—"

Her composure exhausted, Gladys began to sob. "Jehovah God is love," she cried. "Why would He let hideous men walk out of your prison to kill an innocent boy? Why would He put people in charge who would let it happen?!" She rose to her feet.

The reporters were getting all of this, some of them deeply moved themselves, all of them composing new story leads highlighting Gladys's searing pain. The governor's main staff aide tried to push the print reporters back out the door. The reporters didn't give an inch.

Connally eased Gladys down into a chair and pulled up one next to hers. "Mrs. Perry . . . Gladys," he said. "The Lord gives us the freedom to choose— wickedness or righteousness. Job 1: Verses 6 through 12, gives it to us straight: Jehovah permits evil on this earth in order to answer Satan's challenge."

He took her hand in his and looked into her eyes and spoke with a reassuring firmness. "Satan the Devil declared that God could not put men and women on earth who would be true to Him under test, Gladys. He was mocking the Lord. And Satan continues to bring woes now, to turn women and men against God and prove his mockery. But now Job kept integrity. Jesus did. True Christians do now. And we shall, all of us together, with His guiding hand. Matthew 4:1, Peter 1:6. Amen." He squeezed her hands.

Gladys, her eyes filled with tears, said, "Amen."

The governor helped her to her feet and with a nod to his photographer started moving with her toward the door. With flashes going off in the background, he walked with her out the door and down the grand hallways, comforting arm lightly about her shoulders. "It is an amazingly futuristic piece of law enforcement equipment that I've sent out there, Gladys," he said, "expressly to bring back that wayward man and your brave son, Phillip. 'Wonderful and Godly are the works of man.'—Isaiah 65:22. Wait'll you see it. It'd give you confidence just to watch the thing in operation."

Gladys hiccoughed, somehow comforted by this big man.

"We'll have that boy back safe and sound, Gladys," he said as they walked, "and once we do, you promise me you'll bring him up to meet his governor and see the kind of work we are trying to do so that good people like you . . ."

As they moved out of earshot of the reporters restrained behind the ropes, the journalists looked at each other and shook their heads as one. A pro at the top of his game.

"Those Bible lines," Aynsworth of the *Times Herald* said, "they really from the Bible?" He turned to the massed reporters.

"Maybe yes, maybe no," Margaret Hunt of *The Austin Democrat* said, wiping a tear from her eye, "who gives a damn." She elbowed through the other reporters toward the bank of phones.

▪ *THIRTY-FOUR* ▪

As Bradley braked hard, the trailer-pickup rig jack-knifed. The Airstream, traveling at high speed, got crosswise to the pickup and pulled the smaller vehicle at an angle to the direction of travel. The vehicles skidded off the road. Together they rammed through a thicket of small trees, became briefly airborne over a rock ledge, and landed in a bed of mesquite brush near a river bottom. They came to rest side by side.

The Wonderful and Godly work of man, the "amazingly futuristic piece of law enforcement equipment" now lay like an immovable part of the Texas landscape, along with the stony dry wash, the limestone outcroppings, and the everpresent mesquite undergrowth.

One by one the crew emerged, led by Bradley. He stood by the back wheels, running a hand through his hair, chagrined. Red walked past and glanced down to confirm his worst surmise. Yep.

"I think we're stuck, Red," Bradley said. Red kept walking—back through the flattened trees and brush to the road. He walked down the middle of the road in the direction the target vehicle had sailed out of sight.

Sally alone remained in the vehicle, studying a file. This one had a photo not of a felon at the top right corner but of Red—a much younger Red, dressed in a sheriff's uniform. This was Red's file. Sally had requisitioned it from state records at the last minute before hightailing it for Red's office to start the assignment.

An unusual file-pull it was, that of her own boss pro tem. But she did it on a hunch. This was a legendary Texas lawman. *And* a sometime running buddy of the governor himself. It made basic sense to go in there with as good a reading on Red Garnett as she could get. Sally was nothing if not thorough. And she was doing her best to be politically attuned. She was trying to be her father's daughter.

Sally Gerber had the double misfortune of being the second child in her family behind a brilliant older brother whom her father doted on but who died young. She was not a boy, and she was not Hollis II.

Hollis Gerber I was a prominent defense attorney, Texas style—which means swashbuckling, outspoken, powerful. A one-time partner of Racehorse Jones, Hollis took a backseat to no one when it came to political connectedness. And for his chip-off-the-block son, he could see the statehouse in the glimmering future—until Hollis II walked into a propellor blade one summer day at a private airfield where he kept his own four-seater.

Sally, a recalcitrant teenager, was at a Catholic girl's school in Iowa when it happened. Coincidentally, she was about to be expelled for setting the tree outside her dorm window on fire by sitting in it at night, smoking. It seems all the girls sat in the tree late at night and smoked, but it was Sally's idea for each of them to light just one leaf to see what would happen.

Back in Houston she had spent several years striving to be Hollis for her father, to no one's satisfaction. She was out here now trying to become Sally, with her father's blessing. And here she had Red to contend with. She wondered if she was after his blessing.

Her finger scanned down the page and arrived at Red's curriculum vitae, which amounted to his history with different branches of Texas law enforcement, local and statewide.

Her finger stopped at an entry around the middle of Red's career—his stint as a deputy sheriff in Palo Duro County between 1938 and 1942. The record indicated Red worked there through September, 1942. The record also indicated Butch Haynes was arrested in the same county in May, 1942, by the guy Adler implied was Red's partner. There was a crossover here, at least on paper. Surely Red would have mentioned it if he remembered having had contact with their fugitive. Wouldn't he? Yes, she was certain. She could only conclude the two men did not cross paths.

She craned her neck to see Red still walking away down the highway. He stopped and appeared to be staring off on the heading little Phillip Perry had been borne away.

"Uh, Miss Gerber?" Deputy Adler said, appearing by Sally's table.

She looked up at him startled, then girded for some smart-ass comment. "Yes?"

"They teach you that stuff in college, or what?" he asked.

"What stuff."

"That talkin' in tongues, seance thing," Adler said, "where you pretend to be the criminal?"

"Well, yes," Sally said. She was heartened by Adler's apparent shift in behavior, but wary.

"College, I . . . I never . . ." He shook his head, leaning back against a bulkhead. "I'm a straight field cop, school of layin' pipe and nailin' shingles. Came up a clerk in the Fort Worth office. Not too much theory there."

Sally recognized this kind of cop and where he was coming from. "It's really just careful reading of the files and building bridges where gaps exist in the story," she said matter-of-factly. "The trick is turning the stuff every which way, making yourself go through it like you were them. You walk in their mocassins, as the Indians say. After a while you see things."

"Like connect the dots," Adler said.

"Um . . . yeah," Sally said. Close enough.

Adler smiled, nodded. That was plenty enough theory for him for one day.

He pushed himself up off the bulkhead, reached

behind the couch, and pulled out the Lone Star plaque he'd stashed there. He lugged it out the door.

Red stood out in the middle of the road, still gazing at the horizon. Effing John Connally, he was thinking. As if he didn't have an ornery enough bobcat on his back, now Jack Kennedy's hopped on, too. All ready to say, *Ich bin ein Texacaner,* long as we can convince him it ain't too savage down here for the likes of him and that Frenchie wife o' his.

Red stuck a chaw in his gob without blinking or moving his eyes from some spot out there. He was back to thinking about Butch Haynes.

■ *THIRTY-FIVE* ■

Butch sat on the hood of the Ford, staring at the blue sky—staring in his mind's eye at the landscape of his need and desire. He was actually, briefly, content . . . kind of . . . all things considered. He was after it, that need and desire, on its tail, and that put him a thousand times closer than he'd been in a dozen years. Being after it was all he'd ever been, but he'd pretty much decided that was all anybody ever was. His mother, humping in the whorehouse? Was she after it, or was she just stuck, like him in Huntsville? His father, now, he got out, and he lit out. What'd he find? What'd he find that was fat enough to make him write home?

Casper slammed the car door and leaned up against the front fender, looking off and away like Butch.

"Started this road twenty years ago," Butch said. "And it still ain't finished."

Phillip slid his mask up and nodded sagely.

"Appears to me we got a decision to make," Butch

said. It's up to you, Phillip. We can backtrack to the highway or we can try it on foot.''

"Where we goin'?" Phillip asked. He was not the kind of kid to rush into decisions without knowing the what-for.

Butch reached into his back pocket and pulled out a folded postcard. He handed it over to Phillip. The card had to be twenty years old, crumpled, cracking, stained with coffee drips and fingerprints. Phillip unfolded it to reveal a beautiful green valley with a snow-capped mountain behind it.

"It's Alaska, Phillip," Butch said. "Last of the wild frontier.''

"It's pretty.''

"It's beautiful!" Butch said. "That there's Mt. Mc-Kinley, over twenty thousand feet up. It says on the back.''

"You been there?"

"Naw," Butch said. "Just got the one postcard . . . But anyhoo, back to our present dilemma. You feel like a hike?"

"How far?" the boy asked.

"Can't be more'n, oh, say, fifteen hundred miles.''

Phillip looked at him, a tad apprehensive; wanting to be a good sport and all, but still . . .

"Yer prolly' right," Butch said, taking the card from Phillip, sliding off the car, and returning the card to his pocket. "Go give our supplies a check.''

Phillip returned to the front seat of the car and rummaged among the bags and trash paper.

Butch surveyed the countryside—endless, over-grazed, and barren. No hint left of the rich grasslands that once drew horizon-to-horizon-size herds of buf-falo down from the Great Plains. Not even a memory of the Commanches who thrived among them.

A mile or so across the hot dusty plain sat a small ranch house kept company by a windmill and one handsome old sycamore tree. The windmill that drew

water from below the limestone caprock and the few
long sycamore limbs that twisted and waved over a
portion of the house gave the place its only relief from
the parching heat and the relentless West Texas wind.

Phillip reappeared with the once-full candy and provisions bag.

"How's it look?" Butch asked.

"A soda . . . some gum . . . half a Moon Pie,"
Phillip said.

"Rations for one at best," Butch said. "Come on."
Butch strode straight into the rocky field.

Phillip lingered a moment, watching. Then he stuck
the rest of the half-eaten Moon Pie in his mouth and
followed, hurrying to catch up.

■ *THIRTY-SIX* ■

Hay, rocks, sticks, chunks of a broken-up chair
and a spare tire were wedged under the rear wheels of
the GMC pickup. Adler approached with the governor's Lone Star plaque that had been safely stashed
inside the Airstream. Bradley grabbed it and shoved it
under a tire.

Suttle moved back and forth, watching the whole
operation in agony. "Look, guys," he said, "I gotta
say that I, uh, really don't think . . ."

Bradley heaved a hay bale he'd liberated from the
field onto the road shoulder and shoved it up to the
rear of the Airstream. He stuck one end of a sturdy
mesquite fence post over the hay bale and down under
the axle and tested its leverage.

"What?" Suttle said. "Are you crazy?"

"It'll work," Bradley said with great conviction.

"Old marine thing." He turned. "Adler," he called. "Go start her up!"

Adler spun and loped toward the pickup, now reattached to the front of the vehicle.

Suttle, momentarily stunned by this fence-post thing, came to and stumbled after Adler, waving his hand. "No, no!" he shouted. "Stay out of the driver's seat! From now on no one but me drives! Understood?"

Adler turned to Bradley.

"Suit yerself," Bradley said to Suttle, who climbed on board. "Now when I give the signal," Bradley shouted, "step on the gas."

Suttle eased into the driver's seat. Immediately, he took out a handkerchief and wiped off the dash and dials.

"You ready?" came Bradley's shout.

Suttle said a prayer to himself. "Please, Lord . . ." He leaned out and yelled to the rear, "Yeah, okay!"

"Let 'er rip!" Bradley shouted.

The tires began to turn, slowly at first, kicking out some hay and branches. Bradley started applying pressure with the fence post, pushing down with the idea of boosting the Airstream from the muck. Adler jumped to lend a hand and added his weight to the fence post.

The tires spun faster, throwing out more hay, rocks, sticks, pieces of the chair. When the governor's plaque shot backward, too, the spinning tires grabbed solid ground for a few seconds, yanking the Airstream forward five or six feet. Bradley and Adler, straining at the rear, pitched forward as the trailer moved and they dove into the brown sludge. They picked themselves up and looked at each other. New Zealand mud men, *National Geographic* photo essay.

The Airstream settled into a snug new spot, and the pickup pulled in vain.

"All right! All right!" Bradley yelled. "Kill it!"

As the engine stopped, a loud metal crack sounded and the Airstream slumped to one side—causing Sally and her files, inside the RV, to slide a bit.

Bradley peered under the vehicle. The fence post remained sturdily intact, but the axle now had a sharp bend in the middle. The right rear tires were tilted out at a forty-five-degree angle. Bradley and Adler gazed at the offending axle in awe and apprehension.

Suttle, racing around from the front, skidded down on his knees to look. He gasped. "Oh, God . . ."

"Yeah, I'd say it was broken," Bradley said philosophically.

"Oh, yeah, broken," Adler added.

Suttle stood up, shoulders bowed. "I'm fucked," he said in a hoarse wheeze. "What am I supposed to tell Saunders?"

"That's yer call," Bradley said. "I'm just glad I wasn't at the wheel when that axle cracked."

Suttle stared at Bradley, his face a knot of incredulity. He stepped toward Bradley, gathering himself to annihilate the older man.

The phone rang inside. Adler dashed to answer it.

Bradley backed away from the trembling Suttle with arms raised for peace.

Adler stuck his head out the door of the RV and yelled for the chief. "Governor's hot line, Red," he called.

Red turned and walked back toward the slumping RV.

"Governor insists he have the mobile home back for the parade tomorrow," Adler said as the boss walked up. "He's laid out a bunch of publicity about it, apparently. They're calling it a photo event, or some such."

Red spat by the roadside.

" 'Course he wants this thing wrapped up first," Adler added, "since he already announced to the press he loaned his machine to you. As a—" he read from his notes—" 'an up-to-the-minute whiz-bang mobile command post'—those are Saunders's words I'm givin' you."

Red spat again and shook his head. Then he focused, just then noticing Adler's new all-mud look.

Adler saw the chief's expression and tried to brush off the goop, but it just smeared. Bradley walked out from the rear of the RV. Red looked at him—another mud man.

"Uh, Red," Bradley said. "I'm not sure but, uh, Red, I believe the axle's bent . . . a little."

Red sighed and scratched his head. He gave an isn't-it-obvious shrug. "Tell 'em to come and get it," he said to Adler.

▪ *THIRTY-SEVEN* ▪

Butch continued his hell-bent brisk pace across the field of sparse hay, the puffy wind whipping a dust plume in his trail. Butch was charging, pumping himself up for whatever lay out there. The ranch house ahead stood alone against the cloudless sky. It was all Phillip with his short legs could do to keep up.

"Where we goin'?" Phillip asked, out of breath.

"We're goin' trick r' treatin', Phillip," Butch said.

Phillip stopped dead in his tracks. Butch, sensing the boy was no longer following, stopped, spun around and faced him.

"What?" Butch said.

"We ain't allowed to trick 'r treat."

"Huh?"

"My mama don't allow it."

"Trick 'r treatin'?" Butch said in disbelief. "Why not?"

"Against our religion."

"Against yer religion?" Butch said. "What kinda foolishness is that?"

"Jehovah's Witness."

"Well, Christ on a crutch," Butch said. "I ain't never."

"That, too," Phillip said.

"That what, too?" Butch said.

"Cursin'," Phillip said.

"Godamighty, what else?" Butch said.

"Likker, smokin'," Phillip said.

"No shit? Oh, look, sorry . . ."

"And other defilements of the flesh, like homo-in'," Phillip said.

"Do ya' even know what homo-in' is?" Butch asked, amazed.

"No," Phillip said. "Jes' the Bible don' allow it."

"Man, alive," Butch said.

"It's all in the Bible," Phillip said.

Butch shook his head in wonder. "It's jus', what's the point?"

"My mama says him that does the will of God remains forever," Phillip said. "We'll be livin' forever in a rejoicin' world."

"Well now, I don't wanna sour ya on this stuff or anything, Phillip," Butch said, "but that's, uh . . ." He stopped. No point. He looked at the boy. "Tell you what," he said. "That livin' forever stuff, that's for then, this is now. And now I'm askin' you, Phillip. I ain't askin' yer mother, and I ain't askin' Jehovah. Do you wanna go trick r' treatin' or not?"

Butch and Phillip crossed the yard and made their way under the sycamore tree up to the ranch house door.

"Okay, Phillip," Butch said. "All ya gotta do is knock on the door, and when they open it, you say 'trick or treat.' Got it?"

They stationed themselves at the door—Butch hanging back. Butch nodded to Phillip who flipped down his mask, turned, and rang the buzzer.

"Now wait til they come," Butch said low.

A farm wife of about sixty-five opened the inner door and smiled to the two visitors through the screen door.

"Now, Phillip," Butch whispered.

"Trick 'r treat," Phillip said.

"Well, ain't you the cutest lil' ghost I ever did see," the farm wife said. She was diminutive in stature with a nimbus of fine white hair that lifted in the wind. She looked divinely happy to see this little child appear out of nowhere at her door.

Butch kept an eye out for activity in the house behind her, but saw no movement.

"Say it again, Phillip," Butch whispered.

"Trick 'r treat, ma'am," Phillip said.

"Well, seein' that Halloween was yesterday," the woman said, "I guess you'll have to trick me. You missed the caramel popcorn balls I made up special. Children came from all over the county." She opened her hands helplessly—no treats at the inn.

Butch stepped slightly forward and smiled, and pulled up his shirt exposing the revolver stuck in his pants. He kept the shirt raised as the woman looked and the sight registered. He lowered the shirt, still smiling.

The old woman, her seraphic smile wilted, moved back from the door. "Wait right here," she said.

"Good job," Butch said, patting Phillip on the shoulder. Butch's eyes scanned overhead, looking at the wires—at a telephone wire than ran from the house to a nearby pole and on to a distant trunk line.

The elderly woman quickly returned to the door with an armload of anything she could find in the kitchen and pantry. She pushed open the screen door and held out the goods. Phillip gratefully opened his sack and watched as the woman dropped in a loaf of bread, a jar of mustard, candies, jams, butter, a foil package of cream cheese, a package of saltines, and two cans of soup. She added some paper napkins, then reached inside the door, came back with her little cash purse, opened it, and dumped the contents—a couple of dollars and lots of change—into Phillip's bag.

Phillip peered in the bag. "Thankyew," he said and smiled through his mask. He turned and bounded down off the low porch. This trick or treating thing was a steal, he marveled to himself. He opened the bag to show Butch and turned to wave at the generous old lady. She had already shut the door and was locking it.

Butch and Phillip stepped off the porch steps and started toward the weedy field. "Never underestimate the kindness of the common man, Phillip," Butch said. Falling half a step back, he reached behind Phillip, grabbed the phone line where it fed into the house, and yanked. It came loose. He tossed it aside and caught up with Phillip without the boy's catching on.

■ *THIRTY-EIGHT* ■

The showpiece motor home was fast becoming a pig sty. Coffee spills, Coke bottles, overfull ashtrays were everywhere. Adler updated the thumbtacked map and spoke into the mike: "Spur 208 northbound. And 83 at Aspermont coming and going." He moved some tacks and turned to Red. "That it?"

"Yeah," Red said.

Adler reached behind him to set down the mike and didn't see the full cup of coffee that Bradley, trying to make himself useful, had put down for him. The coffee toppled over, running under the radio and onto the floor—the governor's choice pale blue carpet. Suttle dashed back from the front with a towel to wipe it up, but taking a look at the general state of the vehicle's interior, saw futility in trying to empty the ocean with a thimble. He threw the towel aside and returned to the driver's seat to mope and compose his explanation.

Bradley, stripped down to his mud-free undershirt but still caked about the face and head, turned to Red hopefully. "We can call patrol cars in any time you want, Red." Translation: Please let's get the hell out of here before the state boys show up to reclaim their rig.

"Naw," Red said. "Let's just sit tight and see where he turns up." He walked back to the rear, talking to himself: "Ain't in no mood for backin' and forthin'. Ain't dignified. Let him light somewhere."

▪ *THIRTY-NINE* ▪

Butch was loose, horsing across the midwest Texas prairie, tacking this way and that, varying direction and routes, but always and actually tending toward the wild frontier of Alaska. Did he expect to get there? Why not? Eventually. What did he know of the official fury he had unleashed and the juggernaut that had been launched in his wake? And even if he did fully realize, and if he now saw that juggernaut, hung up as it was in a mud bank, why in the name of heaven wouldn't he think he could make it out of Texas and all the way to the Promised Land?

"You sure there's no meat in there?" Butch asked. "Spam maybe, Vienna sausages, anything like that."

"Nawsir," Phillip said.

"Well, I bet you can make us some mustard sandwiches, can't ya?" Butch said.

"Yeahsir."

"Well, go to it."

Phillip broke out the loaf of store-bought bread and laid out four slices on the dashboard.

"How many," Phillip asked.

"Many as you want."

Phillip laid out six more slices. The dashboard was now covered with bread. Phillip pulled out the mustard and opened it, but had nothing to spread it with. He looked around. Butch fished a pack of gum off the seat and gave Phillip a stick. The boy commenced to use it to spread the mustard.

The Ford came over a rise and started down a long hill. At the bottom of the dip in the road, in a copse of native cottonwoods, a family was pulled over having a picnic. Phillip watched them with hungry eyes as the Ford grew even with the family and passed. A mother and father, a boy about seven and a girl a couple of years older. They had a blanket spread in the shade and a mesquite cooking fire going behind the brand new, coffee-brown, heavily laden station wagon.

The dad was filling buns with fat grilled beefburgers. The mom was pulling sodas from a cooler. Each kid was munching from their own bag of chips. They were laughing at something, waiting for what had to be their favorite meal. This was plainly a family on vacation and having a helluva time. Phillip was spellbound.

Something about that family scene fascinated Butch too. He pulled his eyes back on the road as the Ford zoomed up the hill on the other side. As the road crested, something far off caught Butch's eyes. He braked sharply, reversed the car down the hill, pulled two wheels off and set the emergency brake. He reached over and grabbed the first completed mustard sandwich and got out, leaving the Ford running.

"Be right back," he said to Phillip. "Don't be stingy with that mustard, now."

Phillip nodded and continued piling the yellow glop on each of the slices of bread.

Butch walked forward to the crest of the hill again, the tallest land within miles. He took in the 360-degree view. His eyes settled on the highway down the hill and straight ahead—a line of cars idling as they waited their turn to pass a roadblock.

In the Ford Phillip busily spread a second layer of mustard on each sandwich. He sneaked some peeks back at the all-American picnicking family. The Ford moved slightly. Phillip looked around. Butch was still at the top of the hill. The Ford eased a few inches backward again. Then all of a sudden the emergency brake gave completely and the Ford started rolling in earnest.

"Whooaaa! Butch! Butch!" Phillip screamed.

Butch turned to see the Ford picking up steam, reversing down the hill. He exploded after it at a dead run, but the car was already on its way.

"Step on the brake!" Butch yelled. "Put your foot on the brake! The middle one!"

Phillip threw up the sandwiches in his hands and grabbed for the wheel, sliding behind it. He probed for the brake with his foot as he'd seen adults do countless times. His leg was too short by half a foot. He tried to scootch down, reaching with his toe, twisting, trying to see. But as he twisted and his head went below the dashboard, the Ford veered off the road.

Butch, pounding down the road after the Ford, shouted for Phillip to get his head up, and "Turn the wheel left!—That way! Left!"

The white-bread father of the family relaxing by the cottonwood copse, Bob by name, had seen this episode developing from the first. Now his worst nightmare was blossoming into reality; the Ford was veering toward his family and his new Oldsmobile station wagon.

"Everybody run!" he shouted. "Back in the trees! Quick!"

Bob himself ran in the other direction, toward his new car. "Forget the car, Bob!" screamed his wife.

"Are you crazy!" he shouted back as he lunged into the driver's seat. "It's only got a thousand miles on it!" He keyed it frantically and got it going and in gear just as Phillip pulled the steering wheel left enough to swerve the Ford off the highway and through the field. The Ford whipped past the gleaming Olds station wagon with inches to spare—just as Butch came to a heaving halt next to an ashen Bob.

"Bad brakes," Butch wheezed.

"That was close," Bob said, popping the door, jumping out of the car. He gave Butch a relieved smile. "Bob Fielder," he said.

Butch smiled back and shook the man's hand. "Edgar Poe," he said.

"Had me scared silly," Bob said. "Had her but two months. Not even out of break-in period yet."

"She's a beaut, all right," Butch said, admiring her lines and grace. "Say, Bob, what with my brake problem and all, I sure would appreciate a lift. Me'n my boy live about five miles up the road here. I can pick up the car tomorrow."

The Ford, after passing the Family Bob and their new Olds, had enough steam to roll part way up the hill on the other side of the dip. It eventually lost momentum, stopped, and then started back down the hill, Casper the Friendly Ghost still at the wheel. It came slowly at first, but picked up speed, and now it was going at a pretty good clip headed right for Bob and Butch.

Phillip was screaming at the top of his lungs, trying to stay tall enough to steer, but slipping down . . .

Bob swiveled his head in panic, looking for a place to hide.

Butch stepped right to the middle of the Ford's path and stood his ground, staring into Phillip's onrushing face. "The brake, Phillip!" he shouted. "Step on the brake, hard!"

Phillip, clean out of choices, let himself slide to the floor and dove on the brake pedal with both hands, mashing it to the floor with all his strength and weight. The tires squealed, and the Ford came to a skidding halt inches from Butch's kneecaps.

Phillip's face popped up over the dash. Butch gave him a proud smile. "Helluva job, Phillip!" he said. "Never a doubt."

Bob, trembling on top of his luggage rack, crawled down with a big sigh and smile of relief.

■ *FORTY* ■

Eight Texas Highway Patrol cars and four county sheriff's vehicles were gathered at the checkpoint, the intersection of a state two-lane and a county spur in Cottle County. The two Highway Patrol officers manning the line in which the Olds wagon was moving forward were kind of going through the motions of checking licenses and peering into vehicles. They were not at their sharpest as one would expect them to be if the next car could contain a mad-dog killer. Instead they were talking and joking between themselves.

Apparently, the last sighting of the escaped felon and his captive had been way over in Hockle County up on the Llano Estacado west of Lubbock. No way that three-time loser could've gotten this far east in that short a time. This was just practice.

The fly in the ointment of that logic was the last reported sighting was erroneous and had not yet been corrected.

In the station wagon Bob and Mrs. Bob rode the front seat. Butch and Phillip sojourned in the kiddie section way in back while Bob's son, Kelly, and daughter, Patsy, occupied the middle seat. Kelly was explaining to Phillip that the Green Hornet was not an insect any more than Spiderman was a spider. "Jeez, Buzz," he said. "You been on Mars for about ten years?"

"Well, are they real stories?" Phillip asked.

"What?—the Green Hornet?" Kelly said.

"Or are they just made up?"

Kelly just shook his head. "Yep," he said. "A skeezerhead from Mars."

"Yeah, well, did you know that buzzards is armadillos with wings?" Phillip said.

Kelly looked at him uncertainly for a split second, then grinned. "I like that, armadillos with wings," he said. "You got a good sense of humor. Buzzard." They both laughed.

"Sorry for the inconvenience, Edgar," Bob called back. "The kids like the back down like that so they can play."

"No trouble at all, Bob," Butch said.

As Bob pulled the wagon toward the front of the roadblock line, Butch tugged a blanket to his chin and slid down flatter, propping his head between two stuffed animals.

Phillip had his head avidly into a Green Hornet comic book when Officer T. M. Wing leaned an arm on the vehicle and asked for Bob's license.

With a nervous look at the officer's uniform buttons scraping on his paint job, Bob produced his license. "Why the roadblock, Officer?" he said.

"Escaped convict, sir," Officer Wing said. "Just a precaution." He perused the license and glanced casually in the back. It wasn't certain how many life forms he saw back there. "Where ya headed, Robert?" the cop asked.

"Colorado," Bob said. "Vacation."

Looking at the license, the officer said, "Come all the way up from Corpus Christi, how come you're off the interstate."

"Oh ho, new car," Bob said. "Still in the warranty break-in period. Keepin' it under forty."

Butch was dying in the back, wishing sudden muteness on chatty Bob. Phillip had finished with the Green Hornet comic and was fussing with the string on his Casper the Friendly Ghost mask, about to put it back on.

The officer handed back the license. "Have a fine one," he said and stepped back.

"Thanks," Bob said, leaning his arm on the window. "Takin' her up Pike's Peak. Puttin' her through her paces."

The officer nodded, friendly.

"She'll be outa the break-in by then," Bob said.

The officer waved him smartly ahead. Bob pulled away and accelerated oh so gently out of the roadblock and into the countryside. Butch closed his eyes and envisioned Alaska.

▪ *FORTY-ONE* ▪

To the buzzards wheeling high above, the crippled Law Enforcement Special looked like an armadillo with its hinders caught in a gopher hole. Bradley stood off from the vehicle behind some mesquite in his boxer shorts, brushing futilely at the dried mud on his uniform.

Bobby Lee sat on a nearby rock, snickering. He was whittling on a stick, which was starting to resemble something.

"Saw a gorilla in the Dallas zoo had sweeter legs than that," he said.

Bradley said nothing, just swiped vigorously at his pants. He did have kind of skinny legs for his otherwise strapping figure.

"What do broads say?" Bobby Lee asked. "You must be some peehole pirate, standin' there with yer mule up and those snags for legs."

Bradley kept his back to Bobby Lee and kept on brushing.

"You don't suppose that's what's keepin' you from makin' lieutenant, do ya? Bad legs?" Bobby Lee said. "Can bad legs screw up a career as bad as you've screwed up yours? Can't be yer attitude: The world owes me, my pee don't stink—"

Bradley was on him in a flash, hands at his throat trying to get a death grip, the two of them rolling in the dirt.

"Get off me, shithead!" Bobby Lee squealed, fending off Bradley's hands. "Fuckin' loser!"

Adler, standing at the map with the mike in his hands, heard the sudden scuffling and grunts and oaths. He leaned out the door and looked and yelled for Suttle's help. The two men rushed into the mesquite thicket to break up the fight.

It didn't take much. Bobby Lee was ready to disengage immediately. In fact, he never struck a blow, but instead went into a kind of fetal fold with his hands balled up and tucked into his gut until Adler and Suttle rescued him.

He laughed derisively as he stood up, brushed himself off, and got his breath. He dug around in the dirt until he found the piece of whittling he'd been working on.

"You must have a soft fuckin' belly, faggot," Bradley spit at Bobby Lee from the corral of Adler's arms. "I'll remember. Keep yer eye peeled."

In fact, Bobby Lee had a taut, one-hundred-sit-ups-a-day gut. It wasn't his gut he was protecting. Why Bobby Lee didn't fight and why he balled up like a sow bug had to do with his hands. Bobby Lee had a thing about his hands. He went to great lengths to safeguard them and keep them in prime working order. He manicured his nails and cuticles, used tiger balm and an antibiotic salve as hand lotions, and wore black soft-leather gloves when out in the sun or wind for any length of time.

Bobby Lee's hands were his history.

By age ten, growing up in El Paso, Bobby Lee was a "phenom." He had the nickname Slow-hand, for his work with a shortstop's glove on his Little League team. A first-rate contact hitter, too, terrific hand-eye coordination for one so young. The different teams in the older Babe Ruth League vied for Bobby Lee's services, and his father, a wiry dyspeptic scrap wholesaler who made an okay living but knew he was meant for better things, let it be discreetly known that his son's talent was for sale to the highest bidder. Unbeknownst to Bobby Lee when he was assigned to the Conquistadors team across town the next spring, his father, thanks to some serious grinding and double-dealing, walked away with a nice cash kickback.

Bobby Lee was a star in Babe Ruth, too. He was growing taller and stronger. High schools were beginning to salivate over him and there was talk of a pro career. Then two things happened to put a crimp in Bobby Lee's trajectory. He broke some bones in his off-glove hand on a short hopper off a concrete-hard infield. And his father's extortion got leaked to a local reporter. The story didn't come out just because some cash changed hands; kids' sports are a serious business all over Texas. It came out because Bobby Lee's old man had been greedy and had double-crossed the wrong people.

The upshot was Bobby Lee's being banned from organized baseball in El Paso for two years. To hell with it, Bobby Lee said, freaked by the broken bones anyway. He decided to apply his singular eye-hand talents in other directions. By the time he was sixteen he had won the state junior eight-ball championship in San Antonio. And four years later he looked as though he was on his way to making the U.S. Olympic rifle team. But again his father's doings intervened, though in a different way this time.

Bobby Lee's father had become a rabid McCarthyite, obsessed with the country's infiltration by pinkos and Commies. He wanted the borders closed, Castro bombed, and Julius and Ethel Rosenberg hanged. And he took it a step further: He organized a group of Texas-style America Firsters who took it as their sacred duty to burn down a Socialist Party meeting hall and a string of Mexican businesses on the high side of the Rio Grande.

Not enough hard evidence jumped into the government's hands to prosecute Bobby Lee's father—there was a lot of sympathy for the old boy's actions. But Bobby Lee was quietly dropped back from first-team Olympian to second-team, and then to alternate. In the end he didn't even get to go to the Games.

Not long after, he enrolled in the state police academy and moved into law enforcement professionally. He carried with him his phenomenal eye-hand coordination, his father's raw, chauvinist politics, and a corrosive cynicism about looking out for Number One.

Leaden gloom hung over the Law Enforcement Special. Trash covered every inside surface of the vehicle—product of men working in close contact with no one assigned to clean-up. Red was sensitive to rank; he would not assign any one of these high-ranking officers to mop-and-slop work. And the thought of asking Sally to take charge of some policing up, though it had quickly entered his head, just as quickly left it as soon as he walked over to her and started to indicate what an incredible sty the place had become. The look in her eye had stopped the words in his mouth, and he had turned and walked back to his office, resolved to live with garbage.

To pass the time, Red sat, stared at the prairie, and rolled his gold dollar over his knuckles. Or he practiced his unique talent of spitting tobacco juice into an empty Coke bottle from a two- or three-foot distance. Exacting work, and he was world-class at it. Not infallible, though. His misses sank into the brown flecked carpeting that graced that part of the mobile home, with hardly a trace. They did leave a telltale odor, but one that Sally alone seemed to notice. It was enough to keep her away from Red's office, at her own table and files.

Butch's file absorbed her interest still—an addendum page entitled "Juvenile Court Record." It contained the standard prison history chronicled in reverse, starting from postimprisonment parole status filings and working backward through prerelease reports, parole-eligibility reports, inductee reports, to presentencing reports on each of Butch's convictions.

She kept returning to one early report that contained something intriguing and puzzling. She stared at Red. He returned her stare.

"What?" he said.

She decided not to ask. She decided from what she now knew of this living legend in the Texas Ranger boots and Stetson that he would answer this particular question only if it was not asked. Only if he knew that she had the right question and knew enough not to ask it.

Out on the mesquite prairie, Bradley finished his dry cleaning and re-covered his thin legs with his wide-cut trousers. At a distance Bobby Lee sat on a limestone outcropping and finished whittling his artifact, a four-inch-long wooden replica of a high-caliber shell.

Adler, back at the shortwave, kept an eye on both of them through the window. The tension was telling on them all. Conversational exchanges were limited to necessities. Nobody wanted to roil the waters.

Except Red. He was sitting in his favorite chair, gazing out across the brushy, parched landscape and whistling "The Yellow Rose of Texas." Sally looked at him in wonder.

Adler waved a hand in the air—something coming in on the shortwave. He turned to Red. "They've got two highway patrol cars they can give us now," he said.

Red didn't even take his feet down; he was in no hurry. "Have 'em stand by," he said. "We got the best seats in the house right here." He thought for a minute. "Have the guys at the southern roadblocks call in the dogs and move north. Same with the guys from Wichita Falls—move 'em west. Check every road, every farm between Anson and Paducah Corners, and between Sweetwater and Lubbock."

Adler surveyed the map and stuck in thumbtacks signaling those directives. "We got him hemmed in closer than that, don't ya think?" he said to Red.

Red shrugged and picked up humming "The Yellow Rose of Texas."

"I predict we'll have him singing a different tune by nightfall," Adler said, proud of his joke. He looked to Red and Sally. Nobody got it.

∎ *FORTY-TWO* ∎

About forty-two, forty-three miles per hour. Now and then a peak forty-five. The brown Olds station wagon ate up the road oh so slowly under Bob's heavy foot.

Butch relaxed in the back, whistling "Old MacDonald Had A Farm," not a man in any hurry. Bob, in the mood, joined him. Catching the spirit, Mrs. Bob and the kids. Soon the whole damn car was whistling "Old MacDonald Had A Farm."

Patsy, red-haired, freckled and all of nine, got excited and did some bouncing to the music and spilled her 7-UP. Sticky, sugary 7-UP splashed all over the seat back and into Bob's hair.

"You're spilling! You're spilling!" younger brother Kelly sang with delight. Bob and wife spun around, Bob feeling the wetness on the back of his head.

"Oh, Patsy," Mrs. Bob said. "Look at what you've done to your dad's new upholstery." She took the cup from the bouncing girl. She reached back and grabbed the child by the arm and squeezed and jerked. "How many times do I have to tell you? No jumping in the car! No jumping in the car!"

Patsy cried out in pain and fright. Mom gave her a push back into the seat. Bob stared straight ahead.

Butch continued whistling softly, almost eerily, but he watched the unfolding events closely.

Mrs. Bob reached back with tissues and tried to sop the soda stain off the seat. She saw some 7-UP on Bob's hair and was about to mop that, but decided not to invite trouble. Patsy bawled loudly.

"Damn that kid!" Bob growled.

Patsy bawled harder than ever.

Then he softened up. "It's okay, sweetie," Bob said, stroking his daughter on the arm. "The car's going to be all right. Daddy still loves you. Promise you'll be more careful." He turned back to his driving.

Butch, directly behind Patsy and still watching, let his whistling run to silence.

"Yeah, the car'll survive," Bob grumbled to himself, trying to reconcile himself to the inevitable depreciation of his prize asset, thanks to kids. He drove for a while in silence, shaking his head now and then. Finally, Mrs. Bob said with a bitter smile, "So much for the new car smell." Patsy whimpered quietly in the back.

Butch put on his sincere smile and spoke up, looking out at the passing landscape. "This will do fine right here, Bob," he said. "But I do have one more favor to ask."

Five minutes later and the whole complexion of things for the family Bob and the Bobmobile had changed fundamentally. They were standing along the roadside—Mom, Dad, two kids, luggage, coats and guide books, picnic cooler and comic books. The look on their faces said it all. Stranded. Betrayed. Hung out to dry by a guy they had held out the hand of friendship to. Mrs. Bob's eyes were as big as saucers. This kind of thing didn't happen in America.

Butch handed over the last couple of stuffed animals to Patsy. He patted Kelly on the head. And he stuck his hand out to Bob.

"Just a loaner, Bob," he said. "Not to worry. You'll get her back."

Phillip sat in the front seat, watching through the window. He looked neither surprised nor shocked at the sudden shift in arrangements. He had gotten pretty comfortable with the family Bob in the back of the wagon, and the appearance of the pistol again had been a jolt. But the unexpected and the drastic was the expected with Butch, he'd come to know. Besides, he was a kid, and nobody can switch into new modes of reality faster than kids, for whom newness is an everyday thing. What Phillip was uneasy about and hoping to wish away was an outburst of violence like the one that ended the Jerry Pugh reality.

Bob reluctantly grasped Butch's hand and shook it, holding it an extra shake to try to impress on this terrifying man his paramount concern.

"Please, it's new," he said. "Hold it under forty-five tops. Tops . . . At least for the next five hundred miles." There was anguish in the man's face.

"You know I will, Bob," Butch said. He gave them all a snappy salute and jogged around the wagon to the driver's seat, and he and Casper the Friendly Ghost were off.

"Wave, Phillip," Butch said cheerfully as pulled slowly from the shoulder.

Phillip waved. Bob's kids waved back. Phillip started to giggle. "They look funny," he said.

"Maybe," Butch said. "But Bob did the right thing. What if he'd put up a fight? I mighta had to shoot him, and where would that family be then?" A thoughtful half second passed. "Naw, Bob's a fine family man and that's about the best thing a fella can hope to be."

With his speech done, Butch stabbed the gas pedal to the floor. The mighty Olds engine opened its throat and roared and the car screeched rubber on down the highway.

Bob cringed in pain as his pride and joy careened toward the land of the lost.

■ *FORTY-THREE* ■

The main force of Highway Patrol and local sheriffs at Paducah Corners now monitored cars one by one, keeping the seal tight, guaranteeing no leakage past their choke point. They had reacted positively to the news that the west Panhandle sighting was erroneous and that the escaped con might indeed be up their way. They were on the alert, giving each car and truck a thorough going over, ready for any encounter.

Looking up between cars, one officer saw something out ahead of them, past their roadblock, going north. He nudged his partner, grabbed him, made him look . . .

Coming back over the crest of the hill on foot, carrying luggage, hats, coolers, and comics, was the family Bob. Bob in the lead, keeping his head high— The kids still not quite sure what the heck was going on. Mrs. Bob, carrying the two biggest bags, brought up the rear, dragging her tail feathers.

In the immobilized mobile home, Adler dropped his headphones and yelled back to Red. "He got through! At Paducah Corners. Sonuvabith, you were right!"

"What?" Bradley said, waking from a doze.

"Coerced a motorist," Adler said.

Bobby Lee snorted disdainfully. "What's the point of a roadblock?"

Red gave an aggravated sigh and put on his hat. "Well goddamn," he said. "Shout at Amarillo. Tell 'em we got a notion he's headed their way."

Adler jammed the earphones back on and called Amarillo.

Red walked up from the back. "Truth is," he said, "I wish he'd cross the border so we could just put the Feds in charge of the whole thing."

This was a declaration nobody in the vehicle ever expected to hear from Red Garnett. He'd fight the prima donna Feds with all his weapons down to his nail file to keep them from walking all over his cases. The Feds had more money, bigger mouths, and louder PR people than he did, but that's all they had. In his oft-broadcast opinion, Texas Rangers and Texas state cops would clean the plow of the FBI and the ATF on any level playing field. Asked once by a green reporter if he'd like to be an FBI man himself, Red had made himself popular with J. Edgar Hoover by answering that working for the FBI was "a bird's nest on the ground"—too cushy by half.

Now he said, "I got work to do back home."

Adler looked at him to see if he was sick. Sally tried to read his unreadable face.

"I'm hungry," Red said, walking to the open door and stretching, staring out into the late afternoon light. He turned back in. "This thing got any food?"

"Well, uh . . . Ya see . . ." Suttle said, hesitating.

Adler looked at him. "Is there food or isn't there?" He jumped up and went to the fridge.

"Got T-bones in the fridge, Red!" he called in triumph. Only good news they'd had in some time.

Suttle came toward him, hands out. "Uh, uh . . . those were stocked for the governor, men," he said. "I don't think he'd approve of . . ."

Adler was busy mining for other riches. He pulled a plastic bag out of the freezer.

"And look, Red," he said gleefully. "Tater-Tots! Those kind you like."

Red turned and looked. "That so?" he said, shaking his head appreciatively. "John sets a good table, always has."

Suttle looked sick—too defeated even to protest with any vigor. He leaned his head back, squinting down the road, composing his resignation letter.

▪ *FORTY-FOUR* ▪

Butch was pushing the Bobmobile along at good high revs, making about seventy-five out on the plains, thirty-five through the towns in order not to attract attention. Both he and Phillip had tried all the knobs and buttons—electric windows, electric seats, electric aerial, adjustable steering wheel, cruise control. Bob had a nice car here.

"Hell, this car's broke in good. Listen to it," he said to Phillip as he fiddled with the radio. "Can't find zydeco to save my ass." He settled on a south of the border station playing Spanish ballads. He gave it volume and played some lip bugle accompaniment.

Phillip laughed.

"Hey, Phillip," Butch said, "that stuff 'bout not trick 'r treatin' and all causa Jehovah? Ya' get the other days, don'tcha?"

"Nawsir," Phillip said.

"I mean the big ones," Butch said. "Christmas."

"We don't get Christmas."

"Yer shittin' me," Butch said.

"Nawsir," the boy said. "No birthdays, nor parties, neither."

"Now you tell me what's wrong with a birthday party."

"Only two folks in the Bible had birthday parties, Pharaoh and Herod," Phillip said. "They were bad folks." He thought for a moment. "And bein' born into this world of sin ain't no thing to rejoice over. That's the other reason."

"Whew," Butch said and gave the boy a look. "Then you ain't never been to a carnival neither, have ya?"

"Nawsir."

"Not even one," Butch said.

"Not even one."

"Cotton candy?" Butch said.

"Seen that once," Phillip said. "It's red."

"Pink."

"Never ate none though," Phillip said.

"Roller coasters?" Butch asked.

"Seen pictures," Phillip said.

Butch cogitated silently for a few moments, pushing the Olds wagon along through flat pastureland containing a few scrawny head of old-fashioned longhorns. Then he decided, hell yes—a man has to be true to his deepest values.

"You know, Phillip," he said, "you have a goddamned red, white, and blue American right to eat cotton candy and ride roller coasters."

"I do?" Phillip said.

"You really do," Butch answered, pulled the car over.

In two shakes—before he had a chance to decide if this was safe or insane, a hoot or a terror—Phillip was blasting along on the roof of the station wagon, screaming for joy.

Butch had lashed the boy to the wagon's luggage carrier and taken off across the slab-flat West Texas plain like a rocket. With his mouth wide open, his hair flattened straight back by the wind, Phillip howled, laughed, and held on for dear life.

Butch, having at least as much fun below, weighed on the gas and weaved left and right over the whole road, trying his damnedest to hit every hump and bump.

■ *FORTY-FIVE* ■

A bright orange sun poured itself into the purple Davis Mountains. From there to here across the windswept spaces of the Panhandle were nothing but colonies of black-tailed prairie dogs, the coyotes that hunted them, uncounted Texas horned lizards, and ten kinds of rattlesnakes.

There were some cattle; there are cattle everywhere in Texas. And the cowboys moving through with the cattle certain times of the year were the bread and butter of the little spit-grill roadside diner that loomed out of the fading roseate light about the time Butch and Phillip were getting seriously hungry.

The station wagon pulled into the gravel parking lot under the winking red neon sign of Dottie's Cafe. Customers were a welcome sight to the two folks inside. This not being cowboy season, Dottie's people were seeing barely a dozen or so customers a day; they were on the short end of the bread and butter stick.

The bell in the kitchen rang for her twice. But she was busy in the bathroom. What the mirror saw was a once pretty forty-year-old face that at this moment needed some fixing up to be called pretty again. The scrawny and fading but never-without-hope waitress pinched her sallow cheeks, applied some eyeliner and some bright lipstick, and zipped out the door.

"Too much lipstick," croaked Nehemiah, the ancient cook who'd been there frying since Hoover was president, and who, as three-quarters Comanche, claimed all the Panhandle as his. "Look like a 'ho."

"Cowboys like it," chirped the waitress, Eileen, grabbing up the two hamburger plate specials from beside the grill and backing through the swinging doors into the diner.

The diner—a counter, three maroon Naugahyde booths, and a fine layer of grease over everything— was empty save for Butch and Phillip in the middle booth.

Eileen set the two hamburger platters in front of the man and the boy, and the man dug in without ceremony. It had been a long time since his last real meal.

Phillip held up eating and looked at his food uncertainly. The waitress watched, peering at the plate to see if something was wrong.

Finally, Butch noticed, stopped chewing, stayed the motion of his fork.

Phillip bowed his head and prayed, quiet as a mouse. "Thankyew, Father," he said, "fer yer bountiful nature and goodness. Amen."

Butch and Eileen shared a smile and said in unison, "Amen."

"Now dig in, Buzz," Butch said. He grinned at the waitress. "Call him that 'cause he eats like a buzzard. If it's dead, he'll swoop and chow."

Her eyes lit up and she gave an openmouthed smile at Butch's hilarious sense of humor. She leaned on the table and flirted shamelessly with her painted eyes.

"Wisht I'd had a daddy as funny as you," she said. "Mine was just a sour old carp."

That got a smile out of Phillip.

"You Dottie?" Butch asked with his mouth full of cole slaw.

"Eileen," she said. "Dottie died. Her son runs the place but . . . he ain't never here."

"Never," Butch said, interested.

"He leaves at four," she said. "And the cook just left, too." She leaned her elbows on the table. "Amazing old coot," she said. "Seventy-five if he's a day, and he's got a honey over in Muleshoe he drives over to see every night.

"Some guys got it," Butch said with a mashed-potato grin.

"Some guys do," Eileen said, brazenly staring a hole through Butch as she lifted a slice of pickle off his plate, placed it in her mouth, and slowly chewed.

Phillip, eating ravenously, was aware of some off-kilter vibe passing between these people—something he was missing. It was like they were talking to each other in words he couldn't hear. He watched, confused. His mama didn't look at men that way.

Eileen rose up and turned to walk away. She'd planted the seed. That's all a girl could do. Now it was hombre's turn. "If you need me," she said, "I'll be right over here." She slowly sashayed her way behind the counter.

Butch watched her every step. For a small-town girl she didn't miss a trick. A silly smile tickled behind his eyes.

Phillip chewed and watched Butch's eyes. Butch turned his head and caught the boy watching him. "Eat yer food," he said.

▪ *FORTY-SIX* ▪

A sirloin steak hit the makeshift grill beside the Tater-Tot shish kebabs and sizzled to beat the band. Every coyote and bobcat within three counties heard the sound and put his snout in the air trying to catch the scent.

A joint effort of Adler, Suttle, and Bradley, the barbecue pit was created from the abundant boulders of flinty caprock along the riverbed and the rack from the ultramodern stove in the well-stocked RV. The whole thing—chairs, stools, plates from inside—was set up on the bank.

Red smilingly shook a liberal dose of Lea & Perrins onto the flesh. He was in his element, the barbecue chef non pareil when he lived full-time in the Hill Country.

Sally got up and took her files into the motor home; it was getting too dark to read.

Bobby Lee watched her go in and watched her through the window as she moved into Red's office to put some files on the desk, and then kept going into the back bathroom of the vehicle.

Bobby Lee looked at his hands, rubbed them together once, and slid quietly into the RV.

Sally turned on the tiny nightlight in the back bathroom and splashed water on her face. She looked at herself in the mirror. She put a towel over her face to dry, and when she took it away, there was Bobby Lee's face beside hers in the mirror.

"I got you figured," he said with his smile that looked so much like a sneer.

"What do you mean?" Sally asked.

"Women make themselves smart for a reason," he said, "but in yer case you got it wrong."

"What are you talking about?" Sally said, not enjoying this, but not backing down from the guy.

"When they think they ain't pretty enough," Bobby Lee said. "I'm here to tell you not to worry."

"Bobby Lee," Sally said matter-of-factly, "where do you think this is leading?"

"I seen you looking at me, girl." He smiled a sleepy smile: Come into my lair, little vixen . . .

"Excuse me," Sally said and tried to walk around him.

Bobby Lee shifted his position and blocked her. He smiled. "Work and pleasure should naturally go together, don't you think," he said, tilting his head down and peering at her seductively through the top of his eyes.

Sally wasn't the least bit seduced. She tried again to go around him and again he moved.

"Take me, I enjoy my work," he said. "And I *love* pleasure. And"—taking a step toward her—"I got a funny feeling that you and me—"

"I could give a shit what you got a feeling about," Sally said.

"You got a mouth on you, don't you," he said, leering, eyes brightening, as though he was just getting warmed up—as though this was standard seduction, Bobby Lee Kellam style.

The flesh was creeping all over Sally's body. How to get out of this without causing the kind of stink that make people point and say: See, women among men bring trouble.

"Should I scream," Sally said reasonably.

"Should I beat my chest?" Bobby Lee said, inching closer, his smile broadening.

"How you take your steak, Sally"? Red's voice cut through the interior gloom.

They both turned to see Red standing in the doorway, barbecue fork in his hand, Stetson on his head.

"Uh . . . rare," Sally said, vastly relieved.

"Woman after my own heart," Red said.

Her smile of gratitude came out so warm and wide, she almost felt embarrassed. She took the opportunity to move past Bobby Lee toward Red and the door.

"I'll just wipe its ass, herd it through, and cut off a chunk," Red said to her. "How'd that be?"

"Maybe medium rare." Sally grinned. She slipped out through Red's office and into the main room.

Red and Bobby Lee stood eyeballing each other, Bobby Lee's face slightly tinged, eyes popping like a stomped on toad. He could feel it coming.

"You're here for one reason and one reason only," Red said.

"I'm lookin' forward to it," Bobby Lee said with bravado.

"Rattlesnakes on the prairie, I give 'em a walk around," Red said. "In my house I stomp the livin' shit out of 'em."

Bobby Lee flushed scarlet. "Anything else, Chief?" he said.

"Yeah," Red said. "You're in my office."

Bobby Lee gave a weak salute, strode through the main room, and went outside. Red was following him out of his office when the phone rang.

Adler immediately stuck his head in the door of the RV and said, "That's the governor's hot line, Red."

Red calmly walked past Sally, who smiled thanks. Red gave her a one-finger-to-hat salute and went to the hot-line phone. He bent down and yanked out the cord. The ringing abruptly stopped.

"Nuthin' so impolite as callin' at the dinner hour," he said.

▪ *FORTY-SEVEN* ▪

Phillip stripped all the branches off his sprig of parsley and distributed them around the rim of his empty plate. He drank the Real Cream in the little cardboard container. He stared over the top of Butch's half-finished dinner at Butch and the hamburger lady carrying on in that mushy way at the counter.

Butch sat at a barstool with a foolish look on his face, watching Eileen work. Eileen, too, had a kind of foolish smile, and she was more moving things around than working.

Butch leaned over and whispered something sexy in

her ear. She giggled and licked her lips and looked at him, eyes wide.

Butch felt eyes on his back. He turned and looked at Phillip, who immediately turned his look away.

"Buzz, you go ahead and chew on mine if you want," Butch said. He turned back to Eileen, who'd moved down a discreet few feet and was filling ketchup squeeze bottles.

"No thankyew," Phillip called.

Eileen slid back toward Butch. She was making refilling condiment bottles about the sexiest pastime since the hula hoop, somehow squirming while she worked.

"Very polite," she said.

"I try hard," Butch said, low, "but, ya know, since his mama died . . ."

Antenna-ears heard that. "My mama's not dead!"

Butch, a tad annoyed, turned to Phillip and gave him a look. Once again, when he turned back, Eileen had moved off, now into the sugar bowls. Butch watched her move, bend, lick sugar off her fingertips, and wipe her hands on her hips. Every move had a little something extra in it, and Butch appreciated every wiggle. Without moving his eyes away, he called over his shoulder to Phillip, "Okay now, Buzz, you go on out in the parking lot and chunk some rocks or something."

Phillip reluctantly slid out of the maroon Naugahyde banquette and slowly walked out the door. His eyes stayed on Butch and Eileen, showing a medley of confusion, censure, and a hint of jealousy. Say what you will, he had been the center of Butch's attention all day long until they walked into Dottie's Cafe. He was the new "Buzz," he had his own Halloween costume, and he'd had a carnival ride on top of a car without even benefit of a howdah. Who was this lady and what did she want? He chunked a few rocks off into the night.

"So is she dead or not?" Eileen asked, leaning back on the Coke dispenser.

"Well, his biological mother is alive," Butch said, rotating slowly back and forth on his barstool. "Gave him up for adoption to me and my wife. My dead wife, that is. She is, was Phil, er Buzz's stepmother, so she's his mom, was his mom, stepmom, but . . . she's dead." He shrugged at the vagaries of fate.

Eileen smiled only half sadly at those same vagaries. "I'm so sorry," she said. But she seemed to be feeling anything but sorrow. In fact, the whole story seemed to have turned her on past the cut-off point. She leaned on the counter, put her hand behind Butch's neck, and pulled him close for a gentle kiss.

Phillip tossed a bunch of rocks at enemy planes, Commie MIGs and some leftover Jap zeros. Between throws he looked back at the barstools through the diner window. The two grownups were gone. He dropped his handful of rocks and walked over to the window. Inside it was empty. But the doors to the kitchen were still swinging slightly on their hinges.

A one-room office gave off the back of the kitchen. It was an austere spot for trysting—a desk, a few chairs, a floor fan, two rodeo prints, a plastic Remington bronze of the bucking horse and rider. But it had the one essential—a door that Butch and Eileen could close behind them.

Eileen pulled him by the hand into the room and did just that. They were all over each other. Butch lifted her up on the desk and kissed her face and neck. No delicate boudoir seduction this—the room instantly vibrating with barnyard squeals and growls. She tore at his shirt. He ripped it over his head and threw it against one of the two large windows that gave on the side parking lot. Through these windows the sputtering red neon sign cast its nervy light on their frenzied maneuverings.

Butch flipped Eileen over on the desk, pulled the ribbon tying up her girlishly long hair, and unzipped the back of her waitress uniform to the waist. His lips were up and down her nape, her spine, the small of her back.

Phillip, suddenly alone out there in the middle of nowhere, realized he was a touch scared. The highway was empty for miles, the diner deserted. The only hint of life was the buzzing, blinking, damaged neon sign.

He moved over toward the car at the side of the parking lot and turned and saw something. He went toward it.

Butch, prodded by the timeless urgencies of the species, endeavored to love every inch of this female. He suddenly, passionately flipped up her skirt and began kissing her pert and pretty backside. It was the light she was hiding under a bushel, in Butch's modest but delighted and grateful opinion. As he caressed and kissed it worshipfully, Eileen moaned in ecstasy.

Phillip, right outside the window, was like a pacifist at a street fight. He didn't want to watch this but couldn't tear his eyes away. It was the primal scene and he'd never seen it at home. He unconsciously moved down the building to the window directly opposite the desk. He stopped and practically pressed his nose against the glass. Butch and Eileen not two feet away.

Nuzzling, writhing, Butch was rubbing his face all over certain parts of this woman, and there was no mistaking which parts. And now he moved lower, burrowing. Eileen's mane of hair lashed to and fro; she craned her neck, arching it like a swan, moaning like a wildebeest.

She raised her head and in midmoan, stopped, and

stared straight ahead. Butch continued his worship, but only for a beat, sensing the locomotive he was riding had stopped at an unscheduled station. He slid his face from around her rear, a la Kilroy, and he stared, too.

Except for their continuing heavy breathing they could have been an entwined Indian erotic art sculpture from the Kamasutra, staring straight ahead . . .

. . . At Phillip, outside the window, his nose now absolutely pressed to the glass. In fact, if he'd pressed any harder, there wouldn't have been any glass.

Butch and Eileen held their poses for two more heartbeats until Phillip came back to real time. He jerked back and bolted away into the darkness.

Butch was off Eileen in a snap and jumped to the window. "Phillip!" he called.

Eileen, easing her belly down on the desk, said, "Nosy little feller."

Butch tried to catch a glimpse of Phillip out there in the parking lot and panted to catch his breath.

"I keep a cot in the back," Eileen said hopefully.

Butch just kept breathing hard.

▪ *FORTY-EIGHT* ▪

The sky was nothing but stars swimming in West Texas crude. Phillip stood underneath the sputtering neon sign staring up at it, trying to plumb its runic meanings, trying to make sense out of a senseless day and night. His upturned, pained face splashed pink from the neon. Dressed in his Casper costume still, he cut a grotesque little figure.

Butch burst through the cafe door, setting a string

of bells clanging. Pulling on his shirt he blew past the boy and headed for the station wagon.

"Get in the car," he said.

Neighbors kept coming, bringing food, baskets of fruit, bags of canned goods, prepared dishes. It was all people of south Madisonville could think to do to try to soften the pain and share the burden of their neighbor, the soft-spoken keep-to-herself Mrs. Perry.

Even Albert Reeves walked up to the house with a platter of something he'd prepared himself. Gladys interrupted her efforts to get her girls ready for services to answer the door. Reeves handed her his offering and squeezed her hand and left without a word.

In the kitchen Ruth and Naomi scouted the food. They peeked in the three covered dishes. "Tuna casserole . . . tuna casserole . . . tuna casserole!" Ruth said as she opened one after the other. They both laughed weakly. Gladys walked through and put Albert Reeves platter down on the kitchen table, uninterested in food.

Ruth peeked. "Look," she said. "Ribs, barbecue. Phillip's gonna do back flips . . ." Then she realized what she said and put the lid back on and stared at her mother's back, feeling sick.

"God will destroy the present system of things in the battle of Har-Magedon," the elder at the front of the room said. "The wicked will be eternally destroyed."

Gladys, Ruth, and Naomi sat with their Bibles in the Kingdom Hall, seeking strength among the rows of fellow believers. The Bible study theme, chosen for their sake, was "Rejoice because your deliverance is near." "Yes!" the elder said, "deliverance from Satan and his wicked system of things into a peaceful new world!"

Gladys noticed Naomi on the other side of Ruth,

turning pages faster than one usually does in Bible study.

"It was for the joy set before him that Jesus endured the torture stake," the elder said.

Gladys reached over. Naomi was reading *The Brownie Scouts in the Cherry Festival*, inside her Bible cover.

"Naomi!" Gladys whispered, dismayed. "You don't even like that book!"

Naomi began to cry. "I can't read Bible now, Mama," she said. "I'm too scared, I can't think about things." Gladys hugged both her daughters to her and cried.

Once again tearing across the high plains, the Olds carved the briefest wedge out of the encroaching dark with its headlights. Silence in the car. Outside, somewhere to the rear, was the high lonely sound of a train whistle. Phillip slumped, staring straight ahead, now and again sneaking a peek at Butch, who just drove. He just pushed the mint-new wagon as hard as he damn well could, to outrace the lust pounding in his veins.

From behind them a bright white light, chasing, gaining on them. Butch saw it coming, let it come. Phillip was trying to get up his nerve to say something. As he opened his mouth and started to speak, a high-balling passenger train blasted by them, whistling a deafening greeting. The Santa Fe Chief Limited roared past at 105 miles an hour, startling Phillip to silence. He watched a few seconds, then turned to Butch. "You mad at me?"

"No," Butch said, curt.

Further silence in the car as the Santa Fe Chief shrunk down to a point and vanished in the distance, headed for the New Mexico border and points in the West.

"You kissed her, huh?"

"Jus' barely," Butch said, with much regret.

"Why?" Phillip asked.

"Cause it feels good," Butch said, giving the little boy a look. "Ain't you ever seen yer mama kiss a man?"

"No," Phillip said, thinking deep. "You kissed her backside, huh?"

"It's, well, uh, it's kinda hard to explain," Butch said, shifting uncomfortably in his seat. "I know how it musta looked."

The boy was staring at him.

"Hell," Butch said, "I don't know how it looked . . ."

As Butch's voice trailed off, silence overtook the car again. Butch held his breath, waiting, then breathed a sigh of relief not to have to answer any more questions like that. Phillip fiddled with the door handle and stared out at the paralleling train tracks. He turned to Butch. "Do you love her?"

"Who?" Butch said.

"The lady that cooked the hamburgers," Phillip said.

Butch pondered that, then a grin slid across his face. "Yeah, Phillip, I love her," he said. He looked at the boy out of the side of his eyes. "Kissed her butt, didn't I?"

Both man and boy started to laugh.

The station wagon swung off the dirt farm-to-market and onto a smaller, private farm-to-pasture cowpath. After a couple of hundred yards, past a windbreak of gnarled live oaks, Butch pulled off the graded dirt into the field. Shocks bouncing over the dry plowed rows, the station wagon came to rest out on the flat belly of an endless field, under the cushiony black of the Texas night.

Looking around, Butch said, "You wanna drive?"

"Yeah!" Phillip said. The skeptic in him had gotten

off back around Paducah; anything was possible on this trip.

"Jus' kiddin', Buzz," Butch said with a smile. "I'm just gonna stop here for a while and catch forty."

He killed the engine, but kept the radio music on low. They gazed through the windshield at the faint, flat, unending line of the horizon. Of a sudden, the whole length of it became a spiderweb of heat lightning arcing a thousand miles, left to right, bringing a split second of daylight to this southern tip of the Great Plains—an awesome display of the larger forces at work, leaving these mere human watchers feeling diminished. After which darkness wrapped them round again completely.

"Things go our way," Butch said, "we'll be in Alaska in four or five days. Get the jump on winter."

Phillip was not so delighted at this thought as Butch. "It's cold there, huh?"

"Yeah, but we'll get by," Butch said. "Kill a bear for coats, eat whale blubber like it's Spam, that kinda thing."

"How long we stayin'?" Phillip asked.

"I plan to live there," Butch said.

It was obvious that the boy was feeling torn, looking off through the immense darkness homeward.

"But of course you got family in Texas," Butch said, "so you can head back anytime you like."

Not good enough. Still the boy looked sad.

"What is it?" Butch asked.

"I wanna go home now," Phillip answered.

"If you wanted to go home so bad," Butch said softly, reasonably, "why didn't you stay at that store today?"

" 'Cause," the boy said.

" 'Cause why?" Butch said.

" 'Cause I stole," Phillip said. "They'd put me in jail. Prolly go to hell."

Butch chuckled at the notion. "Same difference," he said. "We'll get you home soon, I swear, okay?"

A couple moments of silence, then, "Butch?"

"Yeah, Phillip?"

"I can drive," the boy said.

"Done proved that, ain'tcha?" Butch said. "There's lots and lots of stuff you can do, Phillip." He pointed to the glove box. "Reach in that there. See if Bob's got a notepad or something."

Phillip extracted a small ringed memo pad.

"Good old Bob," Butch said. "Can you write?"

"I can print," Phillip said emphatically.

"Good enough. Now I want you to make a list of everything you ever wanted to do, but wasn't allowed to. Okay?"

"Like what?" Phillip asked.

"Like . . . cotton candy."

"Cotton candy?"

"Hell, I don't know," Butch said. "It's *yer* list." Butch settled in for a catnap. Just as his eyes closed . . .

"Butch?"

"Yeah?"

To the coyotes and the bobcats on the hunt through the live oak for night-prowling vermin, all that could be seen and heard of the car sitting lonely in the massive field under the stars was the small dome light and the low sound of the radio.

"How ya' spell 'rocketship'?"

■ *FORTY-NINE* ■

Contemplating the same stars from a slightly different angle was Red, sipping coffee from his thermos.

Dead-ass asleep and snoring were Bradley and Adler, surrounded by the aftermath of a full-scale Texas barbecue: plates littered with gristle and bone, cigarettes burned down in ashtrays and steeping in half-drunk bottles of cola and mugs of coffee. Suttle was groaning and burping. He had already meticulously picked his teeth clean with a toothpick; now he was going at them with dental floss from his ready bag.

Bobby Lee, too mean to sleep, sat by himself, exercising his fingers and cleaning his nails with his whittling knife.

Sally, sipping from a stay-awake mug, wandered out and found Red sitting on the broken-down back end of the Law Enforcement Special.

"They still asleep?" Red said without looking up from under the cowboy hat.

"Yeah," Sally said.

"Figger to give 'em another hour," Red said, "then grab the patrol cars and head for the Panhandle."

"Home sweet home for you," Sally said casually. "Probably brings back memories."

"Oh, yeah," Red said without thinking. He turned to her. They both knew he slipped. He divulged something—small but something."

"They got a file on me?" Red said, giving her a narrow look.

"It's the 1960s, Red," she said. "They got a file on everybody."

"What's it say?" Red asked.

"That you worked the Sheriff's Department in Palo Duro County," Sally said. "Adler said you were partners with Tom Lamar. Is that the same T. Lamar that's listed as Haynes's arresting officer?"

"Uh-huh," Red said.

"So you were there," Sally said.

"Forty-four years," Red said. "You get to arrest ever'body at least once."

"Maybe," Sally said. "Maybe. But why do I get the feeling this time it's different?"

"It isn't," Red said, looking away down the highway.

Sally thought a bit and decided to go ahead—hell, to charge ahead. "A fourteen-year-old boy does four hard years at juvy camp for a joyride?" she said. "Seems steep."

Red looked at her. "Yeah," he said, flat, unencouraging.

"Routine stuff, huh?" Sally said. She wasn't going to drop it.

Red shifted a bit. He didn't cotton to being prodded by anybody this way, much less a green female. And yet he was letting her get away with it, which was the more unsettling part.

"What about probation?" Sally asked. "The boy had a home and father."

Red tilted his head back and examined the stars. "What's yer file say?"

"That he was a petty thief with something of a rap sheet," Sally said. "But he was young, and he'd stayed clean for a few years. His presentencing report noted he'd taught himself to read and had some smarts and ambition."

A long silence. Sally trusted her instinct and let it ride.

"There are murderers I'd trust with my mother," Red said, "and petty thieves I wouldn't turn my back on." He knew as he said it that it wasn't the whole truth or even a decent explanation. But now wasn't the time or place. He decided to call a halt. "Your precious files are wrong," he said with finality. With his finger he pointed the track of a shooting star.

Sally pulled a good defense-lawyer tactic; she switched tacks completely, but didn't give up. Having the celebrated Red Garnett cornered on a rear bumper in the middle of nowhere was an opportunity that would not come again.

"They say your name is Cecil," she said.

Red had to chuckle a bit. "Jeezus . . ." he said. "Yeah, well, that's definitely the worst of it."

He uncorked his thermos and held it out toward Sally's mug to pour. It was his special coffee-Geritol sludge brew; she knew the importance of this moment. She accepted a dose and took it like a man. She had to stifle a cough. It had the flavor and consistency of diesel fuel.

"Strong . . . but good," Sally said. We all make accommodations. "So, Cecil—"

Red gave her a strong look: Don't go too far, girl.

"Uh, Red," she started over. "What do you do when you're not at work?'

"That's not in the file?''

"Nope," Sally said. It was and it wasn't; she wanted to know how he would put it.

"I got a ranch I never visit," he said, "nieces I hardly know, a tackle box full of dry lures, and a good ole dog that figgers he's the owner and I'm the pet . . . Could have a point, he's there more."

"A confirmed bachelor," Sally said. "Any regrets?"

"I'd like to wet those lures before I die," he said. "Maybe a new dog . . ."

Sally sensed a multitude of other thoughts boiling to the surface—he was a man unaccustomed to facing anywhere but front.

"Yes?" she said.

"Actually I was married once, but nobody knows about it," Red said. "Nobody but you . . ."

"I'll take it to my grave," Sally said.

"A French girl. I was too old to get in the war, but they sent me to Europe after, with the occupation forces. Law enforcement specialist. They sure as hell needed it—countries without governments, people starvin', killin' for food. A big mess. They gave me a translator, girl younger 'n you. Big brown eyes, soft voice, funny accent. One thing led to another . . ."

"And you got married?" Sally asked, unable to suppress her surprise. This was not the Red Garnett of song and story.

"We got married in a fever." Red laughed gently. "Hell, I thought we were in love . . . Fact was I was outa my element. Never been outa Texas afore, more'n a night or two. I was a busted-wing target."

"What do you mean?"

"She saw me comin'," Red said. "I can't blame her." He sipped his sludge trying to decide whether to go on. What the hell, he'd come this far. "Father and brother killed in the war, mother pallin' around with the Krauts and got her head shaved. The girl wanted out."

"What was her name?" Sally asked.

"Danielle," Red said. "I was the land of the free for Danielle. She wanted to come to America and meet Frank Sinatra and live in a house with a toilet you sat on."

"Not such awful things to want," Sally said.

"Maybe not," Red said. "But I found out there was a boyfriend she was fixin' to send for, once she got set up in America and worked this old Texan for what he was worth." He shook his head. "I was old enough to know better . . . I guess you're never too old to make mistakes."

"Or too young," Sally said. "Maybe I've been all wrong about you."

Red gave a half smile. "What's that s'pposed to mean?" he said. "Never mind, don't answer that."

There's personal and then there's personal. "How the hell'd you get into . . . whatever the hell it is you do?"

"My father's a defense lawyer," Sally said. "Hollis Gerber."

"That explains yer mouth," Red said.

Sally laughed. "Instead of Home Ec I studied criminology. When I graduated, my father with the governor's help, they, he and my dad . . . *I* created a position for myself with the prison system."

"What's yer husband think about all this?" Red asked.

"Don't own one," Sally said.

Red glanced at the ring he'd noticed on Sally's wedding finger.

"It was Mom's," Sally said. "I wear this when I'm working. Cuts down on advances."

"Sure worked on Bobby Lee," Red said.

"Symbols don't mean much to some," Sally said.

Red thought a while, watching the big Brazilian bats swooping in and out of the light. A trio of coyotes, a mother and two pups, circled the periphery. Red chunked a rock, and they melted back into the darkness.

"You know, Sally Gerber," he said, "you're not careful you'll wind up just like me—old, tired, with nobody around to love ya."

"Maybe," Sally said, leaning forward. "You think you're too old?"

Red looked at this attractive young woman and for the span of a moment was not too old to wonder. Hell, what if he kissed her? She was inviting and vulnerable; he was powerful in her eyes. She'd probably kiss him back. And then . . . And then, Danielle all over again. And folks would point at this old horse with a girl could be his granddaughter. He laughed at himself. "This job we're on," he said, "like to make me dead before I'm old."

Sally could tell from his eyes some impossible scenario was playing itself out in his head.

The coyotes crouched back in the outcroppings and
howled, hungry for the barbecue they'd tracked up-
wind for miles.

"It's crazy, ain't it," Red said.

"What's that?" Sally said.

"Goin' without sleep chasin' after a three-time loser
and Casper the Friendly Ghost."

"Sleep?" Sally said. "That's what retirement's
for."

"Bite your tongue, missy," Red said. He looked
with horror into his mug of unspeakable brew and took
another long draught.

■ *FIFTY* ■

The memo pad with Phillip's list of things to do
before he died slipped between his legs and the boy
drifted off to sleep. His head lolled to the side, he slid
down and curled up on the seat and sank into sound
slumber.

Butch, his head back and mouth open, slept the
sleep of the exhausted—that is, badly, the mind tor-
menting the soul crying for rest.

Over Butch's hallucinatory dreams played the zydeco that earlier he couldn't find on the radio to save
his ass. Now a baby snapshot of Butch rose in his
mind—a towheaded one-year-old straight from the
angels with a smile for all comers.

Other snapshots, all family pictures, passed into
focus and out.

A picture of a grizzled father standing behind a
mother seated holding an eighteen-month-old baby.

The mother was attractive, slim, with light brown wavy hair, big, warm bedroom eyes. The dad not so attractive, wanting a shave, wanting a lighter attitude. All three standing in front of a small, white-framed house with mismatched pots of begonias and petunias hung from the porch and a clean-swept packed-dirt front yard. Next to the tidy porch leaned the yard broom fashioned from dogwood branches. Next to the dad, half-concealed down by his side was a can of beer.

The face of the eighteen-month old boy child moved close in Butch's sleeping mind—little Butch with sunshine in his smile. The face of the father replaced it, looming—eyes definitely off, anger leaking like battery acid from the eyes.

Another scene—Butch, age six, off to the side. In the center his father and another adult male were both holding deer rifles with one hand and with the other hoisting the antlered head of a twelve-point buck. Chunky-cheeked Butch cradled his air rifle eagerly, wanting to be more a part of the moment.

Butch at age eight came floating by—a boy grown tall and slim, handsome, Phillip's age but looks more grown-up—confident half smile, something knowing in it, hint of innocence lost. Standing with him, posed against a waterside railing with a wide river behind them, was his mother. Delilah Jane still had pretty eyes, but was a little thicker around the middle and, though her smile tried, couldn't project the air of natural-born optimism her earlier photo showed.

Legs in a flouncy skirt materialized, a gaudy sign saying CAJUN QUEEN DANCE HALL—one in a row of New Orleans "night clubs." From the women lounging coyly, not so discreetly, in the upper windows, and the liveried doormen showing photos to would-be customers, one would have to be from the deep bayous not to recognize these as more than night clubs.

Inside Delilah Jane is in a flamboyant, hotly sexy

Latino outfit, a tacky getup, but a worldly sort of Marlene Dietrich sneer helps her carry it off. Three lounge lizards, hands placed on various parts of her body, surround her and hold her up. Is she drunk?—it isn't hard to imagine.

Mother in the same outfit, teaching Butch, age eight, how to dance. His body spells awkward embarrassment, but his face turned up to his mama is devoted.

Butch sits at the bar, surrounded by a motley group of dime dancers, each girl dolled up in a different showy way, but all sleazy.

Another scene of Butch being taught a dance step by his mother; this time her face is slack, she is clearly blitzed.

Butch stirred in the car, shifted position, and moved his head as though bothered by something, then sank into his dreaming state again . . .

Mom dancing again. This time with a patron of the club, a dark-eyed swain with tight black pegged pants, Slim Jim tie and handsy habits, a hand holding Mom's ass.

Mom is kissing the same man—or at least being kissed by the dude. On his arm a tattoo . . . growing larger—A figure of a naked girl framed by the words "Hell-Bent."

Mom sits on the tattooed man's lap at the bar, her head thrown back boozily, a hand on his neck, his hand on her thigh. A man doing things with a woman and vice versa. Butch sits a ways down the bar, alone, watching . . .

In Butch's tormented sleeping mind the images began to replay and overlap and replay again. Butch dancing in Mom's arms . . . the tattooed man dancing with Mom, trying to wrap his tight-panted legs around her . . . Butch sitting with the dime dancers, looking distanced . . . the tattooed arm grabbing Mom's ass, forcing a tongue kiss on the drunken woman . . . the tattooed man on the floor in a pool of blood . . .

Butch stirred again, plagued by the same irritant, a sound, growling, growing louder, intruding on his unconscious. His head lolled in exhaustion. The dreams went on . . .

Policemen pushing the stunned dancers and bar patrons back . . . a detective poking around the body lying in the blood . . . Butch's mom leaning on a nearby barstool, looking dazed as the police photographer and newsmen wandered by . . .

Butch's mom's face comes into close focus—more displaced than horrified, looking like she was waiting for a table to be cleared so she could sit, a bed to be made so she could use it.

The tattooed swain with the patent leather shoes lies toes up on the floor, his mouth a leering smile in death.

In Butch's mind the naked girl tattoo grew larger, the letters of "Hell-Bent" snaked around her tightly and squeezed . . .

The growling grew deafening; the inside of the Olds lit up like noon. Butch started to come out of it.

Blinded by the high-powered lights, he groped under the seat for his gun, instantly bathed in cold sweat—prison searchlights. He squinted for the source, the tower, trying to locate the gun screws, the targets.

Butch's eyes cleared, the reality emerged. A huge combine stood, engine idling, directly in front of the station wagon.

A black man, fifty or so, stepped down from the engine cab and ambled toward the station wagon. He was thin, wiry, and not smiling—a face that said life was more taken up with hard labor than anything to smile at. He walked across the front of the wagon and approached the driver-side window.

Phillip, wide-awake and scared—the huge throbbing combine, the big stranger coming at them—noticed something that scared him even more. Butch had hold of the gun along his right leg, half under it. He was fingering the trigger. Phillip prayed.

The black man stopped opposite Butch's window, back a few feet, and eyeballed the man and the boy sitting in the midst of his field.

"Didn't mean to scare ya," the combine driver said. "I work at night. It's cooler. Ya'alls car break down?"

Butch shook his head to clear the sleep out. "Me 'n the boy was just catchin' some shut-eye in yer field," he said, dazed, friendly.

"Oh, it ain't mine," the man said. "I just works it for Mr. Andrews. Where ya'll from?"

"Drove from Texarkana yesterday," Butch said.

"Quite a haul," the farm laborer said.

"Said a mouthful there," Butch said.

"Well," the man said, "ain't no sense in ya'll sleepin' in the car. Not when I got a fold-out couch sittin' empty."

"Wouldn't want to put you out," Butch said. " 'Sides, we need to get back on the road."

"No trouble t'all," the man said. "Wake you up first light, fill yer belly, and send you on yer way." He stuck his hand out. "Name's Mack."

Butch shook his hand. "This here's Buzz," he said. "Edgar. Edgar Poe."

■ *FIFTY-ONE* ■

The sun came up the color of cat piss in a cloudless pale sky promising a day of flat cruel heat. A Highway Patrol black and white barreled over the desolate caliche plain that Texans call the Caprock, and that under the name the Great Plains stretches all the way north to Canada. The officers in the patrol car and those in the tow truck following felt they'd driven nearly to Canada already and still they hadn't reached their mark.

The governor's proud mobil-operations vehicle lay tilted and immobile by the river bottom—no sign of life among the chairs, stools, and assorted debris of the last night's feeding frenzy. Half a dozen brown buzzards waddled in and out of the mesquite brush, making occasional running, leaping forays into the party scene to clean off a plate.

"We didn't pass it, did we?" said a voice from the backseat of the patrol car. The governor's right-hand man, Saunders, stuck his sleepy head up and craned around.

The two officers, Montgomery, driving, and Hall, the shotgun, looked as though they'd been driving all night, which they had. "No way we coulda passed it," Montgomery said. "Thing that size, it's a standout."

"What's'at?" Hall said, wiggling his finger down the road.

"There it is," Montgomery said. "Yer luxury liner on wheels, Mr. Saunders."

The patrol car and the tow truck slid in behind the RV and stopped. From the first nothing Saunders and the officers saw looked even remotely good. The erstwhile shiny mobile unit had disappeared under layers of dust and mud. The right rear tire was off and lying in the ditch. The weight of the big vehicle rested on an assortment of boards, mesquite limbs, and hay bales. A broken jack lay nearby.

Hall and Montgomery, following Saunders, who was deeply shocked and almost ready to cry, walked up to the vehicle.

"Good Gawd Almighty," Montgomery said. "Governor ain't gonna like this."

Saunders was speechless, striding through the obstacle course of the vehicle's expensive custom furniture just tossed out here on the highway.

He rushed inside. Empty except for more filth, trash, and spillage. Saunders gasped—and grasped the edge of a bulkhead to stop himself from reeling right out the door. The shape the vehicle was in was beyond his worst fears.

"Where the hell are they?" he howled. Everyplace he looked was something worse than the last, an ugly food stain here, a ripped-seam couch there.

A sleepy groan came from the back of the main room. Suttle raised his head from the wreckage. "Uh, uh, they're gone," Suttle said in a raspy voice.

"How long?" Saunders said.

"I don't know. Uh, four, five hours."

Saunders, seriously dejected, shoved trash aside and slumped on the couch. He put his face in his hands and moaned. "Well, goddammit," he said, "did he say anything?"

"Yeah," Suttle said, climbing shakily to his feet and brushing himself off, trying to straighten his clothes.

"What?" Saunders shouted.

"Well, uh, Chief Garnett wanted me to tell you," Suttle said, "that the vehicle gets his seal of approval . . ."

Saunders's face began to redden.

"And that he wants his chair back," Suttle said.

Saunders's face went to crimson then purple.

Montgomery and Hall, waiting outside in the already hot morning, heard a scream. A second later a crash, then Red's chair came flying out through the windshield. The chair bounced once, hit a rock, and split in two.

Away to the west and north, halfway up the Panhandle past Lubbock, two highway patrol cars rocketed along, one following the other.

In the second car Officer Hayden drove and couldn't

help smiling at his shotgun, the still muddy Adler. Adler worked the radio and attempted to triangulate the fugitive's destination on the map he held on his lap. Bobby Lee and Bradley shared the backseat, putting as much distance between themselves as possible. Bobby Lee's leather case rested on the floor between his legs.

In the lead car Officer Delano Jones, a lean hard-nose of twenty-five, drove with a single-minded concentration. Not every day you get to drive a chief of service.

In the backseat Sally said quietly to Red, "Wanna hear what I think?"

Red sat staring straight ahead with his big buff hat on his lap. He nodded.

"The scale is tilting in the kid's direction," Sally said.

"Ya' think so?" Red said. "We're gettin' close to squeeze time. Ya' don't get through without blood but one in ten times."

"Even so," Sally said.

"I'm listenin'."

"Well, it's a chain of reasoning," she said. "The station wagon family described a relationship between Butch and the boy. Not a loving relationship—not fairy-tale stuff, but a kind of mutual respect. Correct?"

"Ain't arguin'," Red said. "But don't go buildin' yer hopes that Butch Haynes's got a daddy instinct. He's got a survival instinct. He's hard, cold, and capable of the worst."

"That's just it!" Sally said. "He wasn't treating the boy as a son in any of the usual ways—doting on him, ordering him around, taking him for granted. He was treating him like he'd want to be treated himself at that age—with respect—as a person with some standing, not just a brainless kid."

"Where's that get you?" Red said.

"If I'm right, he's looking at this kid as little Butch," Sally said. "He's identifying with the kid directly, not as a son or anything like that. Phillip *is* Butch. Which would mean . . ." She looked to see if Red was following her.

"Yeah?" Red said.

"Which would mean that as long as Butch can keep up the fantasy of Phillip as Butch, Phillip is okay."

"What's keepin' it up now?" Red asked, not sure where this was leading, but intrigued despite himself.

"The kid's training is saving him," Sally said. "He's an unusually sweet, polite boy, very accommodating to his elders for a kid his age—product of a mother with strong ideas, product of his religious tradition, who knows? Point is, as long as Phillip keeps that up—keeps going along with Butch, respectful, amenable—he's okay. Butch sustains the fantasy and views him and treats him like he wished he'd been treated. Recapitulating the traumatic past, this time successfully, psychologists say."

Red got it. He also picked up on the lead lining in the silver cloud. "As soon as the boy starts crossing him, screaming bloody murder for his mama, trying to hightail it home, Butch Haynes the psychopath is back. He'll squash him like a road toad."

"Maybe," Sally said. "But I don't think so. The Butch Haynes of the files doesn't do violence for the hell of it. He will lash back in a psychopathic manner, yes. But you have to provoke him. And you have to provoke him pretty good."

"Well, let's pray the boy doesn't do a damn thing to provoke him," Red said. His tone said he'd had enough theorizing—he'd had enough of this whole ugly escapade.

▪ *FIFTY-TWO* ▪

A tin coffeepot, perking, rattled on the stove. A black woman moved the coffeepot off the fire and deftly flipped a skillet, throwing hot grease over the frying eggs to finish the job. Lottie was something over fifty, but the farm and family work of a lifetime gave her an ancient look.

Nor was her work over. Two little black feet dangled from the too-high bathroom toilet. A flush sounded, the little feet hit the floor, and Cleveland, Lottie's six-year-old grandson, padded down the short hall and into the living room.

Cleveland made his way around the pull-out bed and stopped and stared. He stared at Butch, sleeping open-mouthed, snoring lightly, arms thrown up. On the other side, using one of Butch's arms as pillow, was a small form.

Cleveland circled to the opposite side of the bed to observe this smaller form. His head popped up over the edge, and he peered close at the sleeping face of Phillip. He leaned a little closer.

Phillip's eyes blinked open. "Aaaayyyyy!" he shrieked, startled awake and upright.

"Aaaayyyyy!" shouted Cleveland, scared by Phillip.

"Aaaayyyyy!" Butch yelled as he jumped off the bed like a howitzer and was on his feet looking around before the first scream died.

Cleveland lit off for the kitchen and whipped behind the apron strings of Lottie.

She walked into the parlor, smiling. "He wake ya'll up?" she said. Turning her head to the boy, she said, "I tole ya not to do that."

Butch and Phillip, both breathing hard, calming down, laughed at the boy and their own fright.

"No harm, ma'am," Butch said, pulling on his shirt and finding his shoes.

"I'm Lottie," she said with a neighborly smile, "Mack's wife. This here's my grandbaby, Cleveland."

"Cleve, ya' call me," Cleveland said. "I'm six."

"I'm eight," Phillip said. "M'name's Buzz."

Lottie poured Butch a third cup of coffee while Phillip wolfed the last of his burner-top toast. Cleveland, hitting it off well with this mop-headed new boy in his Casper outfit, couldn't wait for him to finish eating.

" 'M'on, man," he said. "We got us a creek down aways. Wanna check it out?"

"Sure thing," Phillip said and was out the door without asking—as instantly into it as if on the yearly summer visit to the cousins.

Mack, done with his long night's work, intercepted them on his way in and brought Cleveland back in. Phillip followed.

"Mornin' to ya'," Butch said.

"Mornin'," Mack said, starting to unsnap his blue bib overalls. "Rest done ya'll some good?"

"You want a plate?" Lottie asked.

"Not jus' yet," Mack said. "Boy, go get my thermos from the truck."

Cleveland, giggling with Phillip at the window, didn't hear.

"Don't ya' hear good, boy?" Mack said, striding over and giving the boy a cuff on the ear. Cleveland yelped and headed straight for the door and the truck, holding his hand over his smarting ear.

Butch and Phillip both looked up at Mack. Sure didn't seem like a fair fight.

"Boy don't got the sense Gawd gave a chicken," Mack snorted and headed down the hall, stripping off his sweaty, dirty shirt.

▪ *FIFTY-THREE* ▪

The air was already hot enough to conjure up shimmery patches of mirage on down the highway. Officer Jones in the lead patrol car saw the signs for the intersection with Route 86 east and west coming up at a four-corners named Turkey. "Want me to stay on 70?" he called back to Red.

"Let's head on over to Amarillo," Red said. "We'll cross him there or wave good-bye at the border."

Sally looked to Red, about to say something. He looked thoughtfully out the window. She waited for another minute before speaking. "I didn't mean to pry last night—about Haynes and all, at Palo Duro, I mean."

"Yes, ya' did," Red said. He continued to gaze out the window.

Sally decided it was time to keep her own counsel. The tension in the car had been building with each mile closer to whatever deliverance or disaster the Panhandle had in store.

Suddenly Red was talking. "Haynes's old man was a petty thief," he said. "What your files don't say was that he was a damn talented career felon with a soft spot for whores. One way or the other, he beat the hell outa ever' person he ever crossed, screwed, or fathered. Judge sends the kid home with his pop, and you bet yer last dollar that within a year he'll have a rap sheet as long as yer arm."

"But he sure didn't," Sally said. "The judge, I mean . . ."

"He would have," Red said, shaking his head in great regret—over what, was not clear to Sally. She waited—he had his own rhythms. Now he was in another place, reliving some time, some turn of events, in pain.

"What're you getting at?" she asked very quietly.

"You make choices in life," Red said. "And the ones you're most sure of, they're the ones that usually come back to bite you on the ass."

"What are you talking about, Red?" Sally asked again.

"I testified against the boy," Red said.

"What's so unusual about that?" Sally said. "You're an arresting officer."

Red was silent for a long time. Then he reached forward and slid the Plexiglas partition closed, cutting off sound to the driver's compartment. Both officers turned and looked at Red and quickly turned back to the front.

"In Texas the bottom line is who ya' know and what they owe ya'," Red said. "That's how I do my job, and that's how you got yours."

"I don't understand . . ." Sally said.

"I bought the judge a sling of T-bones and told him to send the boy up," Red said. "I told him I knew it didn't stack with the boy's crime, but it was the right thing to do. Told him I knew that much about the boy and the boy's home and the place I wanted him sent. And what-all it would do for him that he needed done. Told him I knew all that. The judge went along with me right down the line."

Red shut up and looked out the window. Sally stared at the back of Officer Jones's head.

■ *FIFTY-FOUR* ■

Butch knew he should have been out of Mack's and on the road already, but hell, he and Buzz and Cleve were having a some pretty good fun, and kids need all of that they can get.

He made Cleve bend over and put his hands between his legs. He reached under and grabbed and gave a smart pull and Cleve flipped over in the air. The boy came up laughing hysterically, infectiously. They were all laughing.

"Agin'!" Cleve said. "Do it again'!"

Lottie came in from the kitchen and tousled Phillip's hair as he sat on the couch. "Where's this boy's mother?" she asked.

Butch straightened up and smiled at her. "We left her home this time," he said. "Boy's night out kinda thing."

He did a little dance step and bumped into a small side table. "Say, lookie here," he said. It was an old wood-cabinet phonograph with velvet insides and brass hinges. He gave the turntable a spin with his finger and started peeking through the stack of 78s and singing, "Girl, you run right over me . . ."

"Mr. Andrews give 'em to us when he got hisself a newfangled one," Lottie said.

"Jeezus," Butch said, admiring one. "Nathan Abshire. Now this is music. You know how long it's been since I heard this?"

"That's an oldie all right," Lottie said. "Mrs. Andrews now—her maiden name was Bougeois, half Creole she is—tole me herself, she got a good bit of the blood in her. But Mr. Andrews, he don't like nobody to know, not in these parts. Don't wash. This here's Texas and Texas's still the South, ain't it now . . . Suppose that's why he give us these coon-ass tunes." She laughed a mixture of merriment and cynicism.

In the bathroom Mack dropped his house pants and sat on the throne, taking his rest where he could find it. He reached over and turned on the radio on the wash basin. A farm report came on, and to the familiar drone of cattle prices and cotton quotations, he settled back to the job at hand.

From the living room came the scratchy sound of the 78 player, coon-ass Cajun music.

Straightening up from the record player, Butch looked around with eyes come to life.

"You dance, Lottie?" he said.

"Lawd goodness no," she said.

"Here," Butch said. " 'Jus' follow me." He took the woman in his arms and slowly but surely adjusted her movement to his. After a few rough turns across the bare hardwood floor, they were not too bad together.

Phillip could not help but smile as Cleve just giggled and slapped his leg. Butch and Lottie got smoother, some hard years fell away from both of them, swirling around the room.

"Mr. Poe, you sure can dance." Lottie laughed, moving more nimbly than she ever did except footing away from the diamondbacks and copperheads in the fields.

"Oughta be able to," Butch said. "Was raised in a dime a dance whorehouse."

"Yer foolin' me," Lottie said, about running out of breath but nowhere near ready to quit.

"No ma'am," Butch said. "My mama would dance their asses out of the frying pan into the back room fire." It was a line dredged up from those days, and it took him back.

He noticed Phillip and Cleve watching and giggling and doing some jump-up. "Get on yer feet, Buzz," he called. "You'n Cleve shake a leg."

"Well, go on!" Lottie said.

The boys reluctantly stood and gaped at one another.

"Hell, dance boys!" Butch said, laughing.

The boys grabbed each other's arms and tentatively

moved around each other a bit, imitating the adults. Pretty soon they were doing it in time to the music and laughing and dancing, too.

The record came to an end. They all clapped and giggled and panted. Butch went to flip the record over and heard something from the bathroom, the radio.

Mack sat, still in the contemplative mode, cleaning his fingernails, waiting for nature to take its course. He cleaned the dirt fields from under his fingernails with a Barlow knife and listened as the announcer began a news bulletin.

". . . Update on the manhunt for Robert Butch Haynes, the Huntsville prison escapee. Haynes is armed and extremely dangerous. He is believed to have a hostage with him, an eight-year-old boy. When last seen, he was driving an Oldsmobile station wagon, brown in color, taken from a vacationing family picnicking in Cottle County. Haynes is described as six-feet-one, medium build, with blue eyes—"

A hand reached over and one finger turned off the radio. Mack followed the hand up to Butch's blue eyes, in a face wearing a look of concern. Butch sat down on the edge of the tub across from Mack and reached over and took the Barlow knife away from him.

"We'll be leavin' soon enough," Butch said, the voice of sweet reason. "I'll kill all of you if you try anything stupid."

Mack's heart started racing; he swallowed hard.

"You 'bout finished?" Butch asked. "I think so." He handed the man the roll of toilet paper.

■ *FIFTY-FIVE* ■

"What's Texarkana like, they talk funny over there, don't they?" Lottie said. "I ain't never been down the road that far."

Phillip, caught off guard, looked up at her and blurted whatever came into his head. "Uh, real nice, it's real nice," he said. "I got a dog . . . named Phillip. And coupla cats, uh, Ruth and Naomi . . . and I got a tree house, and ever' year on Halloween we turn my tree house into—"

"Come on, Buzz," Butch said, following Mack in from the bathroom. "Time for us to hit the road."

"Mack? . . ." Lottie said. "Whass wrong, Mack? You look like you seen a ghost." She started toward him.

Cleve, hyper from the dancing, ran up to Butch and spun around. "Do me, agin!" he said. He bent and put his hands between his legs.

"No!" Mack barked. "Boy! Git over by yer mammaw!"

Lottie instantly smelled something serious. She looked from Mack to Butch and reached toward the boy.

"Come on, Mister, do me agin!" Cleve said. He had no inkling the whole fabic of the day was about to be shredded.

Butch smiled and leaned down, about to oblige the boy. But Mack reacted first, smacking the boy and sending him sprawling, as you'd smack a puppy away from a hissing rattler. Cleve landed on the floor, bawling in pain and surprise.

Butch reacted just as quickly. He pivoted and backhanded Mack in the face with major force, enraged. Then he pursued and grabbed the older man and tossed him on the floor like a sack of wheat.

Phillip's heart sank in a sickening rush. He pushed himself back on the couch and sat frozen, watching. Fun to horror in the same instant. He'd seen it enough now; he was beginning to understand—and to get sicker every time.

Butch, the other Butch, had the gun out of his pants and went for Mack on the floor. He bent over the farmer, grabbed him by the throat, and shoved the gun in his mouth. He lifted him as though he was a stuffed doll and chucked him into a chair.

"Why'd ya' wanna go and hit Cleve for?" Butch said, his voice hard and strange. "He didn't move fast enough for ya', is that it?" He shoved his face close to Mack's, their noses inches apart. "Or maybe he gets excited sometimes and don't hear ever'thing ya' say? You make me sick to my stomach." He spat in the older man's face.

He drew back, straightened up, and moved over to Phillip. He handed the boy the .38.

"Point it at 'em," Butch said.

"I don't wanna . . ." Phillip said, fearful.

"Point it!" Butch barked.

Phillip took the gun and pointed it, occasionally wiping away the tears that were slowly running down his cheeks.

Lottie stood trembling by the door to the kitchen. Mack reached over and took her hand.

Butch knelt by the still-sobbing Cleve. "Now, son," he said, "you wanna flip?"

Cleve shook his head no between sobs.

Butch took him gently by the arms and lifted him to a standing position. "Go ahead, put yer hands between yer legs," Butch said, coaxing. "I won't hurt ya'." He gave the boy a kind of twisted smile.

Cleve turned to Mack and ran to him.

Phillip, gun fallen to his lap, watched in growing dread as Butch walked calmly over to the crying child and pulled him away from the old man. Butch led the whimpering boy to the center of the room.

"He don't trust ya' no more," Butch said to Mack. "Ya' gotta earn that, ya' know." He turned to Cleve. "Put yer hands 'tween yer legs, son," he said gently.

Cleve tried to wipe his tears so he could see. He bent over in the flip position. Butch reached down and gave the boy a flip, all the while staring at Mack.

"Again," Butch said. He flipped the boy again. Then a third time. Then a fourth. Staring hard at Mack the whole while, watching the old man's expression—as though he was teaching him something, watching to see he was learning.

Finally, he allowed the still-weeping boy to go to Mack and Lottie. He took the gun out of Phillip's lap.

"Buzz," he said, "go out to the car and get that rope."

Phillip, hands flat on the couch, froze, staring across the room instead of looking at Butch.

"Phillip!" Butch said in a voice that was stern but lacking the venom he had spewed at Mack.

Phillip reluctantly pulled himself off the couch and started for the door. But passing Cleve, their eyes locked, Phillip hesitated, reading the terrified pleading in his new pal's eyes—pleading for something, anything. Phillip put his head down and went out the door.

He crossed the dirt yard past the railroad-tie casing of an old well. He opened the station wagon door and stopped and looked back at the house. He held there for a long moment, trying to sort out if he could do anything, trying to disbelieve this was happening.

■ FIFTY-SIX ■

Butch, gun in hand, pulled the coffee table around opposite Mack in the chair and Lottie and the boy next to him. He sat on it facing them, like the director of a trio.

Looking at Mack, he said, "Now you hold that boy and tell him you love him."

Mack reached up, grabbed Cleve's arms, and set the boy on his lap. "I love you," he croaked, fear in his voice.

"No, old man," Butch said wiggling the gun. "Say it like you mean it."

"This boy knows I loves him, mistah," Mack said, pained.

"Then say it."

"Please, mistah," Lottie said, her voice quavering. "I got a sense about you. I know you a good man." She clutched one of Cleve's hands.

"No'm'am," Butch said, "I ain't a good man. Ain't the worst neither, jus' a different breed."

Lottie put her hand to her mouth to stop her lip from quivering. Shaky-legged, she pulled a cane chair to Mack's and Cleve's side and sat.

Outside the screen door Phillip looked in at the scene—Butch on the low table with his ever-visible gun, his audience seated before him, waiting on his every word, quaking. Most puzzling to Phillip, Butch seemed to be enjoying himself.

"Say it, Mack," Butch said. "Don't cost ya' nuthin'."

"I love you, Cleve," Mack said to the boy, tears in his eyes. He hugged the kid and tears ran down his old scarred face. They were going to meet their Maker, he knew now. It came to him with that smile of pleasure on Butch's face. All three of them—on this day—in this strange horrendous way. He hugged the boy hard.

"Gawd, that's beautiful," Butch said softly. He meant it. Spotting Phillip at the door, he waved him in and took the candy and provisions bag from the boy's hand. He emptied the contents on the coffee table: hard candies, cookies, pretzels, bread, sugar, the old lady's change and dollar bills. And the rope.

Butch picked up the rope, took Mack's Barlow knife from his pocket, and cut off a long shank. Starting with Mack, he began to tie the three people to their chairs.

Phillip, agitated, shifted from foot to foot behind Butch, watching him truss these people like calves. Something worse was coming, he felt it, but didn't know what to say or do. He tried a prayer to Jehovah God, but was too distracted to think through more than Dear Lord . . .

Finished with his tying, Butch moved to the record player and put the same scratchy record on to play. He turned up the volume. He walked back and faced his captive subjects.

"You can go wait in the car," he said to Phillip without looking at him, "or you can watch. You're old enough to think for yourself."

Phillip wanted desperately to run out of there in a burst of fear, but couldn't. Something told his eight-year-old mind, if he went, nothing would stop the truly horrible from happening. If he stayed though . . .

Butch sat down again on the coffee table and eyed his three hostages. He looked like he himself was about to cry. He closed his eyes and rested his chin on the gun barrel while he recited his instructions.

"Shut yer eyes, Cleve," he said. "Mack, you and Lottie hold the boy tight. Shut yer eyes, too."

Phillip started to cry out, but stifled himself. An execution, he's going to murder them. He turned away, then spun back. He was shaking all over.

Butch, his eyes closed, appeared to be in another world, another time and place. A slight smile played across his lips, then disappeared.

"Please, mistah," Lottie said in pitiful tones. "Ain't no use in it."

"We'll give ya' ever'thing we got," Mack said, his anguished face showing he knew he had nothing sufficient to the insanity of the moment, nothing with which to save his family.

Butch was not even hearing their words. He opened his eyes, lifted his chin from the pistol barrel, cocked the gun, and slowly lowered the muzzle toward Mack.

"Our Father which art in heaven," Lottie began tremulously. "Hallowed by they name, thy kingdom come—"

"Shhh . . ." Butch said. "Shhh . . . Shhh . . ."

"Lawd, thy will be done," Lottie went on with terrible emotion. Praying the last prayer for them all. And nobody had a right to stop her or was going to stop her. ". . . here on earth as it is in heaven . . ."

"Shhh . . . Shhh . . ." Butch said again, scowling at Lottie.

"Say it wif me," Lottie pleaded with Mack and Cleve. "Pray the Lawd."

Altogether they prayed. ". . . Give us this day our daily bread . . ."

Jumping up, Butch gave Phillip a strange glance, put the .38 on the floor between them and, scrabbled among the candy wrappers and cookies to find the electrician's tape.

Phillip looked at the cocked gun.

". . . and forgive us, Lawd, our trespasses," the three bound prisoners went on, "as we forgive those who trespass agin' us . . ."

Butch ripped pieces from the roll and slapped one over Lottie's mouth.

". . . And lead us not into temptation . . ." Mack

and Cleve continued. Until Butch slapped tape on their mouths, too, silencing all the praying.

Out of breath, he knelt in front of them and kept his eyes locked on them while reaching around behind and groping for the pistol. It didn't come to hand. He turned to look and saw Phillip, teeth gritted, gripping the revolver in both hands, pointing it directly at Butch.

Butch's expression was blank. Then it transfigured into a faint crooked smile. A smile that conveyed his knowledge that this moment like all the others with Phillip would sort itself out Butch's way and they'd go on as before. He tilted his head in that respectful one-guy-to-another way and opened his hand . . .

Phillip saw the tilt and saw his own fierce resolve and the fraction of a moment he had to act vanishing into nothing, the thing he could do undone forever. Butch opened his hand. Phillip scrunched the trigger, and a deafening blast turned Butch's expression blank once again.

▪ *FIFTY-SEVEN* ▪

Phillip, knocked to the bare floor by the revolver's kick, recovered to his knees, shaking like a leaf.

Butch sank back on his haunches, his hand out, still staring at Phillip. He looked down at his stomach where a stain of brown-red gushed through his T-shirt. He folded a hand over it and looked back to the boy.

The needle on the record, jarred to the end by Phillip's thumping to the floor, found no more music but kept scratching on rhythmically.

"Phillip?" Butch said in a wondering tone, as if he hadn't seen him in years.

The boy, dazed almost to insensibility, stared at the gun in his hand, then at the blood pouring from the side of Butch's stomach. . . then at the taped, terrified faces of Mack and his family. In a flash Phillip was up and running for the door, gun clutched in both hands.

He blasted through the screen door and ran for his life to the railroad-tie well casing. He chucked the gun down the well, skidded behind it, and watched the house for several seconds, listening to his heart pound. Then he turned and ran again, this time up the long rutted drive toward the highway.

Twenty yards down he stopped, looked at the house, and tore back to the station wagon. He scrambled halfway in the window and groped the keys out of the lock. Running again toward the highway, he wound up and threw the keys as far as he could into the weedy field and kept going.

Butch groped to his feet in the living room, his face smoothed over with shock. He moved uncertainly toward the door, then halted. He turned, reaching in his pocket and pulling out Mack's Barlow knife. He held it up, staring at Mack, Cleve, and Lottie. He started toward them.

Lottie began again her mumbled prayer. The end was coming after all. She leaned against the boy and closed her eyes and prayed for swift surcease for them all.

Butch meekly set the knife down on the coffee table. "Thank you for yer hospitality," he said. He moved to the door and stumbled out into the morning glare.

"Phillip," Butch called, searching around with his eyes. No answer, but the sound of morning birds in the alfalfa and the wind whistling through the mesquite thickets behind the house. From horizon to horizon he spotted no movement.

He dragged himself to the station wagon and slid painfully into the front seat. No keys. He checked the seat. Keys? Gun? He pushed the door open and half fell out, holding himself up on the door. He walked all the way around the car, looking for the keys, leaving spots of blood.

He leaned against the car for some moments, gathering strength, trying to gauge his affliction. Then he started down the private dirt road toward the highway, searching the ground at the edge of the grass for the car keys.

He approached the spot where Phillip heaved the keys—where they sat on top of a raised furrow a few yards from the road, the morning sun glinting off them. Butch was searching the field on the other side of the drive, then turning toward where the keys waited when he cramped up. He went down on his knees, groaning.

Phillip ran as fast as he could down the county highway—Casper the Ghost, tears of terror streaking his face, lungs aching. He looked back every so often to see if Butch was following.

Reaching the highway, Butch looked one way, then the other and yelled, "Phillip! I won't hurt ya', I swear!" He started in the direction the curve of the private dirt road took him on the main road as had the boy.

Phillip, running out of steam around the long bend, stopped and leaned against a fence post for a blow. He looked back through the grass and, several hundred yards down, caught sight of Butch struggling forward.

His heart seizing, Phillip crawled through the ditch beside the road and squeezed under the barbed-wire fence. His costume hung up on a barb. He wrenched hard away from the fence with a small cry and left a strip of Casper costume hanging on the wire. He ran into the vast field.

A pickup truck crested a rise and bore down on this curving stretch of road. As the pickup sailed past, the driver, the middle-aged rancher who owned this land, saw a strange sight—Casper the Ghost running like a madman across his field.

"What the hell?" the rancher, Arch Andrews, said as he slowed. "Out in the middle of nowhere. Now who could—" He stopped in midsentence as he came up on Butch and passed him. Something about this man hobbling dazedly along the road made Arch turn and look. The same something made him not do what country people automatically do anywhere: stop to help. Instead, he kept his eye on the man in his mirror and pulled his pickup off the road into Mack's place.

He stopped behind the station wagon with its open door and peered inside—blood on the seat and the ground. He grimaced and walked cautiously up to the house, following a dripped trail of blood up to the stoop.

"Mack? . . . Lottie? . . ." he called. No answer. Arch Andrews had once been shot in the leg by a paranoid old farmer sitting in his house in the dark laying for vandals. Arch had been bringing some kuchen from his mother and thought he'd just slip it in the front door. Now he never went near a house door without an express invitation.

He circled the sharecropper house calling Mack's and Lottie's names. Finally, he peered in through the kitchen screen door. "Mack?" He heard scratching, like a record player going round and round. "Lottie?" he yelled. He thought he heard a groan. He kicked the screen door open and waited. No shotgun blast. He gingerly entered.

Butch, holding his gut and breathing hard, plodded along, calling the boy's name now and again. Then he saw the strip of black-and-white Casper cloth on the barbed wire. He headed toward it. He crossed the ditch and looked over the fence. It was an immense pasture with a scattering of live oaks and cottonwoods. In the center was a big live oak beside a dried-up creek

bed. He bent painfully, stepped through the fence, and
followed the bent-down path he could just make out
through the long grass.

Arch moved through Lottie's kitchen looking all
around. He walked slowly into the living room and
was astounded to see Mack, Lottie, and Cleveland
staring up at him, gagged and tied to chairs.

"That was a helluva thing to do, Phillip," Butch
called as he made his way across the field. "You're a
hero. Prolly be in all the papers tomorrow, how you
saved those folks." He stopped and listened and took
some painful breaths. "Truth is," he said, "I don't
think I woulda killed 'em. I only killed two people in
my whole life. One hurt my mama and one hurt you."
  He heard nothing, but knew the boy was nearby.

■ FIFTY-EIGHT ■

Adler's voice came in over the radio from the
trailing patrol car. Red signaled Officer Jones to turn
up the volume. "Ya'll catch that?" Adler's voice said.
"A town called Happy. Over in Swisher County."

  "How far?" Red asked Jones.

  "Half hour tops," said the officer.

  Red leaned across the seat back and grabbed the
mike. "Any bodies?" He waited, his head slumping
forward as the silence extended.

  Adler's voice came back after what seemed too long
for good news. "No bodies," he said. "Farm family
survived. Rancher said the kid did it, kid crossed him
up good. Haynes is out chasing the boy down. Locals
on the way, they'll get details."

"Ya'll follow us," Red said into the mike. "The fire road along the Prairie Dog Fork'll get us there inside of fifteen." He lowered the mike, then raised it to his mouth again. "And Adler," he said, "get back on the radio and tell whoever gets there first to play it nice and easy."

Sally put her hand on Red's arm to get his attention. "The boy's mother," she said. "We should bring her up if they can get her here."

By now Red knew Sally better than to dismiss her ideas out of hand, but this one sounded rotten. "We're about to get him in a tight, if we're lucky," he said. "Chances are it'll end bloody. Why subject the mother?"

"It's what I call a plus/minus," Sally said. "We're bringin' an army in there—troopers, lights, sirens, guns. That's gonna scare the shit outa the kid more than Haynes who he knows. The mother showing up *could* backfire, but it'll be the only friendly face on our side. Might be needed, might tip the deck."

Red debated for a moment, then raised the mike. "Adler, any way we can get the mother up here fast?"

"Checking," Adler said and clicked off.

In an amazingly short time he came back on. "They're all ready to fly her here on a private."

"Who's 'they'," Red said, suspicious.

"Guvner," Adler said. "He was just waitin' for you to ask. Didn't want to step on yer toes."

Red shook his head. "Politicians," he said to himself. "Go ahead, chopper her in," he said into the mike. "Tell 'em to keep her way back if she gets there before us. Way back."

He signed off and turned to Sally. "The boy crossed him," Red said. "Means he lost his bulletproof shield. He could be dead already."

"If Haynes chases him down in a hurry and is still mad when he finds him, the boy's dead," Sally said. "But if he's calmed down enough not to kill him right off, my bet is he won't kill him and they'll reestablish rapport. It's in both their self-interest.''

Red's expression said he desperately hoped she was right, but doubted it.

"And if he is still alive," Sally said, "and Haynes gets provoked to kill him because *we* show up, that's why we need the mother. To shortstop that. Get the dialogue on family stuff, no law-guns-leniency-prison shit. My hunch is to keep it personal, family. Look at their last two encounters—families. They all somehow survived."

Red raised a skeptical brow—a different brand of law enforcement. Her thought patterns were an optimist's attempt to find a way through the long odds. His assumptions were based on all the times he'd seen people make horrible situations worse just because they could. He eased back in his seat and closed his eyes as the patrol car raced across the countryside.

Sally read Red's pessimism and wasn't at all sure he wasn't right. She stayed on the edge of her seat.

▪ *FIFTY-NINE* ▪

Phillip slid down into the swale by the big live oak. He ran through the brush, watching over his shoulder. Butch's voice floated over the field.

"What say we talk this over," Butch called. "Settle things man-to-man. Then we can be on our way. I'll even let you drive. Knock that off yer list. How'd that be?"

Phillip looked out at the endless pasture spreading before him—and turned back to the big old oak with a full head of leaves. He began to scramble up the tree, keeping the trunk between himself and Butch's voice.

There were climbing knobs most of the way up and a good fat lying-down branch about ten feet off the ground. A boy who just got new sneakers ought to be able to reach that branch with no trouble . . .

A local tan and black was the first to answer the report. Light turning but siren silent per orders from high up, the deputy sheriff's car crept down the private dirt road toward Mack's house. The veiny-faced, scared old rummy of a peace officer had his service revolver out and pointed upright in his right hand while he drove with his left. He stabbed the brake and grabbed his weapon with both hands and pointed it as the screen door banged open and someone emerged.

It was Arch Andrews. The deputy put his weapon away and stepped out to get the facts.

Arch took the deputy by the arm and turned him. "That's his car," he said and pointed back out the dirt road to the highway. "Took off on foot. Up thataway. He's got a pistol. Mack says it looks like a .38." Arch stood back, expecting the deputy to take off smartly in the direction he'd pointed.

"I'll have to get a full report," the deputy said, tugging a notebook from his back pocket.

"Hell, not now, ferchrissake!" Arch said. "Ya got a psychopath chasin' a kid around a field with a gun!"

The deputy took one look out across the vast field with its groves of trees and little arroyos and outcroppings—natural ambushes—and knew he was not meant to be the hero of the day.

"Uh, my orders," he said gravely to Arch, "are to establish a perimeter and more or less beachhead this whole thing for the reinforcements . . . which are right behind me, sir."

Arch snorted in disgust. Mack and Cleve appeared behind the screen door and stared.

Butch stopped to rest within sight of the big oak tree. He looked out on the huge sloping pasture and saw immediately there was no Phillip in it. He started looking carefully up and down the dry creek bed.

The movement of something white caught his eye up in the boughs of the big oak. He turned casually toward it.

▪ *SIXTY* ▪

Flashes of Phillip's arms and legs were visible as he tried to climb to a higher limb.

Butch started forward, slowly moving down into the swale. He made his way through the other trees and brush and, without looking up, sat down to rest underneath Phillip's tree.

"Alaska, Phillip," he said. "Wild and wooly, man against nature. Me personally, I like them odds." He shifted his position, pressing one forearm against his wound to stanch the bleeding. "Did I tell you my daddy lives there?" he asked. "He's the one that sent the picture postcard. Listen here to what he says about it."

He shifted again, slowly, to pull the postcard from his back pocket.

" 'Dear Robert . . .', That's my real name, Phillip. Robert. Jus' like old Bob, the family man," he said. " 'Dear Robert, I just wanted to tell you that me leaving has nothing to do with you'."

Phillip squirmed in the tree, shaking with fright, wanting to run as far from Butch as he could.

At the same time he was seized with something opposite, a curiosity, a yen to listen to the guy, to follow him wherever, to see where that would take him. He moved his head so he could hear better.

" 'Alaska is a beautiful place'," Butch read slowly, suffering through his memories. " 'Colder than hell most all the time. Someday you can come and visit me and we'll maybe get to know each other better'."

Butch gave a short laugh. "Short and sweet," he said. "That's the old man's style. "Cold all the time'—like that's a big sellin' point."

He put his sweaty head back and looked through the leaves of the oak at the hot pale sky. A wind picked up and blew some leaves around and bent the grass a little, but it was a hot south wind with no relief in it.

"He useta' pat me on the head," Butch said, "and tell folks that 'It's some that can live life without askin' about it and it's others has to know why, and this boy here is one of the latters.' "

Phillip was listening, gradually forgetting about being afraid.

Butch had his eyes closed. "That's why I wanted to go up there," he said. "To visit the old man, I guess. Prolly punch him one first, but then maybe we'd end up bein' friends, sit down, have a beer, talk things over . . ."

A spasm pulled him over, and he groaned. He put his hand to his side and looked at it. Blood was oozing all over the place. Painfully, he hitched himself up and returned the card to his pocket.

"We'll just rest a while," Butch said. "Then you can make up yer mind. How's that?"

It was almost as though Butch was talking to himself or to an imaginary companion, not expecting a reply. Phillip, clinging to his branches and looking down, wanted to speak out, wanted to say, don't stop talking, I'm listening, I want to hear about Alaska and the other places you've been.

But he said nothing, just peered down at the foot of

the tree where he could see one of Butch's legs extended, bloodstained pants and a shoe.

A dozen Highway Patrol cars and as many Texas Ranger cars jammed the driveway at Mack's place, lining up all the way back to the highway. Hendricks, the 270-pound, mean-looking F.B.I. Agent in Charge, directed the operation from behind mirrored aviator shades. He sounded as though he wanted to take down this felon personally, with his own hardware, a sawed-off riot gun hanging at his side.

He addressed sixteen or eighteen officers lined up before him in two ranks of almost military precision. "Get all the local deps outa the fields," he growled. "Keep 'em on the roadblocks up on the four corners and down by the 1075 spur. I want 'em handlin' the gawkers, not the guns. Last one of these, some of you boys remember, we had a man shot in the back by a local. He got excited."

The men welcomed the laugh, chance to vent some nervousness.

"Today, nobody gets excited," Lt. Hendricks said. "Nobody shoots without an order from me or Chief Garnett who's gettin' in shortly. The governor's taken an interest. This whole thing's gotta be surgical."

"What's the governor care about this guy?" an officer asked.

"The kid, fer chrissake," Lt. Hendricks said, "he cares about the kid. Like any good politician that wants to be president some day . . . after Lyndon gets his turn."

This drew guffaws from the men.

Mack, Lottie, and Cleve sat on the stoop with Arch Andrews and watched. Mack reached over and took Cleve on his lap and hugged him hard and long.

▪ *SIXTY-ONE* ▪

Butch's eyes stayed closed. A small pool of blood by his side grew larger and began to push through the dust. It reached over the crest of the bank and made a little rivulet of blood rolling slowly and steadily down toward the dry creek bed.

Phillip, spying the dark red stream, couldn't bear it any longer. He maneuvered his way down the tree and dropped to the ground next to Butch.

Butch opened his eyes and smiled. "One thing's for sure now," he said. "I definitely believe in ghosts."

Phillip managed a small smile.

"Never been shot before," Butch said.

"I'm sorry," Phillip said. He sat down next to Butch in the sparse grass on the side away from the blood.

"I know ya' are," Butch said. "Truth is, if it had to happen, I'm glad it was you—as opposed to someone I don't know, I mean. All things considered, I feel pretty good. Could use a beer, though."

"What's beer taste like?" Phillip askcd.

"Oh, it's about the best thing there is," Butch said. "You'd better put that on the list."

Something caught Phillip's eye. He stood up warily and stretched his neck. What he saw were the tops of two Highway Patrol cars rushing past on the dirt road with their lights flashing, kicking up dust.

"You better run," Phillip said.

In the first of those two patrol cars, Sally kept her eye on Red. "I think our chances of this thing ending peacefully are better than you think," she said, pushing the issue for a purpose.

"Ya' do, huh," Red said. He looked as though he was going to his best friend's funeral. All Sally's theorizing had not changed his outlook. A pall hung over him.

"Look, Red," Sally said, speaking low, taking advantage of Officer Jones's being on the car squawk box, coordinating with the locals. "Your thing with Haynes was twenty years ago. Chances are he remembers almost nothing about that, including you—a cop who testified. Other cops testified. You said yourself it wasn't your testimony that sent him up. It was T-bones."

Red gave her a cool look as Officer Jones wheeled the car onto the private dirt road leading to Mack's.

"I remember it like it was yesterday," Red said. "And he remembers 'cause I told him it was me and told him why . . . , I can see 'em right now. That boy's eyes. Not mean and hard, like you'd expect. More like, I don't know, like . . . he was tryin' on my britches, my side of the railing before he decided. Like he decided I coulda done him a lot worse."

The car pulled up among the assembled forces, and Red reached for the door.

"Like what?" Sally asked.

"Like what's gonna happen today," Red said. He pushed the door open and got out. He put his Stetson on against the noon high sun and stepped into the battle.

■ *SIXTY-TWO* ■

"Y̶ou better run," Phillip said to Butch, coming back and kneeling down next to him.

"Naw, Phillip," Butch said. There was no running in him. There was sitting in the shade of this live oak, whisking the flies away and hoping for a fresh breeze.

"I need me a time machine with a loud radio to take me where I'm goin'. Walkin's for squares."

Phillip again saw something out of the corner of his eye and spun around. But it was just the hot wind bending the mesquite brush. Phillip sat down uneasily next to Butch, looking over at the narrow trail of blood flowing down the slope. It was crawling with horseflies.

A perspiring Lt. Hendricks stepped forward in his mirrored shades, back ramrod straight, and saluted Red.

"Hendricks, Chief," he said. "We've met before. I understand you got one of my men with you—Bobby Lee?"

"You got the area cordoned off?" Red asked.

"Water tight," he said. "Like a frog's pussy." A bell clanged in his head. He looked at Sally. "Sorry, missy."

"No doubt an observation based on personal experience, Lieutenant," Sally said. She stared right through his mirrors.

Red couldn't help but smile. "You got him spotted?" Red said.

"By the tree," Lt. Hendricks said. "Halfway down the field." He pointed, then unfolded a piece of paper and showed Red and Sally a hand-drawn sketch: Mack's house, the road, the tree. The grove of cottonwoods and live oaks was marked with a circled X. Target Zero.

"I spaced officers in a circle around them two hundred yards or so away." Hendricks said. "No communications with him yet. Orders to the men to fire in the air if the suspect starts moving."

"Let's head on over there," Red said. He turned to his crew for the second patrol car. "Bradley, gimme a megaphone."

Bradley nodded, then turned to Adler and looked blank.

"In the trunk," Adler said to him low. "Standard issue in every patrol car. How long since they let you out from under a hood and into the field?"

Bradley handed Red the battery-powered megaphone and Lt. Hendricks led the way.

Red asked the question he'd been putting off. "How's the boy?"

"Kid's fine last we saw," Hendricks said. "Haynes is wounded, we don't know how bad. He's losin' blood."

Red waved Hendricks to get his ass in gear and get them to the scene.

Sally brought up the rear. "Holy shit," she said to herself. A hostage who shoots a kidnapper and doesn't kill him? What are the odds for said hostage? She couldn't think of *any*. She felt a shiver of cold despite the sweltering heat. Her body was suddenly perspiring from every pore.

▪ *SIXTY-THREE* ▪

Butch looked longingly at the dry creek bed, as parched as a man could be. "Here's somethin' a boy like you should know," he said. "How to get water if yer ever stranded out in the middle of the plains. Wanna hear?"

"Yeah," Phillip said. He squatted nearby and picked at the fallen leaves.

"*Butch, This is Red Garnett of the Texas Rangers,*" came an amplified voice.

A kind of knowing smile crossed Butch's lips and

vanished. He closed his eyes and leaned his head back against the tree.

"*I know you're hurt*," came Red's voice, wafting disembodied above them. From down in the little gully wash, Butch and the boy saw nothing of the Armageddon preparations forming up in a vast ring around them.

"*We've got damn near one hundred armed men here*," Red's voice said. "*Take a look around and you'll see I'm shootin' ya' straight.*"

"All this for me!" Butch yelled back. "I'm touched, but I'm afraid ya'll gonna have to back it up a step or two! I'm headed to Mexico!" To Phillip he said, "Lyin' to 'em, of course."

Red stood with the megaphone on a little rise just inside the perimeter. Adler, Bradley, and Sally moved up and stood close by.

Sally looked anxious. She tried for the poker-face she saw in the professional lawmen all around her, but in vain. She could have been the boy's mother.

"*Hate to tell ya', Butch*," Red said into the loudspeaker, "*but you're headed in the wrong direction. Tell ya' what. You let the boy go and we'll talk about it. Discuss it over a cold beer.*"

"Beer," Butch said to Phillip. "What'd I tell ya'?" He yelled to Red, "Appreciate the offer, Cap'n, but you know I can't do that! If you and yer pals back outa here, I'll drop the boy at the border!" He let that sink in, then, "If ya' don't I'll shoot him in the head!"

Phillip, betrayed beyond comprehension, gaped at Butch.

"Don't look at me like that," Butch said. "I don't even have a gun. It's just the way this kinda little talk goes. They say a thing and I say a thing back like we're gettin' somewhere. It don't none of it mean a thing. Like two bunches a ladies fightin' over who gets the front pew at church."

Phillip looked a touch mollified.

"What'd'ya' do with the old pistola, anyway," Butch said, ever so naturally—a faint hope remaining.

"Threw it in the well."

"Good thinkin'," Butch said. He meant it.

"**Y**a' think he means it?" Adler asked.

Red, letting the megaphone hang at his side, mulled it over. He two-fingered a new chaw into his mouth and stuck the pouch back in his jacket pocket. He loooked to Sally. "What do you think?"

She hesitated, weary of her own glib theorizing. "Based on what's happened the past two days," she said cautiously, "I don't think he would."

"Turnabout's fair play," Bradley said. "The kid shot him."

Sally shook her head. "The dangerous time was when Butch first caught him in the field," she said. "They got over that, means they're back to being pals. I wouldn't undersell it. They're sorta made for each other in a way."

Bradley let out a guffaw before he could stop himself.

"It's . . . not so simple," she said, giving up on trying to explain. "I think it'd be damn hard for Butch Haynes to shoot this little guy. Jerry Pugh wouldn't've had a problem."

Bradley kept his own counsel.

"One thing's for sure," Red said. "If he gets outa here with the boy, we're right back where we started."

"Other hand," Bradley said, "if he kills the boy, he'll get the chair."

"Shit, he'll get the chair anyway," Adler said. "He's killed two in two days, three countin' Pugh."

"We don't know that he pulled the trigger on either of the innocent victims," Sally said.

"Well, he wasn't at home in his Strato-lounger," Bradley said flatly. " 'Sides, since when the victim gotta be innocent to make it murder? Or you think Casper did it?"

"That's enough," Red snapped. "You two would argue with a mile post. From the trail of blood I got a feelin' it ain't gonna make any difference. Let's just concentrate on getting the boy out for now."

Bobby Lee, carrying his oblong leather case under his arm, appeared at Red's elbow. He had on his black Italian leather gloves, and his hair was freshly slicked back. "Where ya' want me?" he said to Red.

Red looked him up and down. "Can you shoot off a hood?" he said.

"I can lie on my backside and shoot a tick off a longhorn's ass," Bobby Lee said.

Red was unimpressed. "Yeah, well, stay close," he said. "I catch a cold, you sneeze."

A loud thumping shook the air, and a white helicopter with a Texas State insignia on the side came into view. The chopper circled, preparing to land.

"That'd be the boy's mother," Adler said.

"Bring her on over," Red said.

■ *SIXTY-FOUR* ■

Butch and Phillip watched the helicopter flatten out the hay and hurl leaves and stalks around as it flew over close and landed in the field across the road.

"See, Phillip," Butch said. "Dreams do come true. There's yer rocketship."

"Think I'll get to ride it?" Phillip said, but his tone was not excited.

"Today's the day," Butch said.

Phillip looked big-eyed serious, weighted down. He had a growing feeling that the commotion of men and machines they were hearing just out of sight was leading up to something awful. Rocketship and helicopter rides just weren't high in his mind.

"*Butch!*" came Red's amplified voice. "*We got the boy's mama here. She wants to say something.*"

Phillip was visibly stunned by the news. He scrambled up to the crest of the gully wash and squinted, looking for his mama.

"What's wrong, Phillip?"

"It's my mama," Phillip said, his stomach jumping. He craned his neck to see. Suddenly, all was confusion. Through the moving grass he saw a woman back by the road with the cops—could be his mama. He looked back at Butch, their little safe harbor under the tree. Where was he supposed to be? The ground was shifting under him.

"Now ya' got yerself a ghost suit," Butch said, "ya' think she'll let ya' trick 'r treat?"

Phillip scrambled down the dirt slope and came back and squatted near Butch. He shrugged. "I got to do one house," he said. Better than none.

Butch smiled at the boy. He decided it was time to act. "Put yer mask back on," he said.

Another couple of police cars joined the throng. A good three dozen were pulled into the fields or stretched along the road. The air was filled with the dust of many feet and the hubbub of a carnival. Another vehicle, blue light spinning, sped along the county road and came to a stop in the midst of the crowd—A blue-and-white ambulance.

"Incredible," Sally said as the emergency vehicle drove up. "Cops rarely think past the shooting. Who do you suppose—?"

Adler waved his hand to catch her eye and pointed at Red's back.

"Oh . . ." Sally murmured. Surprised again.

"Excuse me," Bobby Lee said, nudging Sally away from the hood of the partol car, giving her a look. He set his leather case on the hood, carefully unsnapped the latches, and opened the container. Inside was a high-powered military rifle broken down in three parts. With practiced precision and showy swiftness, he assembled the weapon in seconds and laid it carefully across the hood.

Bradley watched with curiosity and begrudging respect. Bobby Lee lifted a velveteen bag and pulled out a high-powered scope. The marksman held the lens of the scope to his mouth, breathed on it, and wiped it clean with a special piece of cloth.

He felt eyes and turned to see Sally watching. He smiled at her, cocksure. His dark role in this manhunt had not come home to Sally until this very moment. She turned her head, disgusted and dreading what was about to happen. Was the sharpshooter interested in saving a kid or in notching a big kill? Sally knew it pretty much didn't matter.

Gladys Perry, frazzled, thinner than ever and fighting to keep her composure, was ushered forward to Red's command outpost. Bradley handed her the megaphone. Somewhat in shock, she took it and without waiting for instructions, raised it up and fumbled with it. It squawked loudly, rattling her even more.

Red helped her place her hands on it. "Just push the button and talk normally," he said.

"Is this man insane?" Gladys asked close to tears. "I'm worried about what I'll say; that I'll set him off."

"Just talk to him normally," Red said. "Say what you'd say if he was standin' in yer yard."

Gladys thought for just a moment, then raised the gizmo. She pressed the button Red had shown her, and it squawked something awful again.

"Here," Red said. "I'll hold the thing while you talk."

"Hullo . . . Hullo, please sir," Gladys said into the megaphone. "He's my only son. I'll give you money, whatever I can. Please, let me take my boy home. Let me just—"

The megaphone squawked one long final squawk and shorted out. Red tossed it to Bradley and raised his hands in frustration. Bradley and Adler immediately began taking it apart.

"You're doin' fine," Red said to Gladys. "We'll get another one." He looked expectantly at Bradley.

"I think yer tobacco spit shorted it out, Red," Bradley said, peering around inside the thing.

Phillip had his mask on. Butch dusted him off and admired him with a smile. "You ready to go home?"

"Yeahsir," Phillip said. Now he was sure.

Butch lifted his head up and yelled, "Hey, Capt'n, you got any candy?"

"This one's shot," Bradley said, giving up on the megaphone.

"Well find another one!" Red barked. He cupped his hands and yelled back to Butch, "What?"

"Candy! Halloween candy!," Butch yelled back. "Popcorn balls, caramel apples, gum, shit like that?"

"You hungry?" Red yelled back, giving a puzzled look to Adler.

"You find me some candy," Butch yelled, "and I'll deliver up a ghost."

Red looked at Adler and made a git goin' gesture. "You heard him," he said.

▪ SIXTY-FIVE ▪

Bradley jogged back to the command post. "Don't have another megaphone, Chief," he reported.

Red shook his head and sighed. He watched Adler out at the road, taking up a collection of gum, mints, jelly beans—whatever he could scratch up from attending officers.

Bobby Lee came around from the back of the car and leaned on the hood, placing an eye behind the scope of his lethal-looking rifle.

Gladys started wimpering in fear.

"You all set?" Red asked him.

"You say when, I'll say dead," Bobby Lee said.

"You'll be careful won't you?" Gladys cried "You'll be careful?" She put her hands to her mouth and sobbed. "My baby."

Red glared at Bobby Lee for an extended moment.

Bobby Lee saw the look. But he would have been astounded to know that wrapped up in that look was all of Red Garnett's ambivalence about Butch Haynes and himself and his job and judgment—his role in Haynes's shaping, the ultimate worth of a career that had jettisoned a personal life—for what? To stand in a field and preside over the execution of a misfit or worse, an unforgivable bloodbath? Bobby Lee was just a young shit with a rifle, but to Red he stood for all the dead weight and painful irreversibility of countless miserable choices over the years.

Red removed his hat and smoothed his hair back and replaced the hat. He yelled, "You got yer'self a deal! Candy's waitin'!"

"One more thing!" came the call from Butch. "His old lady's gotta swear to take him trick 'r treatin' every year."

In the little arroyo Phillip was getting upset. That last request. He strained to look for his mama. He was panicky. He was ready to leave.

"Gimme yer list, Phillip," Butch said. Still propped against the tree, he was too weak to stand, but just then realizing the full but fleeting potential of the moment.

"Butch? . . ." Phillip said, pleading.

"Gimme that list," Butch said. Now he had it in his mind.

Phillip pulled it out and handed it over.

Butch snatched it and started reading it to himself, and laughing. He was on a death roll of sorts. Between losing blood and the high merciless sun and being impossibly messed up, he was actually enjoying himself—enjoying this last squeak of insurrection, this macabre scenario he was concocting and unfolding.

Phillip on the other hand was fraying with the tension and starting to sob.

"And . . ." Butch shouted to Red, "she's gotta promise to take him to the fair for roller coasters and cotton candy whenever he wants! . . . or at least once a year!"

"I wanna go home!" Phillip cried.

"And," shouted Butch, checking the list, "when he gets older he gets to drink beer."

"I don't need beer . . ." Phillip wept, getting more and more scared.

"Well, it's on yer list," Butch said to Phillip. He then yelled to Red, "And to go out on dates with girls!" He turned to Phillip. "Not on the list, but you'll thank me later for that little addition."

Butch checked things off on the list. "Done that . . . got to drive . . . gonna ride that rocketship . . ." He looked up at Phillip. "That's about it."

"She's gotta promise!" he shouted to Red. "Or I won't let him go!"

"I wanna go home, Butch," Phillip said, tears

streaming down his face. "My mama's not bad. She gives me those things."

"Don't kid a kidder, Phillip," Butch said, waiting for a reply. He craned up, trying to get a glimpse of Red through the fringe of grass.

Deeply exasperated, Red could not abide how weird this whole thing was getting. He cupped his hands and yelled, "It's a deal!"

The reply from Butch came back. "Make her say it!"

Red looked at Gladys: Well?

She was reluctant; she did not step forward.

Red's face darkened with exasperation.

Phillip, crying anew, got to his feet. "I just wanna go home," he said and started to climb the bank.

Butch reached out and grabbed him by the arm and drew him back down. He pulled the sobbing boy close to him and held him like his own child. "I know jus' how ya' feel, Phillip," he said.

Her face a grimace of pain and agitation, Gladys blurted, "Phillip knows those things are against our beliefs!" She looked to Red, begging for understanding.

Red was fresh out. He detonated. "What kinda foolishness is that?" he spouted. He cupped his hands. "She promises!"

"Make her say it!" Butch yelled.

Red turned and gave Gladys a full-on glare hot enough to wither a Rose Bowl float. It got through. The debate was over. "*I promise!*" she screamed with all her might.

Butch loosened his grip and looked at the wet-eyed boy. "Can we trust her?"

"She's a real good mama," Phillip sobbed, getting to his feet.

Butch reached in his pocket and painfully extracted the remaining wad of stolen bills. "When you get home, hide this," he said. He unzipped the Casper costume, stuffed the bills inside, and rezipped. "If she's lyin', you can buy yer own damn beer."

"Yer not bad, are you Butch?" Phillip asked.

"Yeah," Butch said matter-of-factly. No point in soft-peddling now, with his guts spilling all over the ground. Besides, no illusions. What better rule to leave a kid with? He'd tried to live by it, once it hit him like a brick what his mother was doing for a living in the dance hall, and what his father's business was that made him keep disappearing. Butch had wanted no more shitty surprises. The shitty surprises kept coming, of course, but maybe he was more ready for them, he mused. The events of this day, for instance. Surprising in the details, yes. Who could've predicted being taken out by an eight-year-old. But the outcome itself—no surprise to Butch.

He tried to stretch his neck to see what the assembled masses were preparing across the field.

"Now, Buzz, listen here," he said. "I want ya' to step out there real slow, keepin' yer paws in the air. Then strut right over to them cops and yell 'Trick 'r Treat.' Got it?"

"What are you gonna do?"

"Somethin'll come to mind," Butch said. He stuck out his hand. Phillip shook it, suddenly fearful for his friend.

"Bye, Phillip," Butch said. "It's been one helluva ride." He smiled at the boy and nodded him toward the dirt bank.

"All right, Cap'n!" Butch yelled. "Make way for Casper the Friendly Ghost. The friendliest ghost I know."

He nudged Phillip, who seemed frozen. The boy

walked forward and plodded up the bank toward the field.

"Remember, paws up," Butch said.

Phillip climbed over the lip of the bank and stuck his paws in the air.

▪ *SIXTY-SIX*

Adler, watching through binoculars, couldn't help but smile and chuckle.

"Gimme them things," Red said, taking the binoculars from Adler. He took a look. There was Phillip, marching over the crest toward them, garbed in his full white hood, arms reaching for the sky.

Phillip, reaching level ground, for the first time saw the full strength of the reception awaiting him and Butch—an army. Swirling lights, rifles, pistols, shotguns everywhere, some pointed at him. Troopers—big Stetsons and blank-eyed Ray-Bans—poised to strike from every side.

"Come on," Red said, watching through the field glasses, coaxing. "Keep on walkin'!"

But Phillip had stopped and was standing perfectly still.

Red lowered the glasses. "Why the hell's he stoppin'?" he said. He turned to Gladys. "Call yer boy to come," he ordered her.

"Come on, honey!" Gladys called out, near shock. "Phillip. Keep walking, baby . . ."

The reality came crashing in on Phillip—the amassed police forces, the pointed rifles and shotguns. He turned toward Butch . . . and saw him struggle to his feet by the tree and stagger down to the creek bed, trying to make a run for it. But all the force in his body having run out on the ground, he collapsed.

"Phillip . . . Phillip . . ." Gladys cried out. "Come on, sweetheart, come to me."

Phillip took off at a run—back toward Butch.

"Phillip!" Gladys shrieked.

Red sighed and lowered the binoculars.

Phillip slid down the bank of the little gully and moved over to where Butch on hands and knees was laboring to get up. The boy stood there, uncertain.

"Personally," Butch said, looking up at him, "I think we negotiated you a pretty fair deal, but if there's somethin' else you want . . ."

"They want to kill you?" Phillip asked in disbelief.

"Naw, hell, Phillip . . ." Butch started to lie to the boy, but couldn't. "I know they do," he said, low.

Bobby Lee stroked the trigger of his high-powered weapon. He was smiling, ready, in position.

Red looked again through the binoculars, then lowered them. He shrugged and wiped his brow. "Sonofabitch changed his mind," he said, half to himself.

"How's that?" Adler said.

"He thought better of releasin' the boy," Red said.

"It doesn't necessarily mean that," Sally said.

Red just shook his head. He looked back at Bobby Lee. "Stay on ready," he said to the sharpshooter. He put the binoculars back up and looked. He could make out some movement among the trees.

Phillip held out his hand and helped Butch get up. Butch pushed himself up on a tree trunk with the boy's aid. He steadied himself, dusted some dirt off, grabbed Phillip's hand, and they started up the slope together, heading for the field of combat.

Red picked them up in his binoculars as they came up out of the gully and walked forward slowly together.

"I seen it all now," Red said.

Butch and Phillip, that pained, serious look on his little face, traversed the big field a step at a time. Butch, one hand in Phillip's, the other on his gut, presented an unreadable facade behind his sunglasses.

Red lowered the binoculars, raised his hat, and scratched his head.

"What's he up to?" Lt. Hendricks asked as he sidestepped over to Red, keeping his shotgun pointed in Butch's direction.

"Hell if I know," Red said.

"He's giving himself up," Sally said with certainty.

Lt. Hendricks gave her a sharp look. "Keep in mind," he said, "he still has the gun." He went back to tracking Butch's progress with the double barrels of his side-by-side.

"Butch! Stop and let the boy go!" Red yelled. "Put yer hands up and let the boy go!"

"Oh, please, Phillip!" Gladys wailed at the same time. "Please, mister, let him go . . . Come on, Phillip, come on!"

With all the yelling, Butch and Phillip heard mostly a shouted babble. They walked on, talking together.

"So I guess that's it for Alaska, Phillip," Butch said. "You know, when an Eskimo ain't no use anymore—when he's too old or sick or whatever—a guy in the can told me they put 'em on a chunk of ice and float 'em out to sea. Little ceremony and all, prolly some cold beer, pretzels. Music . . ."

Phillip half smiled at the idea.

"Stop and put your hands on your head!" Red yelled urgently.

"Run, Phillip! Come here, Phillip!" Gladys screamed.

"Come on, come on . . ." Sally urged quietly.

Hendricks glanced Bobby Lee's way. "Chief, you've got an armed killer with an innocent boy out there," he said, prodding.

"You clean?" Red snapped to Bobby Lee.

"As a whistle," Bobby Lee said.

"Keep him locked down," Red said through his teeth. "Don't squeeze till I say when."

In the field Butch and Phillip continued forward at their slow pace, hand in hand. Butch came to a painful halt.

"I wanna give ya' somethin'," he said.

As the target stopped, Bobby Lee steadied down, refining his focus.

"He's stopped," Red said.

"He's gonna make a run for it!" Adler said.

"Give it a second!" Sally hissed.

"Hold him!" Red said to Bobby Lee.

Sally yelled out, "Let the boy go, Butch!"

"If he makes a move, Chief," Hendricks growled, "we should nail him."

Butch went down on one knee and reached slowly, painfully for his back pocket. "Maybe someday," he said to Phillip, "you'll get to go . . ."

"He's goin' for his weapon, Red!" Hendricks shouted.

Red grabbed the binoculars from Adler, leveled them, and saw Butch reaching into his back pocket. He watched the move developing, ready to yell, ready to release fire . . .

Butch, smiling at Phillip, drew his hand from behind his back . . . Sally was sure, the way he was holding it, it couldn't be a gun. "Nooo," she breathed.

Bobby Lee squeezed. *Blammm!* Butch's chest exploded. A ringing echo reverberated across the land. Butch rocked backward, still on his knees . . . and looked at Phillip in amazement.

Phillip screamed, grabbed Butch, and held him up.

"Noooooo!" Sally screamed.

Bobby Lee centered the cross hairs for a second shot, but the boy kept moving in the way.

"Damn, Buzz," Butch said, tasting blood, "shot

twice in the same day." He sighed and collapsed forward into Phillip, knocking him back two steps. The boy fell on his knees. Butch wavered upright for a second or two and toppled on his back.

Phillip moaned and sobbed, kneeling beside him, watching him—the gunshot still ringing in his ears.

Gladys ran forward from behind a police car. A host of officers streamed after her.

"Goddamn it, Hendricks! Keep everybody back!" Red bellowed.

Bobby Lee, lowering the gun from his eye, disengaging, stood up and licked his dry lips. "No need to worry there, Chief," he said. "He can't hurt nobody now."

Red looked at him and looked away.

In the field an officer had reached Butch's side. He was down on his knees doing a careful ground frisk on every side of the fallen man, under him, in his garments. He popped up and yelled to Red, "No weapon, Chief!"

Red turned to Bobby Lee and nearly jumped out of his shoes with a sudden right cross that floored the younger man, sending his precious rifle clattering along the rocky ground.

Hendricks, astonished, jumped in and grabbed Red. He and four other officers moved in and held him back. "Hey, hey, Red, whoa, whoa!" Hendricks said. "What the hell?"

Red settled a bit. Hendricks turned to Bobby Lee, who was struggling up on one knee, stunned, out of it. The shooter wiped at a bloody lip and coughed. He spit out a tooth and looked at it without recognition.

Hendricks looked at Red, whose heart was still pounding, his breath coming short. But his rage was ebbing.

"What the hell was that all about?" Hendricks asked.

Red picked his Stetson off the ground and knock the

dust off it. "I didn't say 'when'," he said. He turned and walked away.

Hendricks took his hat off and mopped his head with his hand, following Red with his eyes. "Goddamn!" he said. He bent to stick a hand under Bobby Lee's arm and help him up.

Adler ran after Red, caught up with him, and stared at him as they walked along. "I thought he had a gun, too, Red," he said. "There was just no way of knowin'."

Red kept his eyes straight ahead and kept on going. Adler stopped, his eyes staying with the tall man.

Sally, who saw the whole thing, watched Red walk away.

His mother helped Phillip to his feet. She held him dearly to her breast. The boy hugged her back just as hard, his bloody Casper costume staining her blouse. Tears coursing down her cheeks, she moved to strip the bloody outfit off him, pulling the zipper down the front. Dollar bills, fives, tens, flopped out and blew around in the hot wind.

Seeing her boy unclothed underneath, Gladys zipped the costume halfway up and started to lead the boy away.

But Phillip balked. He pulled the other way. Gladys turned. He slipped his hand out of hers and moved to Butch's side. He bent down and pulled the postcard from Butch's hand. Butch's eyes, mostly unseeing, fluttered a bit with recognition.

Phillip stood there, staring. A circle of officers, keeping their a distance, jabbered among themselves.

"Probably should get the ambulance, huh?" one officer said.

"They're comin'," a second officer said, craning to see over the crowd.

Gladys gently turned Phillip's shoulders away, took

his hand and led him off. "Lookie there," the second officer said, "a buzzard . . . already."

The men looked up at the black bird flying in lazy circles above them, then down at the prostrate man. A couple of them shook their heads. "Oughta jus' leave him there," a third officer said. "Feed the wildlife."

Butch, his eyes barely open, licked his lips as the muffled voices continued around him. He was in another world. With his fading strength, he lifted his arm and rested it behind his head. His face relaxed.

The officers flinched back just a hair, startled at the movement, the sign of remaining life.

The wind suddenly gusted up and blew some pieces of hay across Butch's face and lodged a dollar bill against his cheek. He didn't notice.

Two state troopers hustled Gladys and the boy past the crowd, the tangle of cars, and across the road. Phillip looked back down the hill two or three times to where Butch was lying.

When the troopers steered them through the adjacent field toward the gleaming bubble of the official state helicopter, Phillip turned his attention forward.

"I'm s'posed to ride it?" he said, his eyes on the machine—eyes that on another day would have lit up like sparklers.

"Today's yer lucky day," the trooper said without a smile. "Ya'll crawl in."

As Phillip clambered up the steps and his mother followed, the blades began to turn.

Phillip pressed his face against the glass bubble as the whirlybird rose, watching . . .

Sally found Red standing behind his patrol car, surveying the field. He pulled out his tobacco pouch and dug for a chaw. She leaned against the car and waited until the chaw had seated in his cheek.

"Where was he headed?" she asked.

Red sighed and didn't say anything, just shook his head without looking at her.

"Come on," she said gently, pushing off the car and half facing him. "You know everything."

"I don't know nuthin'," Red said, his eyes focused somewhere past the rising chopper. "Not a damn thing."

Sally studied him for a few more seconds, then leaned back against the car next to him and stared off in the same direction. Her eyes followed the chopper as it passed over the field of confrontation and the grove of cottonwoods and live oaks.

The roaring helicopter roused a glimmer in the brain of the man bleeding out on the Caprock—fetched him back from his other world. His eyes fluttered open against the sun. He squinted hard, trying to see. A slight smile crossed his dying face as the chopper wiped the sun and sailed into the distance.

Phillip, face and hands against the bubble, searched among the crowd on the ground. His eyes, dazed, near-vacant, picked out the figure lying in the grass. One of the boy's upraised hands clutched the tattered postcard.

Gladys, eyes closed, stony with strain, sat close to the boy, keeping a hand on his back. Phillip watched the receding figure until the chopper swept them beyond sight.

Buzzards intersected the sun several more times and still Butch's eyes squinted and stared. A last swirling gust lifted the dollar bill off his cheek, flipped it over several times in the air, and dropped it in the field.

Butch's eyes squinted directly at the sun and did not move. They were smooth and lifeless.